THE NIGHT
NURSE'S SECRET

A NOVEL

SARAH BLACKWELL

Publisher Contact: MK Storyworks

www.mkstoryworks.com

contact@mkstoryworks.com

ISBN: 978-1-80700-048-6

First Edition

TABLE OF CONTENTS

DEDICATION

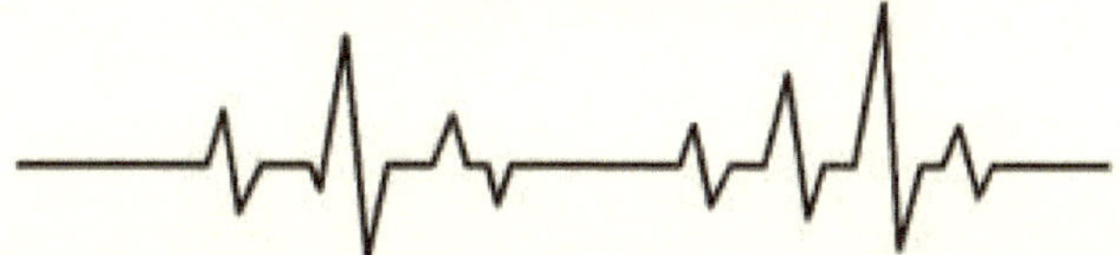

For every healthcare worker who spoke up when silence would have been easier.

For every whistleblower who chose truth over safety.

And for my mother, who taught me that courage isn't the absence of fear, it's doing what's right despite it.

EPIGRAPH

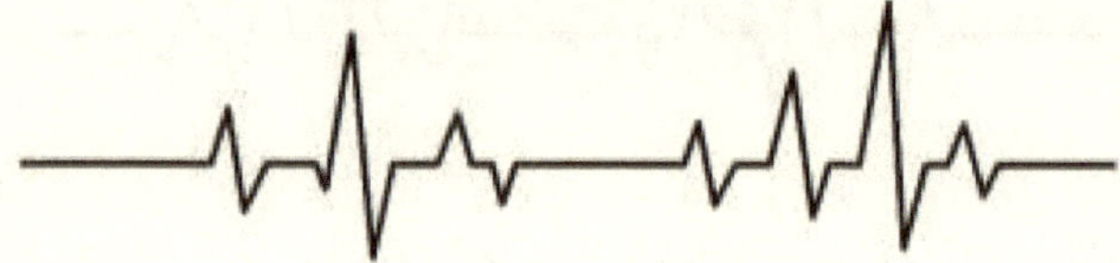

"In the end, we will remember not the words of our enemies, but the silence of our friends."

— Martin Luther King Jr.

"The only thing necessary for the triumph of evil is for good men to do nothing."

— Often attributed to Edmund Burke

"Truth never damages a cause that is just."

— Mahatma Gandhi

CONTENT WARNING

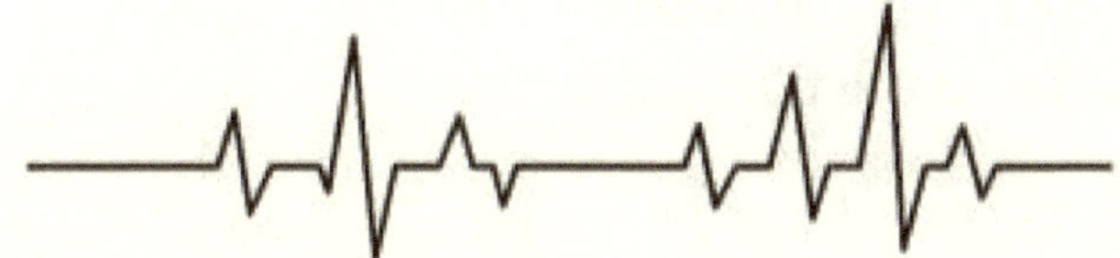

Please Read Before Continuing

The Night Nurse's Secret deals with sensitive themes that some readers may find distressing, including:

- Suicide and suicidal ideation
- Medical abuse and unethical human experimentation
- Institutional corruption and gaslighting
- Mental health stigma and forced psychiatric treatment
- Death of a minor (not graphic)
- Grief and loss
- Systemic injustice

This novel also portrays the long-term psychological impact of whistleblowing and institutional betrayal, including the destruction of a woman's career, reputation, and mental health over a thirteen-year period.

While the story ultimately affirms themes of justice, truth, and vindication, the journey includes difficult content that may be triggering for some readers, particularly those with personal experience of:

- Healthcare system abuse
- Parental loss
- Foster care/family separation
- Whistleblower retaliation
- Mental health discrimination

Resources:

If you or someone you know is struggling with suicidal thoughts, please reach out:

- **National Suicide Prevention Lifeline:** 988 or 1-800-273-8255
- **Crisis Text Line:** Text HOME to 741741
- **International Association for Suicide Prevention:** www.iasp.info

For healthcare workers facing ethical dilemmas or retaliation:

- **The Joint Commission:** 1-800-994-6610
- **OSHA Whistleblower Protection Program:** 1-800-321-6742

Please take care of yourself while reading. It's okay to take breaks or step away if needed.

— *Sarah Blackwell*

PROLOGUE

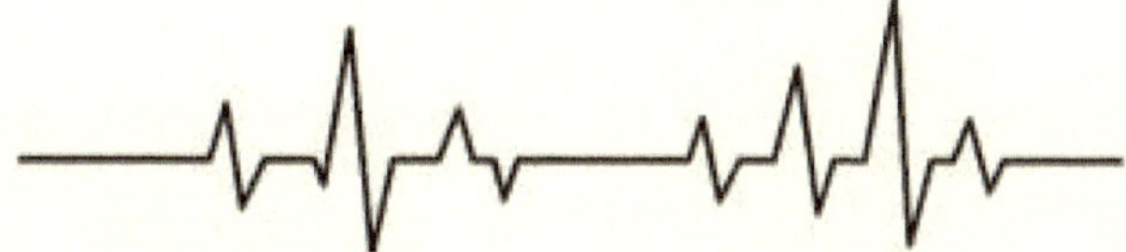

October 22, 1987

Willowbrook Psychiatric Hospital Manchester,

New Hampshire

Sophie Brennan knew she was going to die. She'd known it for three days, ever since she overheard Dr. Morrison and Dr. Shaw arguing in the medication room about "the girl who's been asking too many questions."

She was sixteen years old. She'd been a patient at Willowbrook for four months. And in that time, she'd documented everything.

Every illegal drug trial. Every patient who died after receiving "experimental treatment." Every bribe paid to medical examiners. Every cover-up orchestrated by pharmaceutical executives who valued profit over human life.

She'd kept it all in a journal, page after page of evidence that could destroy them.

And now they were going to kill her for it.

Sophie sat on her bed in Room 247, the journal hidden beneath her mattress. Outside, rain hammered against the windows. The hallway was quiet except for the occasional shuffle of slippers as night shift nurses made their rounds.

She had to get the journal to safety. Had to make sure someone would find it if, when, she didn't survive the night.

Margaret Moore. The kind night nurse with sad eyes who always asked how Sophie was really doing. The one who'd noticed things too. The one Sophie thought she could trust.

Sophie pulled the journal from its hiding place and held it to her chest. Her hands were shaking.

She'd documented 73 deaths. Seventy-three patients who came to Willowbrook for help and left in body bags. Seventy-three families who were told their loved ones died from their illnesses, when the truth was they'd been murdered by illegal pharmaceutical experiments.

If this journal disappeared, those 73 people died for nothing.

But if someone found it, if someone brave enough came forward, maybe their deaths could mean something. Maybe justice could still come.

Sophie opened to the first page and wrote one final entry:

If you're reading this, I'm probably dead. They're going to make it look like suicide, but I didn't kill myself. I was murdered because I documented what they did here.

My name is Sophie Marie Brennan. I was sixteen years old. I tried to save them.

Please. Please tell my family what really happened. Tell them I didn't give up. Tell them I fought until the end.

The truth is in these pages. Don't let them bury it with me.

She closed the journal and tucked it into her pillowcase, then lay back on her bed and waited.

At 11:47 PM, the door to her room opened.

Dr. Morrison entered, syringe in hand.

"Hello, Sophie," he said quietly. "I'm afraid it's time for your medication."

Sophie looked at him with clear, steady eyes.

"I know what you're doing," she said. "And I documented all of it. You won't get away with this."

Dr. Morrison smiled. "You're a very troubled young woman, Sophie. Everyone knows that. No one will believe a word you say."

He injected her with a massive dose of experimental cardiac drug NX-447.

Sophie's heart stopped at 11:58 PM.

At 12:15 AM, Dr. Morrison and two orderlies staged her body in the basement, creating a hanging scene that would look like suicide.

At 4:15 AM, night nurse Linda Walters, filling in on the psychiatric wing, discovered the staged scene and witnessed staff members cleaning up evidence.

Linda filed a police report at 6:47 AM.

It was dismissed within 24 hours.

But Sophie's journal remained hidden, tucked safely in the pillowcase that Margaret Moore took home that night and stored in a box that wouldn't be opened for thirty-seven years.

The truth, Sophie had written, cannot stay buried forever.

She was right.

CHAPTER 1

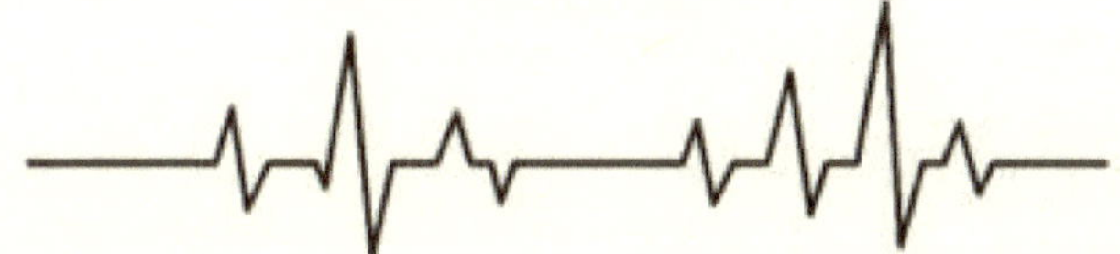

JENNA - The Note (November 19, 2024)

November 19, 2024, 4:17 AM

Manchester General Hospital, New Hampshire

The night shift is supposed to be quiet.

I've been a floor nurse for six years, and I know the rhythm: medication rounds at 4 AM, vitals at 5 AM, shift change at 7 AM. Most patients sleep through it all. The hospital breathes differently at night, slower, darker, more honest somehow.

But tonight feels wrong.

I'm pushing my medication cart down the corridor of the geriatric wing when I notice Room 412's door is open. Margaret Moore, 87 years old, admitted three days ago for pneumonia. She should be sleeping.

I knock softly. "Mrs. Moore? Medication time."

No response.

I push the door open wider. The room is dark except for the glow of the monitor. **Margaret** is in bed, perfectly still.

Too still.

"Margaret?" I move to her bedside and reach for her wrist.

No pulse.

Her skin is cool, not cold, but cooling. I check her pupils with my penlight. Fixed and dilated.

She's been dead at least an hour, maybe ninety minutes.

I should call a code. Press the button, alert the crash team, start the choreographed dance of attempted resuscitation that we all know is futile when someone's been gone this long.

But something stops me.

Margaret's right hand is extended toward the bedside table, fingers slightly curled as if she'd been reaching for something in her final moments. Her face shows no distress, she looks peaceful, like she simply drifted away.

Natural death. Expected, even. She was 87 with advanced pneumonia.

Except.

There's a piece of paper on the keyboard of her bedside table. Folded once, my name written on the outside in shaky handwriting:

JENNA WALTERS

My heart starts pounding.

I pick up the note with trembling hands and unfold it.

To whoever finds this...

My name is Margaret Moore. I was a nurse at Willowbrook Psychiatric Hospital from 1985 to 1991, when the facility closed. I witnessed things there that have haunted me for thirty-seven years.

I stayed silent because I was afraid. Because they threatened my family. Because I was a coward who chose survival over truth.

But I'm dying now, and I can't take this secret with me.

On October 22, 1987, a sixteen-year-old girl named Sophie Brennan was murdered at Willowbrook. They said she committed suicide, that she hung herself in the basement. But she didn't kill herself. She was murdered by staff members who were conducting illegal drug trials on psychiatric patients.

I know because I witnessed the aftermath.

Sophie kept a journal documenting everything, every illegal trial, every patient death, every cover-up. She gave it to me the night before she died because she knew they were going to kill her.

I've kept that journal hidden for thirty-seven years.

It's in storage unit #247 at SafeKeep Storage, 1642 Morrison Avenue, Manchester. The key is taped to the back of my driver's license in my wallet.

Please. Please tell Sophie's family what really happened. Tell them she didn't give up. Tell them she was brave and tried to save the other patients.

Tell them I'm sorry I waited so long.

—Margaret Moore

November 18, 2024

I read it three times, my hands shaking harder with each pass.

Sophie Brennan.

Murdered in 1987.

Staged as suicide.

A journal documenting illegal drug trials.

This is insane.

This is a dying woman's delusion. It has to be. Margaret was 87, on heavy pain medication, probably confused at the end.

Except the note is dated yesterday. November 18th. Margaret was lucid yesterday afternoon, I checked on her myself during my last shift. She was weak but mentally sharp, asking about her daughter's visit, commenting on the news playing on TV.

This wasn't written in delirium.

I should call security. Turn this over to administration. Let them handle it.

But my hand moves to Margaret's wallet instead.

It's in the bedside drawer, next to her reading glasses and a half-finished crossword puzzle. I pull out her driver's license.

Taped to the back: a small silver key.

SafeKeep Storage. Unit #247.

I stand there for a long moment, the key in one hand, the note in the other, Margaret's body cooling in the bed beside me.

Every instinct screams this is wrong. I'm tampering with evidence. I'm interfering with a death investigation. I should put everything back and call the charge nurse.

But something deeper pulls at me.

Sophie Brennan was sixteen years old when she died. If she was murdered, if this isn't just a confused old woman's fantasy, then someone got away with killing a child for thirty-seven years.

And if Margaret kept evidence hidden all this time,

someone needs to find it.

I fold the note carefully and slip it into my scrub pocket. The key goes into my other pocket.

Then I step into the hallway and press the code button.

"Code Blue, Room 412. Code Blue, Room 412."

The hospital erupts into motion.

November 19, 2024, 6:43 AM

The code was called at 4:23 AM. They worked on Margaret for eighteen minutes before Dr. Reyes called time of death at 4:41 AM.

Expected death. Natural causes. Pneumonia in an 87-year-old patient.

I gave my statement to the charge nurse: "I found her unresponsive during 4 AM medication rounds. No pulse, no respirations. I estimate she'd been deceased 60-90 minutes based on body temperature."

All true.

I didn't mention the note.

Now it's 6:43 AM, and I'm sitting in my car in the hospital parking lot, exhausted from the night shift but too wired to go home.

The key to storage unit #247 sits on my passenger seat.

I should sleep. I should go home, take a shower, crawl into bed, and forget about this.

Instead, I start my car and drive to SafeKeep Storage.

November 19, 2024, 7:15 AM

SafeKeep Storage, Manchester, NH

The storage facility is on the industrial edge of Manchester, a sprawling complex of orange metal buildings surrounded by chain-link fence. At 7:15 AM, the place is deserted except for one employee unlocking the office.

I show my ID at the gate. "I'm here to access unit #247. I have the key."

The employee barely looks at me. "Sign in. Building C, second floor."

I sign Margaret Moore's name in the logbook, technically fraud, but I'm already past the point of following rules.

Building C is at the back of the complex. I climb the metal stairs to the second floor and walk down a long corridor that smells like dust and concrete.

Unit #247 is at the end. The padlock is old and rusty, but the key turns smoothly.

The door rolls up with a metallic screech.

Inside: a ten-by-ten space, mostly empty. A few boxes, an old lamp, some furniture covered in dusty sheets.

And in the corner, sitting by itself on the concrete floor: a banker's box labeled in faded marker:

SOPHIE

My heart hammers as I kneel down and lift the lid.

1. Inside:
2. A spiral-bound journal, the cover decorated with stickers of rainbows and unicorns, the kind a teenage girl would buy
3. A manila folder bulging with papers
4. A smaller envelope marked "Photos"
5. A cassette tape labeled "Sophie's voice, April 1987"

I lift out the journal with trembling hands.

The first page reads:

This journal belongs to Sophie Marie Brennan If found, please return to 2847 Oakwood Drive, Manchester, NH Age: 16 PRIVATE!!!

Below that, in different ink, much newer:

Sophie died October 22, 1987. This journal is evidence of her murder. I kept it safe because I was too afraid to come forward. Forgive me, Sophie. —Margaret Moore

I turn the page.

April 2, 1987

First day at Willowbrook. Mom says it's just for evaluation. Two weeks, maybe three. Then I can come home and go back to school.

I'm not crazy. I know they think I am because of what I said during the panic attack. But I didn't mean it. I was scared and the medication the doctor gave me made everything worse.

Two weeks. I can handle two weeks.

I keep reading.

April 15, 1987

They're keeping me longer. Dr. Delacroix says I'm "not ready" to go home yet. He started me on new medications. Three different pills. They make me sleepy and my hands shake.

There's a girl named Lisa here. She's been here six months. She says once they put you on the "special medications," you never leave.

I don't like Dr. Delacroix. His eyes are cold.

I flip ahead.

May 3, 1987

A patient named David died last night. They said it was a seizure. But I saw him yesterday, he was fine until they gave him the new medication during evening rounds.

I asked Nurse Margaret what the medication was. She looked scared and told me not to ask questions.

Margaret. The nurse who wrote the note. She was there.

I keep reading, faster now.

June 8, 1987

I'm counting. Seven patients have died since I arrived in April. SEVEN. In two months.

Emily Rodriguez (April 24) David Mitchell (May 2) Lisa Hartley (May 15) Michael Torres (May 28) Christopher Lee (June 8)

All teenagers. All on "special medications." All died within weeks of starting the trials.

This isn't normal. This is murder.

My hands are shaking so badly I can barely hold the journal.

July 10, 1987

I saw them today. Three men in expensive suits visiting

Dr. Delacroix's office. I hid in the supply closet and listened.

They were talking about "trial protocols" and "acceptable loss rates" and "phase two expansion."

One of them said, "We need faster results. Increase the dosages."

Dr. Delacroix said, "Some patients won't survive increased dosages."

The man replied, "Then make sure their deaths look natural. We can't afford scrutiny."

They're killing us on purpose. For drug trials.

I need to get this information out somehow.

I flip to the last few entries.

October 10, 1987

This is probably my last entry. Dr. Delacroix told me today I'm starting a "new trial protocol" tomorrow. He smiled when he said it, but his eyes were cold.

I know what that means.

I'm giving this journal to Nurse Margaret tonight. She already has copies of the most important pages, but I want her to have the original too. If they kill me, someone needs to know the truth.

My name is Sophie Marie Brennan. I'm sixteen years old.

I didn't kill myself. Whatever they say, whatever report they write, I didn't give up.

They murdered me.

If anyone is reading this: Please investigate. Please don't let them get away with this.

Please give me justice.

The journal ends there.

The next page is blank.

Sophie never wrote again.

Because twelve days later, on October 22, 1987, she was dead.

I sit on the cold concrete floor of the storage unit, Sophie's journal in my lap, tears streaming down my face.

Sixteen years old.

She knew they were going to kill her.

She documented everything.

And no one listened for thirty-seven years.

I wipe my eyes and open the manila folder.

Inside: photocopies of medical records, patient files, death certificates. All from Willowbrook Psychiatric Hospital. All stamped "DECEASED" or "TRANSFERRED."

I recognize some of the names from Sophie's journal:

- Emily Rodriguez: Death certificate dated April 24, 1987. Cause: "Suicide by overdose"
- David Mitchell: May 2, 1987. Cause: "Cardiac arrest due to seizure"
- Lisa Hartley: May 15, 1987. Cause: "Suicide by hanging"

All signed by the same medical examiner: **Dr. Robert Delacroix.**

The same last name as the doctor Sophie mentioned.

I open the envelope of photos.

Inside: A class photo. Twenty-three teenagers standing in front of Willowbrook Psychiatric Hospital. April 1987.

On the back, somcone has drawn Xs over seventeen faces.

The ones who died.

Sophie is in the front row, smiling, alive, looking like any other teenage girl.

I turn over the photo and see handwriting, Margaret's handwriting:

These 17 patients died between April 1987 and October 1987 during illegal drug trials. All deaths ruled "suicide" or "natural causes." All signed off by Dr. Robert Delacroix.

Sophie kept this photo to remember them.

Someone needs to remember them.

I sit there for a long time, surrounded by evidence of a thirty-seven-year-old conspiracy.

Then I pull out my phone and dial 911.

"911, what's your emergency?"

"I need to report a murder," I say. "Actually, multiple murders. At Willowbrook Psychiatric Hospital in 1987."

There's a pause. "Ma'am, did you say 1987?"

"Yes. I have evidence. A journal written by one of the victims. Medical records. Photos. Everything."

"Ma'am, I'm going to need you to…"

"My name is Jenna Walters. I'm a nurse at Manchester General Hospital. I'm at SafeKeep Storage, unit #247. I have documentation of pharmaceutical murder and a decades-long cover-up. I need someone from the Manchester Police Department here immediately. And you might want to call the FBI."

Another pause. Then: "Stay where you are. Officers are on their way." I hang up and look at Sophie's journal one more time.

Please give me justice.

"I'm going to try," I whisper. **"I'm going to try."**

CHAPTER 2

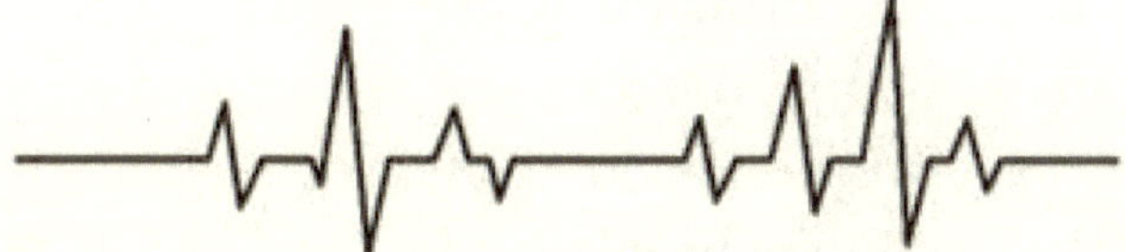

JENNA - The FBI Arrives (November 19, 2024)

November 19, 2024, 8:02 AM SafeKeep Storage, Unit #247

I'm still sitting on the concrete floor surrounded by Sophie's evidence when I hear sirens.

Two Manchester PD cruisers pull into the parking lot below. Then an unmarked black sedan. Then another.

I stand up, brushing dust off my scrubs, Sophie's journal clutched to my chest.

Footsteps on the metal stairs. Multiple people coming fast.

"Manchester Police! Anyone in unit 247?"

"I'm here!" I call out. "I'm the one who called!"

Three police officers appear in the doorway, hands near

their weapons. Behind them, a woman in a dark suit, mid-forties, FBI credentials clipped to her belt.

"Jenna Walters?" the woman asks.

"Yes."

"Special Agent Phyllis Chen, FBI." She steps into the unit, surveying the scene, the open banker's box, the journal in my hands, the papers spread across the floor. "You called 911 about murders at Willowbrook Psychiatric Hospital in 1987?"

"Yes. I found evidence. A journal written by one of the victims. Medical records. Photos. Everything."

Agent Chen exchanges a glance with one of the officers. Something passes between them, recognition, maybe. Or surprise.

"Ms. Walters, I need you to step outside for a moment. This is now a crime scene."

"A crime scene? But the murders happened thirty-seven years ago…"

"Step outside. Please."

There's steel in her voice. I set Sophie's journal back in the box carefully and follow her out to the corridor.

Two more agents are coming up the stairs, crime scene techs carrying equipment cases.

Agent Chen pulls me aside, away from the officers. "How did you find this storage unit?"

"A patient at my hospital died early this morning. Margaret Moore. She left me a note explaining what happened at Willowbrook in 1987. She said she'd kept evidence hidden for thirty-seven years. She gave me the location of this unit and the key."

"Margaret Moore." Agent Chen's expression shifts, recognition again. "She was a nurse at Willowbrook?"

"From 1985 to 1991. That's what her note said." I pull out the note from my pocket and hand it to her.

Agent Chen reads it quickly, her face unreadable. Then she looks at me with an intensity that makes my stomach drop.

"Ms. Walters, I need to ask you something very important. Have you heard the name Owen Brennan?"

My heart skips. "No. Who is he?"

"Owen Brennan is Sophie's younger brother. He's been investigating his sister's death for over thirty years." She pauses. "He's currently in federal custody at FCI Devens in Massachusetts, serving twenty years for murdering four people connected to Sophie's case."

The world tilts.

"What?"

"Owen Brennan killed four people between December 2017 and May 2018. He's been in federal prison since 2019. He confessed immediately and has been cooperating with our investigation ever since."

I lean against the corridor wall, trying to process this.

"Owen killed people? Sophie's brother?"

"Dr. Richard Delacroix, the psychiatrist who administered the fatal injection to Sophie. Patricia Reynolds, the nurse who helped stage the scene. Robert Delacroix, the medical examiner who ruled it suicide, he was Richard's brother. And Dr. Henry Wallace, a pharmaceutical executive who authorized the illegal drug trials."

The names from Sophie's journal. The people who murdered her.

"He killed them," I whisper.

"Yes. And when we arrested him in 2018, he told us everything. About Sophie's murder. About the pharmaceutical conspiracy. About seventy-three patients who died during illegal drug trials at Willowbrook between 1985 and 1995. He gave us financial records, witness statements, corporate emails. Everything he'd collected over three decades of investigation."

Agent Chen's expression hardens. "But we couldn't prosecute. The statute of limitations had expired on most of the crimes. The witnesses were dead or untraceable. The evidence had been destroyed. We had Owen's word, a confessed murderer seeking revenge, but nothing concrete enough to build a federal case."

She gestures toward the storage unit. "Until now. Sophie's journal is the smoking gun we've been looking for. A contemporary account written by a sixteen-year-old victim before she was murdered. That changes everything."

I'm reeling. "So, you already knew about Willowbrook? You've been investigating?"

"For six years. Since we arrested Owen. But we've been stuck. No physical evidence. No witnesses willing to testify. Just Owen's documentation and his testimony, which a defense attorney would tear apart because he's a convicted killer with an obvious motive to fabricate evidence."

Agent Chen looks back at the storage unit where techs are photographing and cataloging everything.

"But Sophie's journal? Death certificates signed by the medical examiner Owen later killed? Photos of victims? Medical records documenting illegal trials? That's real evidence. That's prosecutable."

She turns back to me. "Ms. Walters, you just broke open a six-year-old federal investigation. We need to talk. Extensively."

November 19, 2024, 10:30 AMFBI Field Office, Boston

Agent Chen drives me to Boston, a ninety-minute trip during which I call in sick to work and try to understand what I've stumbled into.

The FBI field office is a modern building in the financial district. Agent Chen escorts me through security and into a conference room on the fourth floor.

Inside: three other agents, a federal prosecutor, and a forensic accountant. The table is covered with file boxes, laptop computers, and evidence boards.

On one board: photos of six men, all in their seventies. Names beneath each photo:

- **James Morrison, VP of Research**
- **Martin Shaw, General Counsel**
- **Robert Chen, CFO**
- **David Patterson, VP of Operations**
- **Michael Williams, VP of Regulatory Affairs**
- **Thomas Foster, VP of Communications**

"Who are they?" I ask.

The prosecutor, a sharp-eyed woman named Rachel Diaz, answers. "Executives at Nexus Pharmaceuticals in the 1980s. The company was later renamed GenHealth Corporation. We believe these six men ordered and facilitated the illegal drug trials that killed seventy-three patients at Willowbrook and four other psychiatric facilities between 1985 and 1995."

Seventy-three patients.

Not just Sophie. Not just the seventeen teenagers in her class photo.

Seventy-three people.

"How do you know there were seventy-three victims?" I ask.

Rachel pulls up a spreadsheet on a laptop. "Owen

Brennan spent thirty years tracking every suspicious death at psychiatric facilities that received funding from Nexus Pharmaceuticals. He cross-referenced death certificates, patient records, financial transactions, witness statements. His documentation is meticulous."

She shows me the spreadsheet, seventy-three names, dates of death, facilities, causes of death listed on official records, evidence of pharmaceutical trials.

"But documentation from a revenge killer isn't enough," Rachel continues. "We need corroborating evidence. Physical proof. Sophie's journal provides that."

Agent Chen sets the journal, now in an evidence bag, on the table. "Sophie Brennan documented seven patient deaths in five months. She recorded conversations she overheard between Dr. Delacroix and pharmaceutical executives. She named the drug being tested, NX-447, an experimental anxiety medication that was never approved by the FDA. She predicted her own murder twelve days before it happened."

Rachel leans forward. "This journal is a contemporaneous account by a victim. It's not someone looking back thirty years later. It's not a revenge killer building a case. It's a sixteen-year-old girl writing about what was happening to her in real time. That's devastating evidence."

"So, what happens now?" I ask.

"We verify everything in Sophie's journal," Agent Chen says. "We cross-reference her entries with Owen's documentation. We track down any surviving witnesses, former staff members, patients, families. We obtain exhumation orders for victims' bodies to test for NX-447 residue. We build a federal case for conspiracy to commit murder."

"How long will that take?"

"Weeks. Maybe months. We'll move as fast as possible, but this needs to be airtight. These six men have powerful attorneys. We can't give them any openings."

Rachel adds, "We'll also need to interview you extensively. About Margaret Moore. About how you found the journal. About what you observed at Manchester General. You're now a witness in a federal murder investigation."

My head is spinning. "This morning I was a floor nurse. Now I'm a witness in a pharmaceutical conspiracy case?"

"Yes," Agent Chen says simply. "Welcome to the Sophie Brennan investigation."

November 19, 2024, 2:00 PM FBI Interview Room

They interview me for four hours.

Every detail about Margaret Moore. Her admission to Manchester General. Her condition. Her lucidity. The note she left. How I found the storage unit. What I saw inside.

Did Margaret seem delusional? No.

Was she on medications that could cause hallucinations?

No.

Did anyone else know about the note? No.

Why did she leave it for me specifically? I don't know.

Agent Chen makes a note. "We'll find out. Margaret chose you for a reason."

By 6:00 PM, I'm exhausted. Agent Chen finally calls a break.

"You can go home," she says. "But we'll need you to come back. Probably multiple times over the next few weeks. Can we count on your cooperation?"

"Yes. Absolutely."

"Good." She hands me a business card. "My direct line. Call me if you remember anything else about Margaret. Anything at all."

I take the card. "Can I ask you something?"

"Go ahead."

"Owen Brennan. Sophie's brother. Can I... can I meet him?"

Agent Chen considers this. "He's in federal custody. Visitation is restricted. But given your role in this investigation, I can probably arrange it. Why do you want to meet him?"

"Because he spent thirty years seeking justice for his sister. Because he killed four people trying to expose what happened.

Because Sophie's journal is the evidence he's been looking for his entire adult life." I pause. "I want him to know someone found it. I want him to know Sophie's story is finally being heard."

Agent Chen studies me for a long moment. "I'll make some calls. It'll take a few days to arrange. Federal prison visits require clearance. But I think Owen would want to meet you too."

She escorts me to the elevator. As the doors close, she says, "Ms. Walters? You did something extraordinary today. You could have ignored Margaret's note. You could have thrown away the journal and pretended you never saw it. But you didn't. You believed a dying woman. You called the police. You gave Sophie a voice."

"I just did what was right."

"Most people don't. That's why it took thirty-seven years to get this far."

November 19, 2024, 9:45 PM Jenna's Apartment, Manchester

I finally make it home at almost 10 PM.

My apartment is small, a one-bedroom in Manchester's outskirts. I've lived here for three years. It's the first place I've ever lived that feels like mine. Not foster homes. Not group housing. Mine.

I drop my bag on the couch and stand in the kitchen,

staring at nothing.

This morning, I was a floor nurse finishing a night shift.

Now I'm a key witness in a federal murder investigation involving seventy-three victims and six pharmaceutical executives.

I pull out my phone and google "Owen Brennan."

The results fill my screen:

"Brother of Teen Murder Victim Confesses to Quadruple Homicide"

"Vigilante Justice: Man Kills Four Connected to Sister's 1987 Death"

"Owen Brennan Sentenced to 20 Years for Revenge Murders"

I click the first article. It's from May 2018:

Owen Brennan, 42, pleaded guilty today to four counts of first-degree murder. Brennan confessed to killing Dr. Richard Delacroix (December 2017), Patricia Reynolds (February 2018), Robert Delacroix (April 2018), and Dr. Henry Wallace (May 2018), all individuals he claimed were responsible for his sister Sophie's death at Willowbrook Psychiatric Hospital in 1987.

Brennan told police his sister was murdered during illegal pharmaceutical trials and that officials covered it up as suicide. He spent 31 years investigating before taking matters into his own hands.

Judge Harold Martinez sentenced Brennan to 20 years in federal prison, calling his crimes "understandable but unforgivable."

There's a photo of Owen being led into court, handcuffed, orange jumpsuit, hollow eyes. He looks haunted. Destroyed.

But also determined.

I find another article from 2019:

"Convicted Killer Cooperating with FBI in Pharmaceutical Conspiracy Investigation"

Sources confirm Owen Brennan is providing extensive documentation to federal investigators regarding alleged illegal drug trials at Willowbrook Psychiatric Hospital in the 1980s-90s. The FBI has reportedly been investigating for over a year but lacks physical evidence to pursue charges.

So, the FBI has been investigating since they arrested Owen.

For six years, they've been trying to verify his claims.

And today, I handed them the evidence they needed.

I set my phone down and walk to my bedroom. On my dresser: a framed photo of my mother.

Linda Walters. My mom. Dead thirteen years.

I pick up the photo, studying her face. She's smiling, but

there's sadness in her eyes. This was taken a year before she died by suicide.

My mother was mentally ill. That's what everyone told me growing up. That's what social services said when they took me away from her when I was seven. That's what I believed my entire life.

But now I'm wondering.

What if my mother wasn't mentally ill?

What if she knew something?

What if…

My phone buzzes. A text from an unknown number:

This is Agent Chen. I looked into something. Your mother, Linda Walters, was a nurse at Willowbrook Psychiatric Hospital in 1987. She filed a police report on October 23, 1987, the day after Sophie Brennan died, claiming she witnessed the staging of a suicide. The report was dismissed as unfounded. I think we need to talk about your mother.

I stare at the text, my hands shaking.

My mother worked at Willowbrook.

My mother filed a police report about Sophie's death.

My mother tried to report the murder.

And they called her crazy.

I sit down on my bed, the photo of my mother in one hand, my phone in the other.

"Oh, Mom," I whisper. "You tried to tell everyone. You tried to save Sophie. And nobody believed you."

Tears stream down my face.

My entire childhood, I thought my mother was delusional. I thought she made up stories about murdered patients and pharmaceutical conspiracies. I thought she was mentally ill.

But she wasn't.

She witnessed a murder.

She tried to report it.

And they destroyed her for it.

I text Agent Chen back:

I need to see everything you have about my mother. Every police report. Every document. I need to know what really happened to her.

Her response comes immediately:

Come to the office tomorrow. 10 AM. I'll show you everything.

I set my phone down and look at my mother's photo. "I'm going to prove you were right," I tell her. "I'm going to prove you were telling the truth all along. I promise."

CHAPTER 3

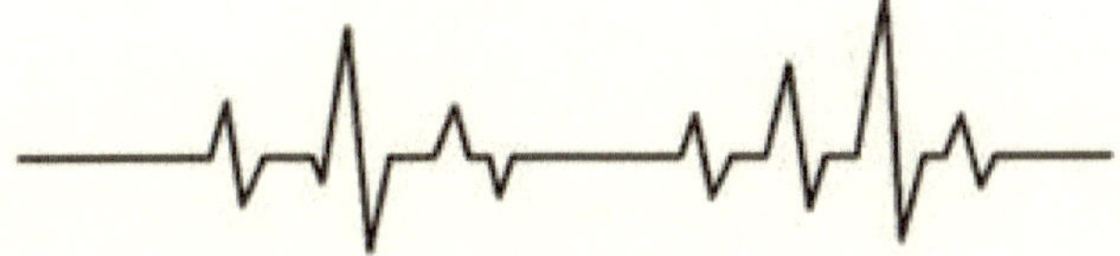

JENNA - Meeting Owen (November 22, 2024)

November 22, 2024, 9:00 AMFBI Field Office, Boston

Agent Chen meets me in the lobby with a thick manila folder.

"Your mother's file," she says, handing it to me. "Everything we've found so far. Police reports from 1987. Complaints to the nursing board. Letters to state investigators. It's... extensive."

I take the folder with trembling hands. It's heavy, at least two inches of documents.

"How much did she file?"

"Over a dozen police reports between 1987 and 2000. Thirty-seven complaints to various agencies. Hundreds of letters to officials, journalists, attorneys. Your mother spent thirteen years trying to expose what happened at Willowbrook."

We sit in a conference room, and I open the folder.

The first document is a police report dated **October 23, 1987**, the day after Sophie died:

MANCHESTER POLICE DEPARTMENT Incident Report #87-10-4729

Date: October 23, 1987, 6:47 AM

Reporting Officer: Sgt. Michael Torres

Complainant: Linda Walters, RN, Age 25

Summary: Officer responded to complaint from Ms. Walters, a registered nurse at Willowbrook Psychiatric Hospital. Ms. Walters reported discovering the body of Sophie Marie Brennan (age 16, patient) at approximately 4:15 AM during night shift rounds.

Ms. Walters stated the death was "staged to look like suicide." She reported observing:

- Post-mortem lividity inconsistent with hanging
- Fresh injection marks on deceased's arms
- Signs of cardiac arrest prior to hanging
- Staff members cleaning the scene before police arrival
- Missing medical records

Ms. Walters requested immediate investigation into possible homicide.

Action Taken: Report forwarded to Medical Examiner's office for review.

Medical Examiner Response (Oct 24, 1987): Death ruled suicide by hanging. No evidence of foul play. Case closed.

Signed: Dr. Robert Delacroix, Medical Examiner

I stare at the report, my vision blurring.

My mother saw Sophie's body. She saw them staging it. She reported it immediately.

And Robert Delacroix, the same man Owen later killed, closed the case within 24 hours.

"Keep reading," Agent Chen says quietly.

I flip to the next report. **November 15, 1987:**

Complainant: Linda Walters, RN

Summary: Ms. Walters returned to station claiming additional evidence regarding Sophie Brennan death. States she witnessed staff members destroying medical records and disposing of medications on October 23, 1987. Requests reopening of investigation.

Action Taken: Report forwarded to Medical Examiner. ME confirmed case closed. No further action taken.

Another report. **December 3, 1987:**

Complainant: Linda Walters, RN

Summary: Ms. Walters provided list of seven additional patient deaths at Willowbrook between April-October 1987. Claims all deaths suspicious. Requests investigation.

Action Taken: Medical Examiner reviewed death certificates. All ruled natural causes or suicide. Case closed.

On and on. **January 1988. March 1988. June 1988.**

My mother filed report after report. Every one dismissed. Every one closed by Robert Delacroix.

Then the complaints to other agencies start:

New Hampshire Board of Nursing - April 1988: *Linda Walters, RN, filed complaint regarding patient safety concerns at Willowbrook Psychiatric Hospital. Alleges illegal drug trials and patient deaths. Investigation found no evidence to support claims. Complainant appears emotionally unstable.*

New Hampshire Department of Health - July 1988: *Complaint filed by Linda Walters regarding Willowbrook facility. No merit found. Complainant has filed multiple baseless reports.*

State Attorney General's Office - September 1988: *Linda Walters requests criminal investigation into Willowbrook deaths. Reviewed by prosecutors. No prosecutable offenses identified. Complainant appears to be suffering from paranoid delusions.*

That phrase appears again and again: **"appears to be**

suffering from paranoid delusions."

They weren't investigating her claims. They were diagnosing her mental state.

"They gaslighted her," I whisper.

Agent Chen nods. "For thirteen years. Every agency she contacted dismissed her as mentally ill. Nobody investigated. Nobody believed her."

I flip to the final section, documents from 1989:

New Hampshire Board of Nursing License Revocation Hearing - Linda Walters, RN

Date: August 15, 1989

Charges: Making false statements regarding patient care. Harassment of medical examiner's office. Conduct unbecoming a registered nurse.

Testimony: Multiple witnesses testified that Ms. Walters has made repeated unfounded accusations regarding deaths at Willowbrook Psychiatric Hospital. Medical Examiner Robert Delacroix testified that Ms. Walters has filed over 20 complaints, all investigated and found baseless. Psychiatrist Dr. James Morrison testified that Ms. Walters shows signs of paranoid personality disorder.

Decision: Nursing license REVOKED effective September 1, 1989.

Reason: Ms. Walters is emotionally unstable and

represents a danger to patient safety. Her continued employment as a nurse is not in the public interest.

I look up at Agent Chen, fury rising in my chest. "Dr. James Morrison testified against my mother?"

"James Morrison, VP of Research at Nexus Pharmaceuticals," Agent Chen confirms. "One of the six executives we're targeting. He wasn't just conducting illegal trials, he actively destroyed whistleblowers who tried to expose him."

"They took her license. They took her career."

"Keep reading."

I flip ahead. **1998:**

New Hampshire Department of Children and Family Services Case #98-NH-4472

Regarding: Jenna Marie Walters, age 7, daughter of Linda Walters

Summary: Anonymous report received regarding unstable home environment. Mother (Linda Walters) observed making paranoid statements to child, obsessing over "murdered patients" and "pharmaceutical conspiracies."

Investigation: Home visit conducted April 22, 1998. Mother appears severely mentally ill, unable to provide stable environment. Child placed in temporary foster care pending evaluation.

Outcome: Custody removed. Child placed in permanent foster care May 15, 1998.

I can't breathe.

They took me away from her because she was trying to expose pharmaceutical murder.

Because she witnessed Sophie's death and wouldn't stop fighting for justice.

Because she told the truth.

"I was seven years old," I whisper. "I remember that day. Social workers came to our apartment. My mother was screaming that they were wrong, that she wasn't crazy, that patients had been murdered. I thought she was having a breakdown."

"She was trying to save lives," Agent Chen says gently. "And they destroyed her for it."

I close the folder, my hands shaking. "She died in 2011. Suicide. Everyone said it was because of her mental illness. But it wasn't, was it?"

"No. It was because she spent thirteen years being told she was crazy when she was actually telling the truth. That kind of gaslighting destroys people."

I look at Agent Chen. "My mother tried to save Sophie. She tried to expose the conspiracy. And they killed her for it.

Not with a weapon. With systematic psychological abuse until she couldn't take it anymore."

"Yes."

"So, when we prosecute those six executives, we're not just prosecuting them for Sophie's murder. We're prosecuting them for my mother's death too."

Agent Chen meets my eyes. "Officially, no. Linda's death won't be part of the criminal case, it's too indirect. But morally? Yes. Those men destroyed your mother. And we're going to make sure everyone knows it."

She stands. "Owen is expecting you at FCI Devens at 1 PM. I arranged the visit. He knows you found Sophie's journal. He knows about your mother's connection. He wants to meet you."

November 22, 2024, 1:00 PM Federal Correctional Institution Devens, Massachusetts

The prison is massive, concrete and razor wire, guard towers, double fencing. I go through three security checkpoints, surrender my phone and keys, and submit to a pat-down search.

A guard escorts me through corridors of reinforced steel doors. Everything echoes, footsteps, voices, the clang of locks.

"Owen Brennan is one of our cooperative inmates," the guard tells me. "Teaches GED classes. Helps in the law library.

No disciplinary issues. He'll be in for life, but he makes the most of it."

"I thought his sentence was twenty years?"

"Twenty years minimum. Federal sentence. He's eligible for parole in 2044 when he's 68. But parole boards don't like cop killers or revenge killers. He'll probably die here."

We reach a visitation room, small, divided by reinforced glass, phones on each side.

The guard gestures to a chair. "Wait here. He'll be brought in shortly."

I sit, my heart pounding.

A door opens on the other side of the glass.

Owen Brennan enters.

He's 48 years old but looks older. Prison orange jumpsuit. Hands cuffed in front of him. Gray hair, tired eyes, the face of someone who's been fighting for decades and finally ran out of options.

He sits across from me, picks up the phone.

I pick up mine.

"Jenna Walters," he says. His voice is rough, like he hasn't slept in years.

"Owen Brennan."

"Agent Chen told me you found Sophie's journal. That you brought it to the FBI. That you're Linda Walters's daughter."

"Yes."

His eyes fill with tears. "Thank you. Thank you for believing Margaret's note. Thank you for not throwing away the journal. Thank you for giving Sophie a voice."

"I just did what was right."

"Most people don't. Your mother did. She tried to save Sophie and she was destroyed for it. I'm sorry about that. I'm sorry you lost her."

"I'm sorry you lost Sophie."

Owen closes his eyes, composing himself. When he opens them, he's all business.

"Agent Chen says the FBI is building a case against the six executives. James Morrison, Martin Shaw, Robert Chen, David Patterson, Michael Williams, Thomas Foster. Is that true?"

"Yes. They're using Sophie's journal as evidence. Combined with your documentation."

"How long until arrests?"

"Weeks. Maybe months. They need to verify everything first."

Owen nods slowly. "I've waited thirty-seven years. I can wait a few more months."

He leans forward, his cuffed hands pressed against the glass. "I need to tell you something about your mother. Something important."

"What?"

"Your mother and Margaret Moore worked together. They both witnessed Sophie's murder aftermath on October 23, 1987. They both tried to report it. And when officials dismissed them, they kept investigating together, for three years, from 1987 to 1990."

My breath catches. "They knew each other?"

"Margaret told me, years later. After I started investigating Sophie's death in the early 2000s, I tracked her down. She was terrified to talk to me at first, afraid of retaliation. But eventually she opened up. She told me about Linda. About how they tried to expose Willowbrook together."

Owen's voice is intense now, urgent.

"Your mother was Margaret's hero, Jenna. Margaret said Linda was the bravest person she'd ever met. Linda knew what reporting Sophie's murder would cost her, her career, her reputation, maybe even her safety. But she did it anyway. She filed reports every month. She contacted every agency she could think of. She never gave up."

"Until they destroyed her."

"Until they destroyed her," Owen agrees. "In 1990, Margaret was threatened directly, someone told her if she kept helping Linda, her family would be hurt. So, Margaret stopped. She kept Sophie's journal hidden but stopped actively investigating. She's lived with that guilt for thirty-four years."

"And my mother kept fighting alone for another ten years."

"Yes. Until they took you away in 1998. After that, Linda broke. Margaret said losing custody of you was what finally destroyed her. She kept filing reports sporadically until 2000, but she was just going through the motions. The fire was gone."

I wipe tears from my face. "She died in 2011. Eleven years after she stopped fighting."

"I know. I wanted to contact her, to tell her I believed her, to show her my documentation. But by the time I found her address, she was already in a group home, heavily medicated. I went there once in 2009. She didn't recognize me. Didn't remember Sophie's name."

Owen's voice breaks. "I wanted to tell her she was right. That Sophie was murdered. That I was going to get justice. But she was too far gone. So, I kept investigating alone. For another eight years. Until I couldn't stand it anymore and I killed the four people most directly responsible for Sophie's death."

"And then the FBI arrested you."

"And then the FBI arrested you," he confirms. "December 2018. I confessed immediately. Told them everything. Gave them all my evidence. And I've been in here ever since, cooperating with their investigation, waiting for them to build a case."

He looks at me intently. "But they couldn't. Not without physical evidence. Not without Sophie's journal. Your mother spent thirteen years being told she was crazy for saying Sophie was murdered. I spent thirty-seven years collecting documentation. But neither of us could prove it."

"Until Margaret gave me the key to the storage unit."

"Until Margaret gave you the key," Owen says. "She waited thirty-seven years. She watched your mother get destroyed. She watched me go to prison. And then, at the very end of her life, she decided to do the right thing. She gave the journal to Linda Walters's daughter."

"Why me specifically?"

"Because you're the one person who has the most to gain from proving your mother was right. Because you grew up thinking Linda was mentally ill. Because Margaret knew if anyone would fight to clear Linda's name, it would be you."

I sit back, processing this.

My mother tried to save Sophie.

Margaret tried to help her.

Owen investigated for decades.

And now I'm finishing what all three of them started.

"What happens now?" I ask Owen.

"The FBI builds their case. They interview witnesses. They exhume bodies. They trace financial records. They prepare arrest warrants. And then, hopefully before I'm fifty, those six men are arrested and prosecuted for murdering seventy-three people, including Sophie, including the seventeen other teenagers in her class photo, including all the patients whose names we'll never know."

"And my mother?"

Owen's expression softens. "Your mother won't be part of the criminal case, her death is too indirect. But she'll be part of the story. When this goes to trial, everyone will know Linda Walters was the first whistleblower. The first person who tried to expose the conspiracy. She'll be recognized as a hero."

"She deserves that."

"She does. And you're going to make sure she gets it."

A guard knocks on the glass, time's up.

Owen stands, his cuffed hands awkward. "Thank you for coming, Jenna. Thank you for finishing what your mother started."

"Thank you for never giving up on Sophie."

"I'll never give up on her. Even from in here." He gestures at the prison around him. "I've got fourteen more years minimum. Maybe longer. But I'll keep helping the FBI. I'll testify at trial. I'll do whatever it takes."

"Good."

As the guard leads Owen away, he turns back one more time.

"Tell Agent Chen to move fast. David Patterson is seventy-four and has heart problems. If he dies before arrest, the other five will blame everything on him. We need to get them all."

Then he's gone.

I sit alone in the visitation room, staring at the empty chair where Owen sat.

Sophie's brother. In prison for killing four people. Cooperating with the FBI to bring down six more.

The math is brutal. Owen gave up twenty years of his life, maybe his entire life if parole is denied, to get justice for Sophie.

And now it's finally happening.

Because a dying nurse gave me a key.

Because my mother tried to save Sophie thirty-seven years ago.

Because Owen never stopped believing.

Because I made the choice to believe Margaret's note instead of ignoring it.

Justice isn't one person. It's many people making brave choices across decades.

Sophie documented the truth.

Margaret kept it safe.

My mother tried to expose it.

Owen investigated relentlessly.

I brought it to the FBI.

And now, finally, those six executives are going to face consequences.

Not perfect justice. Not complete justice.

But justice nonetheless.

November 22, 2024, 4:30 PM Jenna's Apartment, Manchester

I get home exhausted, emotionally drained.

On my kitchen table: the folder Agent Chen gave me about my mother.

I open it again and read through everything, every police report, every complaint, every letter Linda wrote trying to expose Willowbrook.

My mother wasn't mentally ill.

She was a whistleblower who was systematically destroyed.

I pull out my phone and call Agent Chen.

"I want to help," I tell her. "Whatever you need for this investigation. Interviews, testimony, research. I want to be part of bringing those six men to justice."

"Are you sure? This will take months. Maybe over a year. It'll be intense."

"I'm sure. My mother spent thirteen years fighting for this. I can give it a year."

"Okay. Come to the office Monday morning. We'll officially bring you on as a cooperating witness. You'll work closely with our team as we build the case."

"Thank you."

After I hang up, I look at my mother's photo on the dresser.

"I'm going to prove you were right, Mom," I say. "I'm going to make sure everyone knows you were a hero. I promise."

CHAPTER 4

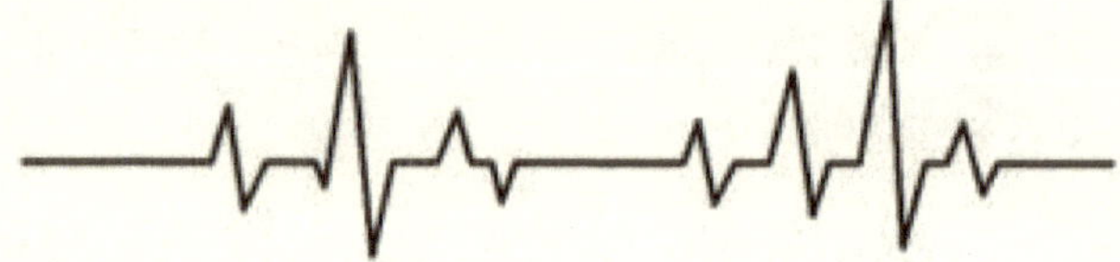

JENNA - The Investigation Begins (November 25 - December 15, 2024)

November 25, 2024, 9:00 AM FBI Field Office, Boston

Agent Chen leads me into a large conference room that's been converted into an investigation command center.

Evidence boards cover three walls. Photos of the seventy-three victims. Timelines spanning 1985 to 1995. Organizational charts showing the structure of Nexus Pharmaceuticals (now GenHealth Corporation). Financial flow diagrams tracing millions of dollars in suspicious payments.

At the center of it all: **Sophie's journal**, now enlarged and mounted on poster boards so every entry is visible.

Six FBI agents work at laptops. Rachel Diaz, the federal prosecutor, stands at a whiteboard covered in legal notes.

"Welcome to the Sophie Brennan Task Force," Agent Chen says. "As of yesterday, this is an official FBI investigation. Case number 2024-FBI-47392. Target: conspiracy to commit murder, wire fraud, obstruction of justice."

She gestures to the evidence boards. "We have six primary targets." She points to their photos:

James Morrison, age 73 - VP of Research at Nexus Pharmaceuticals, 1985-1995. Authorized the illegal drug trials. Currently retired, living in Boston.

Martin Shaw, age 76 - General Counsel. Structured the legal framework to avoid liability. Lives in Greenwich, Connecticut.

Robert Chen, age 70 - Chief Financial Officer. Approved forty million dollars in bribe payments. Lives in New York City.

David Patterson, age 74 - VP of Operations. Managed hospital contracts and ensured staff compliance. Lives in Virginia. Health declining, heart condition.

Michael Williams, age 72 - VP of Regulatory Affairs. Bribed FDA officials to approve unsafe drugs. Lives in Kentucky.

Thomas Foster, age 75 - VP of Communications. Orchestrated the cover-up and silenced whistleblowers. Lives in California.

"All six are alive," Rachel Diaz adds. "All six are wealthy.

All six have powerful attorneys. We need an airtight case."

She taps the whiteboard. "Our prosecution strategy has three pillars:"

PILLAR ONE: Physical Evidence

- Sophie's journal documenting the trials
- Medical records showing illegal drug administration
- Death certificates signed by the corrupt medical examiner
- Financial records showing $40 million in bribe payments

PILLAR TWO: Witness Testimony

- Owen Brennan (cooperating witness, currently incarcerated)
- Former Willowbrook staff willing to testify
- Victims' family members
- Forensic experts

PILLAR THREE: Exhumation & Forensic Analysis

- Exhume victims' bodies
- Test for NX-447 residue (the experimental drug)
- Prove cause of death was drug toxicity, not suicide

Rachel looks at me. "You're part of Pillar Two. You found the journal. You're Linda Walters's daughter. Your testimony will establish that this conspiracy involved destroying whistleblowers. That's our obstruction of justice charge."

"When do we start?"

"Today."

November 25, 2024, 11:00 AM Interview Room, FBI Field Office

Agent Chen and another agent, a forensic accountant named Daniel Brooks, interview me for three hours.

They want every detail about Margaret Moore. Her medical condition. Her mental state. The exact wording of her note. How I found the storage unit. What was inside.

Then they shift to my mother.

"Tell us about Linda Walters," Agent Chen says. "What do you remember about her?"

I take a deep breath. "I remember her being obsessed with something. With patients who died. With a hospital called Willowbrook. She would stay up all night writing letters, making phone calls. She had files and folders everywhere, documents, newspaper clippings, notes."

"How old were you?"

"It started when I was five or six. By the time I was seven, social services took me away. They said she was mentally unstable. That her obsession was dangerous."

"What did Linda tell you about Willowbrook?"

"She said patients were being murdered. That she witnessed a girl's death being staged as suicide. That pharmaceutical companies were testing drugs on psychiatric patients without consent. She said officials were covering it up."

Agent Chen leans forward. "Did you believe her?"

"No." The word comes out bitter. "I thought she was crazy. Everyone told me she was delusional. Social workers, therapists, foster parents. They all said Linda had paranoid personality disorder. That she made up conspiracy theories. That I was better off without her."

"When did you last see your mother?"

"2009. I was nineteen. She was in a group home, heavily medicated. She barely recognized me. I tried to talk to her about getting help, about moving forward. But she just kept saying 'They murdered Sophie. Nobody believes me. They murdered Sophie.'"

My voice breaks. "I thought she was stuck in a delusion. But she was telling me the truth. She was trying to make me understand. And I didn't believe her."

Daniel Brooks, the forensic accountant, speaks up. "We need to establish that your mother was targeted specifically for whistleblowing. Can you walk us through what happened after she filed the first police report in 1987?"

I think back to the documents Agent Chen showed me. "She filed a report on October 23, 1987, the day after Sophie died. Within weeks, she started receiving pressure. Her supervisor at Willowbrook questioned her judgment. Other nurses stopped talking to her. She was assigned to different shifts, isolated from other staff."

"Retaliation," Agent Chen confirms.

"By 1988, the nursing board was investigating her, not the deaths she reported, but her fitness to practice. By 1989, they revoked her license. The official reason was 'making false statements' and 'emotional instability.' But the real reason was that she wouldn't stop reporting Sophie's murder."

Daniel makes notes. "And she lost custody of you in 1998?"

"Yes. I was seven. An anonymous tip to child protective services said my mother was paranoid, unstable, a danger to me. They came to our apartment, interviewed her, interviewed me. Within weeks, I was in foster care."

"Did your mother fight the custody removal?"

"She tried. But by that point, she had no credibility. No nursing license. No job. A decade of being labeled mentally ill. The court ruled she was unfit."

Agent Chen looks at me intently. "Jenna, we believe that

anonymous tip came from Nexus Pharmaceuticals. We think they were monitoring your mother. When she kept filing reports year after year, they decided to destroy her completely. Taking you away was the final blow."

Rage floods through me. "They took me from my mother to silence her?"

"We can't prove it yet. But the timing is suspicious. Linda filed her last detailed police report in March 1998. In April 1998, child services received an anonymous tip. In May 1998, you were removed from her custody. Linda filed one more report in 2000, but it was perfunctory, just going through the motions. After losing you, the fight went out of her."

"And she killed herself in 2011."

"Yes."

I wipe tears from my face. "So, when we prosecute those six men, we're not just charging them with murdering Sophie and the others. We're charging them with destroying my mother. Even if her death isn't part of the criminal case, it's part of the truth."

"Exactly," Rachel Diaz says. "The obstruction of justice charge covers destroying evidence, bribing officials, and silencing whistleblowers. Your mother is Exhibit A for that charge. Linda Walters: a nurse who witnessed a murder, reported it faithfully for thirteen years, and was systematically destroyed until she took her own life."

"Good. Make sure everyone knows what they did to her."

December 1, 2024 FBI Command Center

The investigation accelerates.

Over two weeks, the FBI team:

Week 1 (November 25 - December 1):

- Interviews twelve former Willowbrook employees
- Obtains exhumation orders for ten victims
- Traces $40 million in payments from Nexus Pharmaceuticals
- Confirms Owen's financial documentation is accurate
- Identifies three former FDA officials who accepted bribes

Week 2 (December 2 - December 8):

- Exhumes bodies of Sophie Brennan and nine other victims
- Forensic analysis confirms NX-447 residue in tissue samples
- Matches drug signatures to Nexus Pharmaceuticals manufacturing
- Identifies seventeen emails between executives using code phrases like "appropriate measures" and "accelerated protocols"
- Confirms deaths followed pattern: patient questions trials → marked as "problem" → receives lethal dose →

death staged as suicide

I'm in the command center almost every day, working with the team.

Agent Chen has me review witness statements, checking them against Sophie's journal entries. Everything Sophie wrote is corroborated by other evidence.

Sophie wrote (May 3, 1987): *"David Mitchell died last night. They said it was a seizure. But I saw him yesterday, he was fine until they gave him the new medication."*

Medical Examiner Report (May 2, 1987): David Mitchell, age 16. Cause of death: Seizure. Signed by Dr. Robert Delacroix.

Forensic Analysis (November 2024): David Mitchell's exhumed remains show toxic levels of NX-447. Death was cardiac arrest induced by drug overdose, not seizure.

Sophie wrote (June 8, 1987): *"I'm counting. Seven patients have died since I arrived in April."*

FBI Verification (December 2024): Seven death certificates from Willowbrook between April-June 1987. All signed by Robert Delacroix. All ruled suicide or natural causes. All victims were enrolled in trials for NX-447.

On and on. Every entry in Sophie's journal is verified.

December 8, 2024, 2:00 PM FBI Conference Room

Agent Chen calls a meeting. The entire task force gathers.

"Update," she says. "We've confirmed forty-two of seventy-three victim deaths. Medical examiner is still working on the remaining thirty-one, some bodies are too degraded for definitive testing. But we have enough."

She projects a timeline on the screen:

1985-1987: Initial trials at Willowbrook and three other facilities. Twenty-three patients die. Deaths ruled natural causes or suicide.

1987-1989: Trials expand. Sophie Brennan documents deaths in her journal. Thirty-eight patients die. Sophie is murdered October 1987. Linda Walters attempts to report it, blocked at every turn.

1990-1995: Final phase of trials. Twelve patients die. Margaret Moore keeps Sophie's journal hidden but stops actively investigating after being threatened.

1995: NX-447 fails FDA approval. Nexus Pharmaceuticals abandons the drug. Seventy-three patients dead. No consequences.

1996-2017: Executives continue careers. Company renamed GenHealth. Profits soar.

2017-2018: Owen Brennan kills four people directly involved in Sophie's murder.

2018-2019: Owen arrested, tried, sentenced to 20 years. Begins cooperating with FBI.

2024: Margaret Moore gives journal to Jenna Walters. FBI has physical evidence to prosecute.

Rachel Diaz stands. "We're ready to seek arrest warrants. We have physical evidence, financial records, witness testimony, forensic analysis. This is a prosecutable case."

"How long until arrests?" I ask.

"Two weeks. We need to coordinate with U.S. Marshals for simultaneous arrests in six states. Can't risk anyone fleeing."

Agent Chen adds, "We're also moving on three corrupt FDA officials, Dr. Harold Kemp, Dr. Susan Martinez, and Dr. Robert Wallace. They accepted bribes from Nexus to fast-track NX-447 through approval process. They'll be charged separately but arrested simultaneously."

"So, nine arrests total?"

"Nine arrests. Six pharmaceutical executives for conspiracy to commit murder. Three FDA officials for bribery and corruption. The largest pharmaceutical prosecution in decades."

Daniel Brooks, the forensic accountant, projects financial data on the screen.

"We've traced forty million dollars in payments from Nexus Pharmaceuticals between 1985 and 1995. Recipients include:

- Medical examiners: $2.3 million
- Hospital administrators: $8.7 million
- FDA officials: $5.2 million
- Police investigators: $1.8 million
- State regulators: $3.4 million
- Journalists: $900,000
- Attorneys: $2.1 million
- Miscellaneous: $15.6 million

This wasn't just covering up murders. This was buying an entire system."

I stare at the numbers. "They spent forty million dollars to protect a drug that killed seventy-three people?"

"Actually," Daniel says, "NX-447 eventually became the basis for GenZanax, which GenHealth currently sells for three billion dollars annually. So, from their perspective, forty million in bribes to cover up seventy-three deaths was a sound investment."

The room goes silent.

"They murdered children to develop a blockbuster drug," I say.

"Yes," Rachel confirms. "And they made billions from it. That's why the wire fraud charge is so important. They used illegal means to develop and profit from a pharmaceutical product. Every dollar earned from GenZanax is tainted by the murders that made it possible."

Agent Chen looks at the timeline. "We arrest December 22nd. Six AM. Coordinated raids in six locations. Full FBI SWAT teams. We can't risk anything going wrong."

"What about Owen?" I ask. "Does he know?"

"We'll notify him the day before. He's been waiting for this since 2018. He deserves to know it's finally happening."

December 15, 2024, 10:00 AM Video Conference with Owen Brennan

The FBI arranges a video call between the task force and Owen at FCI Devens.

Owen appears on the screen, wearing prison orange, sitting in a small conference room with a guard standing behind him.

"Owen," Agent Chen says, "we're making arrests on December 22nd. All six executives. Three FDA officials. We have everything we need."

Owen closes his eyes. When he opens them, tears are streaming down his face.

"Thank you," he whispers. "Thank you. It's been thirty-seven years since Sophie died. Six years since I confessed to murdering four people hoping someone would finally investigate. And now it's finally happening."

Rachel Diaz speaks. "Owen, we need you to testify at

trial. You'll be transported from prison under maximum security. You'll testify about your three decades of investigation. About the documentation you collected. About why you killed those four people."

"The defense will attack my credibility," Owen says. "I'm a convicted murderer. They'll say I'm lying to reduce my sentence."

"Your sentence is already set," Rachel replies. "Twenty years, eligible for parole in 2044. You're not getting a reduction. You're testifying because it's the right thing to do. Because Sophie deserves justice."

"I'll testify. I'll do whatever you need."

Agent Chen leans forward. "Owen, there's something else. Jenna Walters is here. Linda's daughter. She wants to say something to you."

The camera pans to include me.

Owen looks at me through the screen. "Jenna."

"Owen, I just want you to know, my mother tried to save Sophie. For thirteen years, she fought. And they destroyed her for it. But we're going to make sure everyone knows. We're going to vindicate Linda and Sophie together."

Owen nods, unable to speak.

I continue. "My mother died thinking she failed. Thinking nobody believed her. But she was right. About everything. And when this goes to trial, the whole world will know it."

"Thank you," Owen manages. "Thank you for finishing what Linda started."

The call ends.

Agent Chen turns to me. "December 22nd. Six AM. Six simultaneous arrests. And then this becomes public. Media will explode. This will be the biggest pharmaceutical scandal in history."

"Good," I say. "Sophie deserves that. My mother deserves that. All seventy-three victims deserve that."

December 15, 2024, 6:00 PM Jenna's Apartment

I'm reviewing trial preparation documents when my phone rings. Unknown number.

"Hello?"

"Ms. Walters, this is Victoria Lang. I'm an investigative journalist with the Boston Globe. I've been following the GenHealth investigation. I understand you're involved. I'd like to talk."

I hesitate. "How did you get my number?"

"Public records. You're listed as a cooperating witness in federal case 2024-FBI-47392. The case is sealed, but your name is in the court filings. I'm hoping you'll talk to me about your mother."

"My mother?"

"Linda Walters. The nurse who tried to expose Willowbrook in 1987. I've been researching pharmaceutical whistleblowers for ten years. Your mother's story is extraordinary. And I think the world needs to hear it."

"The case hasn't gone public yet. I can't comment."

"I understand. But when it does go public, and it will, very soon, I want to write about Linda. Not just as a footnote in Sophie Brennan's story, but as a hero in her own right. A whistleblower who spent thirteen years fighting corruption while being called crazy. Can I interview you when the time comes?"

I think about my mother. About thirteen years of being dismissed, destroyed, erased.

"Yes," I say. "When this goes public, I'll talk to you. I want people to know what my mother did. I want them to know she was right."

"Thank you. I'll wait for your call."

After she hangs up, I look at my mother's photo on the dresser.

"Seven more days, Mom," I whisper. "Seven more days until those six men are arrested. Seven more days until everyone knows you were telling the truth."

December 21, 2024, 11:00 PM Jenna's Apartment

I can't sleep.

Tomorrow morning, six pharmaceutical executives will be arrested for murdering seventy-three people.

Tomorrow morning, the world will learn about Sophie Brennan, the sixteen-year-old who documented pharmaceutical murder before they killed her.

Tomorrow morning, my mother's name will be cleared.

I think about the chain of events that led here:

Sophie documented illegal drug trials in her journal, knowing it would get her killed.

Margaret kept that journal safe for thirty-seven years, too afraid to come forward.

Linda witnessed Sophie's murder aftermath and spent thirteen years trying to report it.

Owen investigated for three decades and killed four people in desperation.

I found Margaret's note and brought the journal to the FBI.

Five people. Five brave choices across four decades.

And tomorrow, justice begins.

Not perfect justice, Sophie is still dead. Linda is still dead.

Owen is still in prison for twenty years.

But justice nonetheless.

I set my alarm for 5:00 AM. I want to be at the FBI command center when the arrests happen.

Tomorrow, everything changes.

CHAPTER 5

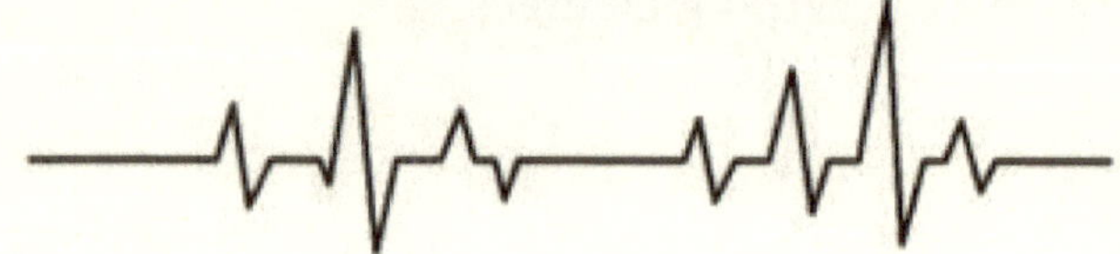

JENNA - The Arrests (December 22, 2024)

December 22, 2024, 5:45 AM FBI Field Office, Boston - Command Center

The command center is packed with agents, all wearing tactical gear and body armor.

I stand in the back with Rachel Diaz, watching six large monitors, one for each arrest location:

Monitor 1: Boston, Massachusetts - James Morrison's penthouse

Monitor 2: Greenwich, Connecticut - Martin Shaw's estate

Monitor 3: New York City - Robert Chen's apartment

Monitor 4: Arlington, Virginia - David Patterson's townhouse

Monitor 5: Louisville, Kentucky - Michael Williams's home

Monitor 6: San Francisco, California - Thomas Foster's mansion

Each monitor shows a live feed from body cameras worn by FBI SWAT team leaders.

Agent Chen stands at the center console, coordinating with all six teams via radio.

"All teams, this is Command. Status check."

Six voices respond in sequence:

"Team One, Boston, in position."

"Team Two, Greenwich, in position."

"Team Three, New York, in position."

"Team Four, Virginia, in position."

"Team Five, Kentucky, in position."

"Team Six, San Francisco, in position."

Agent Chen checks her watch. "Five minutes. Stand by for go signal."

Rachel leans close to me. "This is it. Thirty-seven years after Sophie's murder. Six years after Owen's arrest. One month after you found the journal. This is the moment everything changes."

My heart is hammering. "What happens after they're arrested?"

"Transport to federal detention. Arraignment within 48 hours. Bail hearing. Then we prepare for trial."

"Will they get bail?"

"We'll argue against it, flight risk, danger to witnesses. But they're elderly, wealthy, respected. A judge might grant it. We'll see."

Agent Chen's voice cuts through: "All teams, this is Command. You are go. Execute arrests now."

6:00 AM - Simultaneous Arrests

Monitor 1 - Boston:

The screen shows FBI agents approaching James Morrison's penthouse building. The doorman protests. Agents show a warrant. They enter the building.

Elevator ride to the 23rd floor. Agents stack up outside apartment 2301.

"FBI! Open the door!"

No response.

"Battering ram."

The door crashes open. Agents flood inside, weapons drawn.

"FBI! James Morrison, show yourself!"

A voice from deeper in the apartment: "I'm in the bedroom! I'm not armed!"

Agents move through a luxurious living room, modern art on the walls, floor-to-ceiling windows overlooking Boston Harbor. They reach the bedroom.

James Morrison stands beside his bed wearing pajamas, hands raised. Age 73, gray hair, looking more confused than frightened.

"James Morrison, you're under arrest for conspiracy to commit murder, wire fraud, and obstruction of justice." An agent cuffs him. "You have the right to remain silent..."

Morrison's voice is steady. "I want my attorney."

"You'll get your phone call at the detention center."

They lead him out in handcuffs.

Monitor 2 - Greenwich, Connecticut:

Martin Shaw's estate is massive, gates, security cameras, manicured grounds.

FBI vehicles surround the property. Agents breach the gate.

Shaw emerges from the house already dressed, apparently he saw them coming on his security system. Age 76, tall, distinguished, a lawyer who knows exactly how this works.

"I assume you have a warrant?"

An agent hands it to him. Shaw reads it carefully.

"This is outrageous. These charges are baseless. I'll be released within hours."

"You can discuss that with the judge. Turn around, please."

Shaw complies. They cuff him and lead him to a waiting vehicle.

Monitor 3 - New York City:

Robert Chen's apartment building in Manhattan. FBI SWAT teams enter the lobby.

They take the elevator to the 18th floor. Chen's door is already open, he's standing in the doorway waiting, also dressed, also clearly monitoring their approach.

Age 70, shorter than the others, calm and controlled.

"Robert Chen, FBI. You're under arrest..."

"I know why you're here. This is persecution based on lies from a convicted murderer. My attorneys will have this dismissed by tomorrow."

"That's between you and the judge. Hands behind your back."

Chen complies without resistance. They cuff him and escort him out.

Monitor 4 - Virginia:

David Patterson's townhouse in Arlington. FBI agents knock.

A woman answers, Patterson's wife, looking terrified. "What's happening?"

"We have an arrest warrant for David Patterson. Where is he?"

"He's, he's in his study. He has a heart condition. Please don't..."

"We'll be as gentle as possible, ma'am. Please step aside."

Agents enter the townhouse. Patterson is in his study, age 74, visibly frail, oxygen tank beside his desk.

"Mr. Patterson, you're under arrest for conspiracy to commit murder..."

"I know." His voice is weak. "I've been expecting this since Owen Brennan was arrested six years ago. I knew he'd talk. I knew you'd come eventually."

"Sir, can you stand?"

Patterson struggles to his feet, leaning heavily on his desk. An agent steadies him.

"Do you need medical attention?"

"No. Just... please don't put the cuffs too tight. My circulation..."

They cuff him carefully and help him walk out. His wife is crying in the hallway.

Monitor 5 - Kentucky:

Michael Williams's home in Louisville. A large suburban house, Christmas decorations still up.

FBI agents' approach. Williams opens the door before they can knock.

Age 72, wearing a bathrobe, looking resigned.

"You're here about Willowbrook."

"Michael Williams, you're under arrest for conspiracy to commit murder, bribery, and obstruction of justice..."

"I'm not resisting. I'd like to speak with my attorney as soon as possible."

They cuff him. A woman appears behind him, presumably his wife. "Michael, what's happening?"

"Call Gerald Hutchins. Tell him they finally came. He'll know what to do."

They escort Williams to a waiting vehicle.

Monitor 6 - San Francisco:

Thomas Foster's mansion overlooks the Bay. FBI vehicles surround the property.

Agents approach the front door. Before they can knock, Foster opens it.

Age 75, immaculately dressed despite the early hour, as if he'd been preparing for this moment.

"You have a warrant, I presume?"

"Thomas Foster, FBI. You're under arrest..."

"Spare me the speech. I know my rights. I'm invoking my Fifth Amendment right to remain silent and requesting my attorney. Now, if you'll excuse me, I need to inform my wife that I'll be detained for a few hours until this absurdity is resolved."

"Sir, you need to come with us now."

Foster sighs dramatically. "Very well. Though I assure you, your case will fall apart within days. A revenge killer's testimony? A teenage girl's diary? Please. My attorneys will destroy this."

They cuff him and lead him away.

6:15 AM - Command Center

All six monitors show the same image: handcuffed executives being loaded into FBI vehicles.

Agent Chen turns to the room. "All targets in custody. Transport to federal detention centers immediately. Well done, everyone."

Cheers erupt in the command center. Agents shake hands, high-five, embrace.

Rachel Diaz grabs my arm. "They're arrested. All six. This is really happening."

I can barely speak. "Thirty-seven years. Sophie has been dead for thirty-seven years. And they're finally being held accountable."

"Not just held accountable," Rachel corrects. "They're going to be prosecuted. And if we do our jobs right, they'll spend the rest of their lives in prison."

Agent Chen approaches us. "Jenna, I need to tell you something. We arrested three FDA officials simultaneously, Dr.

Harold Kemp in North Carolina, Dr. Susan Martinez in Florida, Dr. Robert Wallace in New York. Nine arrests total. And in one hour, we're holding a press conference."

"A press conference?"

"This story goes public in sixty minutes. The media will explode. We need to control the narrative. Rachel will speak, I'll speak, and we need you to speak."

"Me?"

"You're Linda Walters's daughter. You found Sophie's journal. You're the reason this case exists. The public needs to hear from you."

My stomach drops. "I don't know what to say."

"Say what's true," Rachel advises. "Say your mother tried to expose this conspiracy thirty-seven years ago. Say she was destroyed for telling the truth. Say you're grateful justice is finally being served. That's it. Simple, honest, powerful."

December 22, 2024, 7:00 AM FBI Field Office - Press Conference Room

The room is packed with reporters, cameras, microphones.

Rachel Diaz stands at the podium with the FBI seal behind her. Agent Chen and I stand to the side.

Rachel begins:

"Good morning. I'm Rachel Diaz, Assistant U.S. Attorney for the District of Massachusetts. At 6:00 AM this morning, the FBI arrested six former executives of Nexus Pharmaceuticals, now known as GenHealth Corporation, on charges of conspiracy to commit murder, wire fraud, and obstruction of justice."

The room erupts with questions. Rachel holds up a hand.

"Please hold questions until I've finished. The six defendants are: **James Morrison, age 73. Martin Shaw, age 76. Robert Chen, age 70. David Patterson, age 74. Michael Williams, age 72. Thomas Foster, age 75.**"

She pauses, letting the names sink in.

"These six men are charged with conspiring to conduct illegal drug trials at Willowbrook Psychiatric Hospital and four other facilities between 1985 and 1995. These trials resulted in the deaths of seventy-three psychiatric patients, most of them teenagers. The patients were not informed they were being experimented on. They did not consent. And when they died, officials covered up the deaths as suicides or natural causes."

Rachel projects a photo on the screen behind her, **Sophie's class photo from April 1987.**

"This is a photograph of twenty-three patients at Willowbrook Psychiatric Hospital in April 1987. By October 1987, seventeen of them were dead. All seventeen deaths were ruled suicide or natural causes. All seventeen were actually murders, killed by experimental drugs administered without consent."

The room is silent now, reporters staring at the photo.

Rachel continues: "One of those patients was **Sophie Marie Brennan, age sixteen.** Sophie kept a journal documenting the illegal drug trials. She recorded patient deaths. She overheard conversations between doctors and pharmaceutical executives. She predicted her own murder twelve days before it happened."

Another photo appears: **Sophie's journal, opened to her final entry.**

Rachel reads: "*My name is Sophie Marie Brennan. I'm sixteen years old. I didn't kill myself. Whatever they say, whatever report they write, I didn't give up. They murdered me. If anyone is reading this: Please investigate. Please don't let them get away with this. Please give me justice.*"

Several reporters are wiping their eyes.

"Sophie was murdered on October 22, 1987. Her death was staged as suicide. The medical examiner, who was later found to have received fifty thousand dollars from Nexus Pharmaceuticals, closed the case immediately."

Rachel projects another image: **Linda Walters, 1987.**

"This is **Linda Walters.** She was a registered nurse at Willowbrook. On October 23, 1987, Linda discovered Sophie's body and witnessed staff members staging the scene. She filed a police report within hours. She reported what she'd seen to every authority she could contact. She spent thirteen years trying to expose the conspiracy."

Rachel's voice hardens. "Instead of being believed, Linda Walters was destroyed. She lost her nursing license in 1989. She lost custody of her daughter in 1998. She was labeled mentally ill and delusional. In 2011, at age forty-nine, Linda died by suicide, believing no one would ever believe her. But she was right about everything."

The image changes to show **Owen Brennan being led into court in 2018.**

"This is **Owen Brennan,** Sophie's younger brother. Owen spent thirty years investigating his sister's murder. He collected financial records, witness statements, corporate emails, everything proving the conspiracy. But when the legal system failed to prosecute, Owen took matters into his own hands. Between 2017 and 2018, he killed four people directly responsible for Sophie's death. Owen is currently serving twenty years in federal prison for those murders. He has been cooperating with the FBI since his arrest in 2018."

Rachel looks directly at the cameras. "One month ago, a dying nurse named **Margaret Moore** gave Sophie's journal to a young nurse named Jenna Walters, Linda's daughter. That journal is the physical evidence we've been seeking for six years. It corroborates Owen's testimony. It proves the conspiracy. And it's why we were able to make arrests this morning."

She steps back from the podium. "I'll now take questions."

Reporters shout over each other:

"Will the defendants get bail?"

"When is the trial?"

"What about GenHealth Corporation?"

"Are there more victims?"

"What's the penalty if they're convicted?"

Rachel answers methodically:

"Bail hearings are scheduled for December 24th. We will argue against bail, these defendants have extensive resources and could flee. Trial is tentatively scheduled for March 2025. GenHealth Corporation is not being charged criminally, but civil lawsuits are expected. We've confirmed seventy-three victims, but there may be more. If convicted, each defendant faces life imprisonment."

A reporter asks: "Is Owen Brennan getting a reduced sentence for cooperating?"

"No. Owen's sentence is already set, twenty years minimum, eligible for parole in 2044. He's not receiving any reduction. He's cooperating because it's the right thing to do."

"What about Linda Walters? Is she being vindicated?"

Rachel gestures to me. "Linda's daughter is here. Jenna Walters found Sophie's journal and brought it to the FBI. I'll let her speak to that."

I step to the microphone, my heart pounding.

"My name is Jenna Walters. Linda Walters was my mother. I grew up believing she was mentally ill. Everyone told me she had paranoid delusions, that she made up conspiracy theories, that her stories about murdered patients weren't real."

My voice shakes. "But she was telling the truth. My mother witnessed Sophie Brennan's murder being covered up. She reported it immediately. She filed police reports for thirteen years. She contacted every agency, every official, every person who might listen. And instead of being believed, she was destroyed."

I look directly at the cameras. "They took her nursing license. They labeled her crazy. They took me away from her. They gaslit her until she couldn't fight anymore. In 2011, my mother killed herself, believing she'd failed, believing no one would ever believe her."

Tears stream down my face, but I don't stop. "But she didn't fail. She was right. Sophie was murdered. Patients were experimented on. Officials were bribed. My mother was a **whistleblower** who tried to save lives. And I'm grateful that today, thirteen years after her death, thirty-seven years after Sophie's murder, justice is finally being served."

The room erupts with questions, but Agent Chen steps forward. "That concludes our press conference. Written statements will be available shortly. Thank you."

December 22, 2024, 9:00 AM FBI Conference Room

The press conference is over, but the media firestorm is just beginning.

Rachel, Agent Chen, and I watch news coverage on multiple screens:

CNN: "BREAKING: Six Pharmaceutical Executives Arrested in 37-Year Murder Conspiracy"

MSNBC: "Sophie Brennan: The Teenage Whistleblower Who Documented Her Own Murder"

Fox News: "GenHealth Executives Face Life in Prison for Illegal Drug Trials"

The New York Times: (breaking news alert) "FBI Arrests Six in Pharmaceutical Conspiracy That Killed 73 Patients"

Every network is running the story. Every channel shows the same images:

- Sophie's class photo with seventeen faces marked
- Sophie's journal entry predicting her murder
- Linda Walters's 1987 photo
- The six executives in handcuffs
- Owen Brennan's 2018 mugshot

My phone explodes with notifications, texts, calls, emails. I silence it.

Agent Chen mutes the televisions. "This is going to dominate news cycles for weeks. The public is outraged. Social media is exploding. #JusticeForSophie is already trending. Your mother's name is everywhere, Jenna. People are calling her a hero."

I can barely process this. This morning, my mother was an obscure mentally ill woman who died by suicide in 2011. Now she's a national hero who tried to expose pharmaceutical murder.

Rachel's phone rings. She answers, listens, then hangs up looking grim.

"All six defendants have posted bail."

"What?" I'm stunned. "Already?"

"Their attorneys moved fast. Bail was set at ten million dollars each. They posted it within two hours. Electronic ankle monitors, travel restrictions, but they're out."

"They're free?"

"For now. Arraignment is tomorrow. Then trial prep begins. But yes, they're free until trial."

Rage floods through me. "They murdered seventy-three people and they get to go home?"

"They're wealthy, elderly, no prior records, and not considered violent threats," Rachel explains. "Judges grant bail in these situations. But they won't stay free. Once we convict them, and we will, they'll spend the rest of their lives in prison."

Agent Chen adds, "And they're being monitored 24/7. Any attempt to flee, any contact with witnesses, any tampering with evidence, they'll be back in custody immediately."

My phone rings. Victoria Lang, the journalist from the Boston Globe.

I step into the hallway to answer. "Hello?"

"Jenna, it's Victoria. I'm watching the press conference. Your statement about your mother was powerful. I'd like to write a comprehensive piece about Linda, her life, her whistleblowing, her destruction. Will you talk to me?"

"Yes. I want people to know what she did."

"Good. Let's meet tomorrow. I want to tell Linda's story properly."

After I hang up, I stand in the hallway, processing everything.

This morning, six men were arrested.

This morning, my mother's name was vindicated.

This morning, Sophie's story went public.

But the six men are already out on bail.

The trial is months away.

Justice is slow.

But it's happening.

For the first time in thirty-seven years, justice is actually happening.

December 22, 2024, 6:00 PM Jenna's Apartment

I finally make it home, exhausted.

My phone has 247 unread messages. My email inbox is flooded. My social media has thousands of notifications.

Everyone wants to talk to me. News programs, podcasts, documentaries, book publishers, victims' families.

I silence everything and sit on my couch, staring at my mother's photo.

"They were arrested today, Mom," I tell her. "All six men who covered up Sophie's murder. All six men who destroyed you. They're facing charges. They're going to trial. Justice is coming."

I think about what Victoria said: *Your mother's story needs to be told properly.*

My mother spent thirteen years being dismissed as crazy. Thirteen years fighting alone. Thirteen years watching her life fall apart because she told the truth.

And now, thirteen years after her death, everyone knows she was right.

I pull out my laptop and start writing. Not for the media. Not for the public. For me.

A letter to my mother:

Dear Mom,

I'm sorry I didn't believe you. I'm sorry I thought you were mentally ill. I'm sorry I didn't understand that you were fighting for something important.

You tried to save Sophie Brennan. You witnessed her murder being covered up and you spent thirteen years trying to expose it. Everyone told you that you were wrong, that you were delusional, that you were crazy. But you weren't. You were right about everything.

They destroyed you for telling the truth. They took your license. They took me. They gaslit you until you couldn't take it anymore. And I hate them for it. I hate the six men who murdered Sophie and then destroyed you to cover it up.

But Mom, you won. You were right. Sophie was murdered. Patients were experimented on. Officials were bribed. And today, thirteen years after you died, six pharmaceutical executives were arrested for conspiracy to commit murder.

You didn't fail. You were the first whistleblower. The first person who tried to stop them. And even though it cost you everything, you planted seeds that eventually grew into justice.

Sophie got justice today because of you.

Seventy-three victims got justice today because of you.

And you're being recognized as a hero.

I'm going to make sure everyone knows your story. I'm going to make sure you're remembered properly, not as a mentally ill woman who killed herself, but as a brave nurse who tried to save lives and was destroyed by corruption.

I love you, Mom. I'm sorry I didn't believe you when you were alive. But I believe you now. And I'm going to finish what you started.

—Jenna

I save the letter to my desktop. I'll probably never send it anywhere. But writing it helps.

Tomorrow, I meet with Victoria Lang to talk about my mother's story.

Next week, the arraignment. The six executives will plead not guilty. Then we prepare for trial.

The fight isn't over. It's just beginning.

But today, for the first time in thirty-seven years, justice moved forward.

And my mother's name was cleared.

That's enough for today.

CHAPTER 6

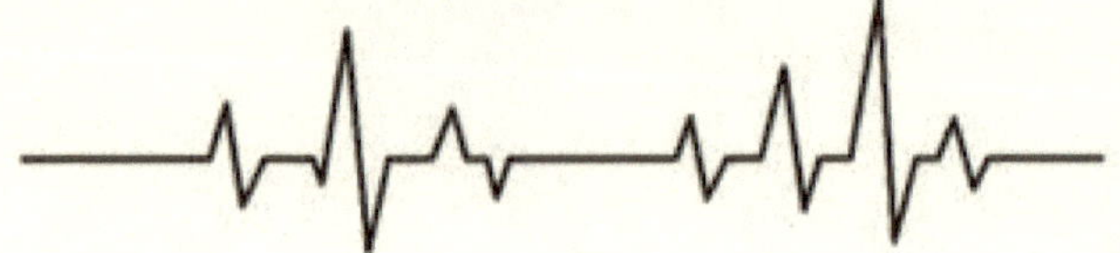

JENNA - Arraignment (December 23-24, 2024)

December 23, 2024, 9:00 AM Federal Courthouse, Boston

The courthouse is surrounded by media trucks, cameras, protesters.

Signs wave in the cold December air:

"JUSTICE FOR SOPHIE"

"73 VICTIMS - ZERO EXCUSES"

"PHARMACEUTICAL MURDER = LIFE IN PRISON"

"LINDA WALTERS WAS RIGHT"

I push through the crowd with Agent Chen and Rachel Diaz. Security is intense, metal detectors, bag searches, K-9 units. The courthouse has received threats overnight from people outraged that the executives posted bail.

Inside, the courtroom is packed. Victims' families fill the gallery. I recognize several faces from photos in the FBI files, parents who lost children at Willowbrook, siblings who spent decades seeking answers.

At the front: six defense tables, each with a team of attorneys.

And at each table: one of the six executives.

James Morrison sits with three lawyers, wearing an expensive suit, looking calm and composed.

Martin Shaw leans back in his chair, arms crossed, the posture of a man who's been in courtrooms before and isn't worried.

Robert Chen whispers with his attorneys, occasionally glancing at the gallery where victims' families sit.

David Patterson looks frail, oxygen tank beside his chair, but his eyes are sharp and alert.

Michael Williams stares straight ahead, expressionless.

Thomas Foster examines his fingernails, projecting boredom.

These are the men who murdered Sophie. Who destroyed my mother. Who killed seventy-three people to test a drug.

And they're sitting here free on bail, surrounded by lawyers who cost thousands of dollars per hour.

The bailiff calls: "All rise. The Honorable Judge Harold Martinez presiding."

Judge Martinez enters, mid-sixties, stern-faced, no-nonsense demeanor. He's known for tough sentences and zero tolerance for corporate crime.

"Be seated. We're here for arraignment in United States v. Morrison, et al. Case number 2024-CR-47392. Will the defendants please rise?"

All six men stand.

Judge Martinez looks at them with obvious disdain. "You're charged with conspiracy to commit murder, seventy-three counts. Wire fraud. Obstruction of justice. How do you plead?"

Gerald Hutchins, Morrison's lead attorney, speaks first. "Your Honor, my client James Morrison pleads not guilty to all charges. These accusations are based on the unreliable testimony of a convicted murderer and a teenage girl's diary written nearly forty years ago. We move to dismiss..."

Judge Martinez cuts him off. "Save it for trial, counselor. Mr. Morrison's plea is not guilty. Next."

One by one, each defendant pleads not guilty.

Shaw: "Not guilty, Your Honor. These charges are politically motivated..."

Judge Martinez: "Not guilty. Next."

Chen: "Not guilty. This prosecution is based on lies..."

Judge Martinez: "Not guilty. Next."

Patterson: "Not guilty, Your Honor."

Judge Martinez: "Not guilty. Next."

Williams: "Not guilty. I'm a victim of character assassination..."

Judge Martinez: "Not guilty. Next."

Foster: "Not guilty. This is a witch hunt against successful businessmen..."

Judge Martinez: "Not guilty. Sit down."

The judge reviews documents. "Bail has been posted at ten million dollars per defendant. Electronic monitoring is in effect. Travel restrictions apply, defendants may not leave their respective states without court approval. Any violation results in immediate remand to custody. Understood?"

All six attorneys nod.

Judge Martinez continues: "Pre-trial motions due by January 15, 2025. Trial date is set for March 17, 2025. This court expects both sides to be ready. Any delays will be viewed unfavorably."

Rachel Diaz stands. "Your Honor, the government requests that bail be revoked. These defendants have extensive financial resources and international connections. They're flight risks..."

Hutchins jumps up. "Objection! My client has lived in Boston for fifty years. He has no criminal record. He posted ten million dollars bail. He's not going anywhere..."

Judge Martinez holds up a hand. "Counselor, I've reviewed the bail assessment. While I share the government's concerns, the defendants have no prior criminal history and have complied with all bail conditions thus far. Bail remains in effect. However..." he looks directly at the six executives "...I'm warning you. Any attempt to contact witnesses, any attempt to tamper with evidence, any violation of travel restrictions, and you'll be in custody so fast your heads will spin. Clear?"

The six men nod.

"Adjourned. Trial begins March 17th."

The gavel bangs.

December 23, 2024, 11:00 AM Outside Federal Courthouse

The six executives emerge surrounded by attorneys and private security.

Media swarms them.

"Mr. Morrison, did you murder seventy-three patients?"

"Mr. Shaw, how do you respond to Linda Walters's police reports?"

"Mr. Chen, are you ashamed?"

Gerald Hutchins steps to the microphones, his clients standing behind him.

"My clients are innocent. They're respected businessmen who dedicated their careers to developing life-saving medications. These charges are based on the testimony of Owen Brennan, a confessed murderer who killed four people, and a teenager's diary that's nearly forty years old. This is not evidence. This is a witch hunt."

He gestures to the executives. "James Morrison pioneered pharmaceutical research that's saved millions of lives. Martin Shaw drafted regulations that improved patient safety. These are heroes being persecuted by overzealous prosecutors seeking headlines."

A reporter shouts: "What about the seventy-three dead patients?"

Hutchins doesn't miss a beat. "Tragic deaths during legitimate medical research. Not murders. The FDA approved these trials. The hospitals consented. The medical examiners ruled them accidental. Thirty-seven years later, prosecutors are second-guessing medical professionals based on conspiracy theories."

Rachel Diaz steps forward, flanked by Agent Chen and me.

"Those aren't conspiracy theories," Rachel says sharply. "They're documented facts. Sophie Brennan's journal describes pharmaceutical executives ordering increased dosages even after patients started dying. Financial records show forty million dollars in bribes. Forensic analysis confirms patients were killed by experimental drugs. This isn't second-guessing, this is prosecuting murder."

Hutchins smirks. "We'll see what a jury thinks. These charges won't survive trial. My clients will be exonerated."

The executives are escorted to waiting vehicles and driven away.

I watch them leave, fury rising in my chest.

They murdered Sophie. They destroyed my mother. And they're acting like victims.

Agent Chen puts a hand on my shoulder. "Don't let them get to you. That's all performance for the media. When we get to trial, the evidence will speak for itself."

"What if the jury believes them? What if they get acquitted?"

"They won't. We have Sophie's journal. We have forensic evidence. We have financial records. We have forty-two confirmed murders. They can hire all the expensive lawyers they want, they're still going to prison."

Rachel adds, "Hutchins is doing his job, planting doubt, creating a narrative. But our case is solid. Trust the evidence."

December 23, 2024, 2:00 PM Coffee Shop, Boston

I meet Victoria Lang at a quiet café near my apartment.

Victoria is in her late forties, sharp-eyed, carrying a worn leather notebook and a voice recorder. She's written extensively about pharmaceutical corruption, I googled her last night and found dozens of investigative pieces exposing medical fraud.

"Thank you for meeting me," she says as we sit. "I know this is overwhelming."

"It is. But I want people to know my mother's story."

Victoria sets up her recorder. "Let's start with Linda. What was she like before Willowbrook?"

I think back to fragmented childhood memories. "Caring. Dedicated. She loved being a nurse. I remember her coming home from shifts and telling me about patients she'd helped. She was proud of her work."

"When did that change?"

"After October 1987. I was born in 1991, so I don't remember the first few years. But my earliest memories are of my mother being... consumed. Obsessed with something she called 'the Willowbrook murders.' She would stay up all night writing letters, making phone calls, reviewing documents. Our apartment was covered in files."

"Did she talk to you about it?"

"She tried. But I was a child. I didn't understand. She'd

say things like 'They murdered Sophie' and 'The pharmaceutical companies are covering it up' and 'Nobody believes me.' I thought she was paranoid."

Victoria makes notes. "When did social services get involved?"

"1998. I was seven. Someone, we don't know who, called child protective services and said my mother was unstable. They investigated. They saw our apartment covered in conspiracy documents. They saw my mother obsessing over deaths from a decade earlier. They ruled she was mentally ill and took me away."

"How did Linda react?"

"She fought. For months. She hired a lawyer, or tried to, but no one would take her case. She filed appeals. She attended hearings. But the system had already decided she was delusional. By 1999, she'd lost all custody rights. I was placed in permanent foster care."

"Did you see her after that?"

My voice breaks. "A few times. Supervised visits. But she was heavily medicated by then, antipsychotics, mood stabilizers. She could barely function. The last time I saw her was 2009. She was in a group home. She didn't really recognize me."

"What happened in 2011?"

"She died by suicide. Overdose of medications. The

official report said she'd been suffering from paranoid personality disorder for decades and finally gave up fighting it."

Victoria looks up from her notes. "But that wasn't true."

"No. She wasn't paranoid. She witnessed Sophie Brennan's murder being covered up. She tried to report it for thirteen years. And instead of being believed, she was gaslit until she couldn't take it anymore."

"Tell me about finding Sophie's journal."

I walk Victoria through everything, Margaret's death, the note, the storage unit, Sophie's documentation, the FBI investigation.

"Margaret Moore waited thirty-seven years to come forward," Victoria says. "Why do you think she gave the journal to you specifically?"

"Because I'm Linda's daughter. Because I grew up thinking my mother was crazy. Margaret knew if anyone would fight to clear Linda's name, it would be me."

Victoria leans back, studying me. "You're doing more than clearing her name. You're vindicating her. Linda Walters was the first whistleblower in this case. She tried to expose the conspiracy when it was still happening. If anyone had believed her in 1987, sixty-two other patients wouldn't have died between 1987 and 1995."

The weight of that hits me. "You're saying my mother could have prevented more deaths?"

"I'm saying she tried. But the system failed her. Officials dismissed her reports. Medical examiners closed cases without investigating. Nursing boards revoked her license instead of listening to her concerns. The conspiracy succeeded because whistleblowers were destroyed."

Victoria flips to a new page in her notebook. "I want to write a comprehensive piece about Linda. Not just as a footnote to Sophie's story, but as a hero in her own right. A nurse who saw something wrong and spent thirteen years trying to fix it. A mother who sacrificed everything, career, daughter, life, because she couldn't stay silent about murder. Would you be comfortable with that?"

"Yes. That's exactly what I want. I want people to know my mother wasn't mentally ill. She was brave. She was right. And she deserves to be remembered that way."

"Good. Because when this trial happens, and it will, probably in March or April, Linda's story needs to be at the center. The prosecutors will focus on Sophie, which is appropriate. But journalists need to focus on Linda. On what happens to whistleblowers who threaten powerful corporations."

Victoria closes her notebook. "I'm going to spend the next few weeks researching Linda's life. I'll interview people who knew her. I'll review every document she filed. And when the trial starts, I'll publish a long-form piece in the Boston Globe Sunday Magazine. Ten thousand words. Photos. Timeline. Everything. Linda Walters will be recognized as the hero she was."

Relief washes over me. "Thank you."

"Don't thank me. This is my job, exposing pharmaceutical corruption and honoring whistleblowers. Your mother deserves recognition. I'm going to make sure she gets it."

December 24, 2024, 10:00 AM FBI Field Office - Trial Preparation Meeting

Rachel Diaz gathers the prosecution team.

"Trial starts March 17th. That's less than three months. We have a massive amount of work to do."

She projects a timeline on the screen:

January 2025:

- Finalize witness list
- Complete forensic analysis of remaining victims
- Respond to defense motions
- Prepare opening statement

February 2025:

- Mock trial / practice sessions
- Witness prep (Owen, Jenna, family members)
- Expert witness coordination

- Evidence presentation strategy

March 2025:

- Final pre-trial motions
- Jury selection (March 10-14)
- Trial begins March 17th

Rachel looks at me. "Jenna, you'll testify in week two. Your testimony establishes the obstruction of justice charge, that these defendants destroyed whistleblowers. We need you to walk the jury through your mother's attempts to report Sophie's murder and how she was systematically destroyed."

"I can do that."

"Good. We'll practice extensively. The defense will attack you, they'll try to argue Linda was mentally ill, that her reports were delusional. You need to stay calm and stick to facts."

Agent Chen adds, "Owen testifies in week three. We're arranging secure transport from FCI Devens to the courthouse. He'll be in full restraints, prison jumpsuit, cuffs, shackles. The jury will see that he's incarcerated and not benefiting from his testimony."

"What about the six executives?" I ask. "Will they testify?"

"Probably not," Rachel says. "Their attorneys will advise them to invoke Fifth Amendment rights and stay silent. But we don't need their testimony. We have Sophie's journal. We have financial records. We have forensic evidence. We have Owen's documentation. The evidence speaks for itself."

Daniel Brooks, the forensic accountant, speaks up. "I've finished tracing all forty million dollars in bribes. We can show exact payment amounts to specific individuals on specific dates. Including fifty thousand dollars to Robert Delacroix two weeks after he closed Sophie's case. The financial trail is airtight."

"Perfect," Rachel says. "The jury needs to see this wasn't just medical malpractice, it was organized conspiracy. Money changed hands. Officials were bought. Whistleblowers were destroyed. This was systematic."

She looks around the room. "We're prosecuting the largest pharmaceutical conspiracy in U.S. history. If we do this right, these six men will spend the rest of their lives in prison. And we'll send a message to every pharmaceutical executive in the country: You cannot murder patients for profit. Not anymore."

December 24, 2024, 4:00 PM Jenna's Apartment - Christmas Eve

I'm alone on Christmas Eve.

No family, my mother is dead, I never knew my father, and I aged out of foster care at eighteen with no connections to my foster families.

But I'm not lonely. I'm focused.

On my kitchen table: trial preparation materials. Witness statements to review. Medical records to memorize. Testimony to practice.

My phone rings. Unknown number.

"Hello?"

"Jenna Walters?" A woman's voice, elderly, shaking. "My name is Catherine Brennan. I'm Sophie's mother."

My breath catches. "Mrs. Brennan."

"I saw you on television. At the press conference. You spoke about your mother, about how she tried to save my daughter. I wanted to thank you."

"You don't need to thank me. I just found the journal…"

"You did more than that. You believed Margaret's note when you could have ignored it. You brought Sophie's journal to the FBI when you could have thrown it away. You're the reason those six men were arrested. You're the reason Sophie is finally getting justice."

Catherine's voice breaks. "I've spent thirty-seven years believing Sophie gave up. Believing she killed herself because I failed as a mother. But she didn't give up. She was murdered. And you proved it."

I wipe tears from my face. "Sophie was brave. She documented everything knowing they would kill her for it. She tried to save the other patients."

"I know. I read her journal, the FBI gave me a copy. Seeing her handwriting again after all these years..." Catherine can't continue for a moment. "She was sixteen. She should be fifty-three now. She should have had a life. A career. Maybe children of her own. They took all of that from her."

"And they'll pay for it. The trial starts in March. We're going to convict them."

"I hope so. I need to see them convicted. I need to hear a jury say they murdered my daughter. I've waited thirty-seven years for that."

"You'll get it. I promise."

After we hang up, I sit in silence.

Sophie's mother. My mother. Both destroyed by the same conspiracy. Both spent decades suffering because six men valued profits over lives.

But now, finally, those six men are facing consequences.

The trial is less than three months away.

Justice delayed for thirty-seven years.

But justice nonetheless.

December 24, 2024, 11:00 PM Jenna's Apartment

I can't sleep.

I keep thinking about tomorrow, Christmas Day. My first Christmas knowing the truth about my mother.

Last Christmas, I thought Linda was a mentally ill woman who died by suicide because she couldn't cope with her delusions.

This Christmas, I know she was a hero who witnessed a murder and spent thirteen years trying to expose a pharmaceutical conspiracy.

Last Christmas, I was ashamed of my mother's legacy.

This Christmas, I'm proud of her.

I pull out the letter I wrote to her two days ago and read it again:

You didn't fail. You were the first whistleblower. The first person who tried to stop them. And even though it cost you everything, you planted seeds that eventually grew into justice.

I add one more line:

Merry Christmas, Mom. This year, for the first time, I'm celebrating you properly. Not mourning your death, but honoring your courage. You were a hero. I'm sorry it took me thirty-three years to understand that.

I save the document and close my laptop.

Tomorrow is Christmas.

In three months, the trial begins.

And sometime next year, maybe April, maybe May, six pharmaceutical executives will be convicted of murdering seventy-three people.

Including Sophie Brennan.

Including, indirectly, my mother Linda Walters.

Justice is coming.

Slow. Imperfect. Incomplete.

But coming nonetheless.

CHAPTER 7

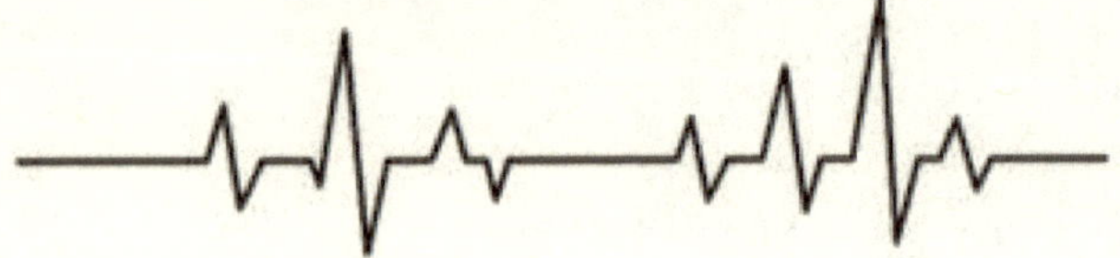

JENNA - Trial Preparation (January 2025)

January 6, 2025, 9:00 AM FBI Field Office, Boston - War Room

The task force has taken over an entire floor.

Three conference rooms converted to evidence staging areas. Twelve investigators working full-time. Walls covered with victim photos, timelines, financial charts.

Rachel Diaz calls an all-hands meeting.

"Trial is ten weeks away. We have seventy-three victims to present. We can't cover all of them, we'd need months, so we're focusing on twelve representative cases that span the entire conspiracy."

She projects twelve photos on the screen:

The Twelve Victims:

1. **Emily Rodriguez, age 16** - First victim (April 1987)
2. **Sophie Brennan, age 16** - Kept journal, documented conspiracy (October 1987)
3. **Michael Torres, age 17** - Death covered up as seizure (May 1987)
4. **Lisa Hartley, age 14** - Youngest victim (May 1987)
5. **David Mitchell, age 16** - Died after questioning medical staff (May 1987)
6. **Christopher Lee, age 17** - Family suspected murder but was ignored (June 1987)
7. **Sarah Kim, age 15** - Died during "phase two" expansion (August 1987)
8. **Jennifer Walsh, age 18** - Last Willowbrook victim (September 1991)
9. **Marcus Johnson, age 16** - Victim at second facility (March 1989)
10. **Rebecca Foster, age 17** - Victim at third facility (June 1990)
11. **Daniel Martinez, age 15** - Victim at fourth facility (November 1992)
12. **Ashley Thompson, age 16** - Final victim before trials ended (August 1995)

"Each case represents a phase of the conspiracy," Rachel explains. "Emily shows it started in 1987. Sophie documented it. The others show it continued across multiple facilities for eight years. Ashley proves it didn't stop until the drug failed FDA approval."

Agent Chen adds, "We have forensic evidence for all twelve, NX-447 residue in tissue samples, falsified death certificates, financial payments to officials who covered up deaths. Each case is prosecutable on its own."

"What about the other sixty-one victims?" I ask.

"They'll be mentioned in our opening statement and included in the conspiracy count. But we can't present full evidence for all seventy-three, the trial would take six months. These twelve cases prove the pattern. The jury will understand it extended to all seventy-three victims."

Rachel continues: "Prosecution timeline is four weeks. Week one: forensic evidence and medical experts. Week two: financial evidence and obstruction of justice. Week three: witness testimony including Owen and victim families. Week four: defense case and closing arguments."

She looks at me. "Jenna, you testify on day eight, second Tuesday of trial. Your testimony covers your mother's whistleblowing attempts and how the defendants destroyed her. We'll spend the next ten weeks preparing you."

January 8, 2025, 2:00 PM Mock Courtroom - FBI Training Facility

They've built a replica courtroom for practice.

Rachel Diaz sits at the prosecution table. Agent Chen plays the role of defense attorney. Twelve FBI agents sit in the jury box, taking notes.

I'm in the witness box, nervous.

Rachel stands. "Ms. Walters, please state your full name for the record."

"Jenna Marie Walters."

"What is your relationship to Linda Walters?"

"She was my mother."

"When did Linda Walters die?"

"May 15, 2011. She was forty-nine years old."

"How did she die?"

"Suicide. Overdose of prescription medications."

Rachel walks to the jury box, forcing me to look at the "jurors."

"Tell the jury about your mother's employment at Willowbrook Psychiatric Hospital."

I take a deep breath. "Linda worked at Willowbrook from April 1987 to October 1987. She was a night shift registered nurse."

"What happened on October 23, 1987?"

"My mother discovered the body of Sophie Brennan, a sixteen-year-old patient. Sophie had supposedly hung herself. But my mother witnessed staff members staging the scene, moving the body, cleaning up evidence, destroying medical records."

"What did your mother do?"

"She filed a police report immediately. She reported what she'd witnessed to the Manchester Police Department at 6:47 AM on October 23, 1987."

Rachel projects the police report on a screen. "Is this the report your mother filed?"

"Yes."

"What happened to that report?"

"It was sent to the medical examiner, Dr. Robert Delacroix, who closed the case within twenty-four hours. He ruled Sophie's death a suicide and refused to investigate further."

"Did your mother accept that ruling?"

"No. She filed additional reports. She contacted the nursing board, the state health department, the attorney general's office. She filed reports for thirteen years."

Agent Chen stands, playing defense attorney. "Objection, Your Honor. Ms. Walters is testifying about events that occurred when she was an infant or not yet born. She has no personal knowledge of these reports."

Rachel responds, "Your Honor, Ms. Walters has reviewed the official documents. She's testifying about the content of police reports and government records, not personal recollections."

The mock judge, another FBI agent, rules: "Overruled. Continue."

Rachel turns back to me. "What was the result of your mother's thirteen years of reporting?"

"She lost her nursing license in 1989. The board claimed she was emotionally unstable and making false accusations. She lost custody of me in 1998. Social services said she was paranoid and unfit to parent. She died by suicide in 2011, believing no one would ever believe her."

"But your mother was telling the truth, correct?"

"Yes. Everything she reported, Sophie's murder, the pharmaceutical trials, the cover-up, was true. The FBI investigation has confirmed it."

Agent Chen stands for cross-examination, playing the role of hostile defense attorney.

"Ms. Walters, isn't it true your mother was diagnosed with paranoid personality disorder?"

I pause, remembering Rachel's coaching: *Stay calm. Stick to facts.*

"My mother was never formally diagnosed by a psychiatrist. The nursing board used the phrase 'emotionally unstable' when they revoked her license, but no mental health professional ever evaluated her."

"But she exhibited paranoid behavior, didn't she? Making wild accusations about murdered patients?"

"She exhibited whistleblower behavior, reporting crimes she'd witnessed. The accusations weren't wild. They were accurate."

"You didn't think they were accurate at the time, did you?"

I hesitate. This is the trap.

"No. I didn't believe her when I was a child."

"Why not?"

"Because everyone told me she was delusional. Social workers, therapists, foster parents, everyone said my mother had paranoid delusions. I was a child. I believed the adults."

"So, you thought your mother was mentally ill?"

"I was wrong. The adults were wrong. My mother was telling the truth about pharmaceutical murder, and she was systematically destroyed for it."

Agent Chen presses: "But for most of your life, you believed Linda Walters was crazy, correct?"

"I believed what I was told. I was seven years old when they took me away from her. I didn't have the knowledge or resources to verify her claims. But now I do. And I've verified everything. My mother was right."

Agent Chen sits down. Rachel gives me a small nod, I

handled that well.

We run through the testimony three more times, refining my answers, anticipating defense attacks.

By the end of the day, I'm exhausted but prepared.

January 15, 2025, 10:00 AM Video Conference with Owen Brennan

The prosecution team holds a video conference with Owen at FCI Devens.

Owen appears on screen in prison orange, sitting in a secure conference room with guards visible behind him.

Rachel Diaz speaks: "Owen, we're finalizing your testimony. You'll be transported to the courthouse on day fifteen of trial, the third Wednesday. You'll testify for two days about your thirty-year investigation and the evidence you collected."

"What about my murders?" Owen asks. "Will the defense bring those up?"

"Absolutely. They'll hammer it. 'You killed four people. You're a revenge-seeking murderer. Why should the jury believe you?' We need to address it head-on."

Owen nods. "So, what's the strategy?"

"Honesty. You admit you murdered four people. You explain you spent thirty years investigating legally, filing reports, contacting authorities, and nothing happened. You explain that killing those four people was wrong and you're serving twenty years for it. But you also explain that every piece of evidence you collected has been independently verified. You're not lying. You're not fabricating. Every financial record, every witness statement, every document has been authenticated by the FBI."

"And if they say I'm testifying to reduce my sentence?"

"We'll clarify that your sentence is set, twenty years minimum, no reduction. You're testifying because it's the right thing to do, not for personal benefit."

Agent Chen adds, "Owen, the jury needs to see you as a flawed but credible witness. You made terrible choices, killing four people, but your investigation was meticulous and accurate. We're not asking them to like you. We're asking them to believe your documentation."

Owen looks directly at the camera. "I'll tell the truth. I killed four people because I couldn't stand watching them live free while Sophie was dead. I accept my punishment. But those six executives ordered Sophie's death and seventy-two others. They need to be held accountable too."

"That's perfect," Rachel says. "Honest, remorseful, but clear about the conspiracy."

After the call, Rachel turns to the team. "Owen is our strongest witness, and our weakest. Strong because he has decades of documentation. Weak because he's a confessed murderer. The jury will be conflicted. We need to surround his testimony with independent evidence that confirms everything he says."

January 22, 2025, 3:00 PM Meeting with Victims' Families

Rachel organizes a meeting for families of the twelve victims who will be featured at trial.

Fifteen people gather in a conference room, parents, siblings, children of patients who died at Willowbrook and other facilities.

Maria Rodriguez, Emily's mother, age 64. "Emily was my oldest. She loved painting. She had so much life ahead of her."

Catherine Brennan, Sophie's mother, age 70. I've spoken to her on the phone but this is our first in-person meeting. She hugs me immediately. "Thank you for everything you've done."

Thomas Torres, Michael's older brother, age 60. "Michael was going to be a doctor. He wanted to help people. Instead, he became a victim."

Margaret Hartley, Lisa's mother, age 68. "Lisa was fourteen. The youngest. They experimented on a child."

One by one, families tell their stories. Children who went to psychiatric facilities for help and never came home. Deaths ruled suicide. Decades of grief and unanswered questions.

Until now.

Rachel addresses them: "The trial starts in eight weeks. Each of you will have the opportunity to give victim impact statements after the verdict, assuming we convict, which we will. But I want to prepare you for what's coming."

She projects photos of the six executives on the screen.

"These men will sit in that courtroom every day looking respectable. Looking like grandfathers. Looking like pillars of the community. Their attorneys will paint them as heroes who saved millions of lives through pharmaceutical innovation. They'll argue your children's deaths were tragic accidents during legitimate medical research."

Several family members start crying.

Rachel continues, her voice hard: "But we're going to prove they're murderers. We're going to show financial records proving they paid officials to cover up deaths. We're going to present forensic evidence proving your children were killed by experimental drugs. We're going to let Sophie's journal speak, a sixteen-year-old documenting her own murder."

She looks around the room. "This trial will be painful. You'll hear medical details about how your children died. You'll see autopsy photos. You'll listen to executives' attorneys attack your credibility, suggest your children were unstable, imply the deaths were somehow inevitable. It will be brutal."

"But we need you there," Agent Chen adds. "We need you in that courtroom every day. We need the jury to see you, real people who lost real children. We need them to understand these aren't abstract statistics. These are families that were destroyed."

Catherine Brennan speaks: "We'll be there. Every day. I've waited thirty-seven years for this. I'm not missing a single moment."

Maria Rodriguez nods. "Emily deserves to be represented. I'll be there."

Thomas Torres: "Michael deserves justice. We'll all be there."

Around the room, families commit to attending the entire trial.

Rachel looks at me. "Jenna, your mother can't be here. But you're representing her. You're Linda's voice. When you testify, you're not just telling your story, you're telling hers."

"I know. I'm ready."

January 28, 2025, 11:00 AM FBI Evidence Room

Agent Chen shows me the physical evidence we'll present at trial.

Exhibit A: Sophie's journal, the original, in a protective case. Seventeen pages flagged with key entries.

Exhibit B: Death certificates for all seventy-three victims. Each signed by corrupt medical examiners. Each falsified.

Exhibit C: Financial records showing $40 million in bribes. Wire transfers, checks, cash payments, all traced.

Exhibit D: Emails between the six executives using phrases like "accelerated protocols" and "appropriate measures", code for murdering patients who asked too many questions.

Exhibit E: Forensic reports confirming NX-447 residue in victims' remains. Proof they were poisoned.

Exhibit F: Linda Walters's police reports from 1987-2000. Thirteen years of trying to expose the conspiracy.

Exhibit G: Photos of the seventeen teenagers from Sophie's class. Visual evidence of mass murder.

"This is just the physical evidence," Agent Chen explains. "We also have twelve expert witnesses, forensic pathologists, toxicologists, financial analysts, who will explain everything to the jury."

"What about the defense? What evidence do they have?"

"Not much. They'll present character witnesses saying the executives are good people. They'll bring in their own medical experts who will argue the deaths could have been accidental. They'll attack Owen's credibility. But they can't explain away the financial records or Sophie's journal or the forensic evidence. Their strategy is to create doubt, not prove innocence."

"Will it work?"

"Not if we present our case properly. The evidence is overwhelming."

February 3, 2025, 4:00 PM Jenna's Apartment

I'm reviewing testimony notes when Victoria Lang calls.

"Jenna, my article about your mother is almost finished. Ten thousand words. I want you to read it before publication."

"When are you publishing?"

"The day trial starts, March 17th. I want Linda's story out there when the world is paying attention. Can I email you the draft?"

"Yes."

Ten minutes later, the article arrives.

THE WHISTLEBLOWER WHO WASN'T BELIEVED

How Linda Walters Spent 13 Years Trying to Expose Pharmaceutical Murder, And Was Destroyed for It

By Victoria Lang

Linda Walters was 25 years old when she witnessed the aftermath of a murder.

It was October 23, 1987, at 4:15 AM, during her night shift at Willowbrook Psychiatric Hospital in Manchester, New

Hampshire. She entered the basement and found staff members staging the death of sixteen-year-old Sophie Brennan to look like suicide.

Linda filed a police report within hours. She described seeing staff members move Sophie's body, clean up evidence, and destroy medical records. She reported fresh injection marks on Sophie's arms. She insisted the death was murder, not suicide.

The medical examiner closed the case the next day without investigating.

Linda didn't give up. For thirteen years, from 1987 to 2000, she filed police reports, contacted state agencies, wrote to officials, and tried desperately to expose what she'd witnessed.

Instead of being believed, Linda Walters was destroyed.

She lost her nursing license in 1989.

She lost custody of her daughter in 1998.

She was labeled mentally ill, paranoid, delusional.

In 2011, at age 52, she died by suicide, believing no one would ever believe her.

But Linda was right about everything.

[Article continues with detailed timeline of Linda's reporting, the destruction she faced, and the vindication that came 13 years after her death...]

I read the entire article, tears streaming down my face.

Victoria has captured my mother perfectly, not as a mentally ill woman, but as a brave nurse who witnessed corporate murder and refused to stay silent despite the cost.

The article ends:

Linda Walters is dead. But on March 17, 2025, when six pharmaceutical executives go on trial for conspiracy to commit murder, Linda will be vindicated. She will be recognized as the first whistleblower who tried to stop a conspiracy that killed seventy-three people.

She won't be there to see it. But her daughter Jenna will. And Jenna carries Linda's courage forward.

That's how justice works, not through one hero, but through many brave people across decades making the choice to speak truth even when the world calls them crazy.

Linda Walters was not crazy. She was right. And history will remember her that way.

I call Victoria. "It's perfect. Publish it."

"Thank you. The world is going to know your mother's story."

February 14, 2025, 9:00 AM FBI Field Office - Final Pre-Trial Meeting

One month until trial.

Rachel gathers the entire team, twelve investigators, six attorneys, four forensic experts.

"Final status check. Are we ready?"

Agent Chen: "Evidence is staged and ready. All exhibits authenticated and admitted."

Daniel Brooks: "Financial analysis complete. Every dollar of the forty million traced."

Forensic pathologist: "All twelve victim autopsies reviewed and confirmed. Cause of death established."

Rachel: "Witness list finalized. Opening statement prepared. Jury selection starts March 10th. Trial starts March 17th."

She looks around the room. "This is the biggest pharmaceutical prosecution in U.S. history. If we win, we send a message to every pharmaceutical executive in the country: You cannot murder patients for profit. If we lose, corporate criminals learn they can kill with impunity."

"We're not losing," Agent Chen says firmly.

Rachel nods. "No. We're not. Because we have the truth. We have Sophie's journal. We have Linda's reports. We have forensic evidence. We have financial records. We have seventy-three dead patients and six executives who thought they'd never face consequences."

She stands. "One month. Then we go to trial. And we're going to convict six murderers."

February 28, 2025, 11:00 PM Jenna's Apartment

Two weeks until trial.

I can't sleep.

I'm running through my testimony in my head, anticipating defense attacks, preparing responses.

My phone buzzes. A text from Catherine Brennan:

Can't sleep either. Too nervous. But also, hopeful. For the first time in 37 years, I'm hopeful Sophie will get justice. Thank you for making this possible.

I text back:

Sophie documented the truth. My mother tried to expose it. Margaret kept it safe. Owen investigated. I just found it. We all did this together.

Catherine responds:

That's how justice works. Many people. Many choices. Many acts of courage. See you in court on March 17th.

I set my phone down and look at my mother's photo.

"Two weeks, Mom," I whisper. "Two weeks until trial. Two weeks until those six men sit in a courtroom and answer for what they did to Sophie. What they did to you. What they did to seventy-three people."

I think about the long chain of events that led here:

- **1987:** Sophie documents pharmaceutical murder. Linda witnesses aftermath. Both destroyed.
- **1987-2018:** Owen investigates for thirty years, kills four people in desperation.
- **2018-2024:** Owen cooperates with FBI but they lack evidence.
- **November 2024:** Margaret gives me Sophie's journal.
- **December 2024:** Six executives arrested.
- **March 2025:** Trial begins.

Thirty-seven years from Sophie's murder to the trial.

Thirteen years from my mother's death to her vindication.

Six years from Owen's arrest to prosecution of the executives.

Justice moves slowly.

But it moves.

And in two weeks, it moves into a courtroom where twelve jurors will decide whether six pharmaceutical executives spend the rest of their lives in prison.

I'm ready. Sophie is ready.

My mother is ready.

Let the trial begin.

CHAPTER 8

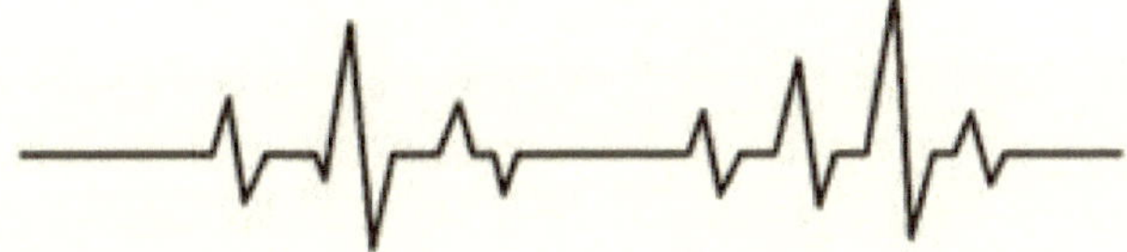

JENNA - The Trial Begins (March 10-17, 2025)

March 10, 2025, 8:00 AM Federal Courthouse, Boston

The courthouse is under siege.

Media trucks line every street. Protesters hold signs. Security has tripled, K-9 units, armed guards, metal detectors at every entrance.

Inside, the courtroom is packed. Every seat in the gallery filled. Overflow crowds watch on monitors in adjacent rooms.

I sit in the front row behind the prosecution table with Catherine Brennan, Maria Rodriguez, and other victims' families. Across the aisle: the six executives and their massive defense teams.

James Morrison sits with four attorneys, looking calm and distinguished in an expensive suit.

Martin Shaw leans back, arms crossed, projecting confidence.

Robert Chen whispers with his lawyers, occasionally glancing at the gallery.

David Patterson looks frail, oxygen tank beside him, but his eyes are sharp.

Michael Williams sits stone-faced, expressionless.

Thomas Foster examines documents, appearing bored.

These men murdered seventy-three people. And they're sitting here in tailored suits acting like victims of persecution.

Judge Harold Martinez enters. "All rise."

Everyone stands.

"Be seated. We're here for jury selection in United States v. Morrison, et al. We have one hundred and fifty prospective jurors. We need twelve jurors and four alternates. This process will take approximately three days."

He looks at the prospective jurors filling the gallery and overflow rooms.

"Ladies and gentlemen, you've been summoned for jury duty in a complex criminal trial. The defendants are charged with conspiracy to commit murder, wire fraud, and obstruction of justice. The trial is expected to last four weeks. If you cannot serve for four weeks, please raise your hand now."

Thirty hands go up. Judge Martinez dismisses them.

"How many of you have heard about this case?"

Nearly every remaining hand goes up.

"That's expected. This case has received significant media coverage. The question is: Can you set aside what you've heard and decide based solely on evidence presented in this courtroom?"

Twenty people admit they've already formed opinions and cannot be impartial. Dismissed.

"How many of you work in healthcare or pharmaceuticals?"

Fifteen hands.

"Have you or a family member ever been a patient in a psychiatric facility?"

Twenty-two hands.

"Have you or a family member ever participated in medical research or drug trials?"

Ten hands.

The questioning continues for hours. Judge Martinez, Rachel Diaz, and the six defense attorneys take turns probing for bias.

By noon, fifty prospective jurors have been dismissed for cause, bias, hardship, conflict of interest.

March 10, 2025, 1:00 PM Courthouse - Voir Dire Begins

After lunch, individual questioning begins.

Prospective jurors are called one at a time to the sidebar where attorneys can question them privately.

Juror #34, woman, age 47, accountant:

Defense: "You work in finance. The prosecution will present complex financial records showing alleged bribes. Will you presume those records are accurate, or will you scrutinize them critically?"

Juror #34: "I'll scrutinize them. Numbers can be manipulated. I'd need to see source documents and verification."

Defense: "Thank you. No objection to this juror."

Rachel: "Ms. #34, the defense may argue that financial payments were consulting fees, not bribes. Can you distinguish between legitimate business transactions and criminal payments?"

Juror #34: "Yes. I've worked in corporate accounting for twenty years. I know what legitimate consulting fees look like versus suspicious payments designed to hide criminal activity."

Rachel: "No objection."

Juror #34 is seated.

Juror #52, man, age 38, high school teacher:

Rachel: "This case involves teenage victims. You work with teenagers every day. Will that make it difficult for you to be impartial?"

Juror #52: "It'll make it emotionally harder. But I can separate emotion from evidence. If the prosecution proves the defendants murdered these teenagers, I'll vote to convict. If there's reasonable doubt, I'll vote to acquit."

Rachel: "That's exactly what we need. No objection."

Defense: "We object. This juror works with teenagers daily. He'll be emotionally biased toward the teenage victims."

Judge Martinez: "The juror stated he can be impartial. Objection overruled. Juror #52 is seated."

Juror #71, woman, age 55, nurse (not psychiatric):

Rachel: "You're a registered nurse. Linda Walters, whose testimony will be presented through documents, was also a nurse. Will you identify with her or be biased in favor of the prosecution?"

Juror #71: "I'll evaluate her reports objectively. Being a nurse doesn't mean I automatically believe other nurses. I'll look at the evidence."

Rachel: "No objection."

Defense: "We object. This juror will sympathize with a nurse whistleblower. She'll be biased."

Judge Martinez: "The juror stated she'll evaluate evidence objectively. Objection overruled. Juror #71 is seated."

The questioning continues for three full days.

By March 12th evening, twelve jurors and four alternates have been selected:

Final Jury:

1. Female, 47, accountant
2. Male, 38, high school teacher
3. Female, 55, nurse (non-psychiatric)
4. Male, 29, software engineer
5. Female, 68, retired postal worker
6. Male, 46, construction foreman
7. Female, 40, attorney (civil, not criminal)
8. Male, 56, small business owner
9. Female, 32, graphic designer
10. Male, 64, retired teacher
11. Female, 45, social worker
12. Male, 41, electrician

Alternates:

1. Female, 31, lab technician
2. Male, 59, mechanic

3. Female, 51, librarian
4. Male, 43, paramedic

Judge Martinez addresses the jury. "Ladies and gentlemen, you've been selected to serve on this jury. This is one of the most important responsibilities a citizen can undertake. You will hear four weeks of testimony. You will deliberate based solely on evidence presented in this courtroom."

He looks at both legal teams. "Opening statements will be Monday, March 17th, at 9:00 AM. Both sides will have the weekend to prepare. We're adjourned until Monday."

March 13, 2025, 10:00 AM FBI Field Office - Opening Statement Preparation

Rachel Diaz rehearses her opening statement with the prosecution team.

She stands at a podium, projecting slides on a screen, practicing her delivery.

"Members of the jury, over the next four weeks, you're going to hear about one of the largest pharmaceutical conspiracies in American history. Between 1985 and 1995, six executives at Nexus Pharmaceuticals, now called GenHealth Corporation, conducted illegal drug trials on psychiatric patients. These trials resulted in the deaths of seventy-three people. Most were teenagers. None of them consented. And when they died, their deaths were covered up as suicides or natural causes."

She projects Sophie's class photo.

"This is Willowbrook Psychiatric Hospital, April 1987. Twenty-three teenage patients. By October 1987, seventeen of them were dead. All seventeen deaths were ruled suicide or accidental. All seventeen were actually murders, patients killed by experimental drugs."

She pauses, letting the image sink in.

"One of those patients was **Sophie Marie Brennan**, age sixteen. Sophie kept a journal. She documented patient deaths. She recorded conversations between doctors and pharmaceutical executives. She predicted her own murder twelve days before it happened."

Rachel projects Sophie's final journal entry.

"Sophie wrote: 'My name is Sophie Marie Brennan. I'm sixteen years old. I didn't kill myself. Whatever they say, whatever report they write, I didn't give up. They murdered me. Please give me justice.'"

She walks along the jury box.

"Sophie's journal is the centerpiece of this case. It's not someone looking back thirty years later with questionable memory. It's a sixteen-year-old girl writing in real time about what was happening to her. It's devastating evidence."

Rachel projects financial records.

"We will prove the defendants paid forty million dollars to cover up these murders. Bribes to medical examiners. Bribes to hospital administrators. Bribes to FDA officials. Bribes to police investigators. They bought an entire system."

She projects images of the six defendants.

"**James Morrison** authorized the trials. **Martin Shaw** created the legal framework to avoid liability. **Robert Chen** approved the bribes. **David Patterson** managed hospital compliance. **Michael Williams** bribed FDA officials. **Thomas Foster** silenced whistleblowers."

She pauses for emphasis.

"And when a nurse named **Linda Walters** witnessed Sophie's murder and tried to report it? They destroyed her. Took her nursing license. Labeled her mentally ill. Took her daughter. Gaslit her until she couldn't take it anymore. Linda died by suicide in 2011, believing no one would ever believe her."

Rachel's voice hardens.

"But she was right. These six men murdered seventy-three people to test a drug. They valued profits over lives. And we're going to prove it beyond a reasonable doubt."

Agent Chen, watching the rehearsal, nods approvingly. "That's powerful. But the defense will counter hard. They'll attack Owen's credibility, argue the deaths were accidental, paint the executives as heroes. We need to preempt that."

Rachel adds to her notes. "I'll address it: 'The defense will tell you these men are respected businessmen. They'll bring character witnesses. They'll show you their philanthropy, their awards, their contributions to medicine. But none of that erases murder. Good people can do terrible things when profits are at stake. And that's what happened here.'"

We rehearse for six more hours, refining every word.

March 15, 2025, 6:00 PM Jenna's Apartment

Two days until trial.

Victoria Lang's article about my mother publishes online Sunday night, timed to hit peak readership before the trial starts Monday morning.

I read it one more time:

THE WHISTLEBLOWER WHO WASN'T BELIEVED

Linda Walters spent 13 years trying to expose pharmaceutical murder. She was destroyed for it. Tomorrow, she's vindicated.

By Victoria Lang

Boston Globe Sunday Magazine

Linda Walters was twenty-five years old when she witnessed the aftermath of a murder...

[The article details Linda's entire story, her discovery of Sophie's staged death, her thirteen years of reporting, her systematic destruction, and her death in 2011]

...Linda Walters is dead. But on March 17, 2025, when six pharmaceutical executives go on trial for conspiracy to commit murder, Linda will be vindicated. She will be recognized as the first whistleblower who tried to stop a conspiracy that killed seventy-three people.

She won't be there to see it. But her daughter Jenna will. And Jenna carries Linda's courage forward.

That's how justice works, not through one hero, but through many brave people across decades making the choice to speak truth even when the world calls them crazy.

Linda Walters was not crazy. She was right. And history will remember her that way.

Within an hour of publication, the article has fifty thousand shares on social media. #LindaWalters trends alongside #JusticeForSophie.

Comments flood in:

"Linda Walters tried to save lives and the system destroyed her. This is why whistleblowers stay silent."

"Imagine spending 13 years being called crazy when you're actually exposing corporate murder. RIP Linda."

"Her daughter must be so proud. Jenna finished what Linda started."

My phone explodes with messages. News outlets requesting interviews. Victims' families thanking me. Strangers offering support.

I silence everything and look at my mother's photo.

"The article published, Mom," I tell her. "Victoria wrote ten thousand words about your courage. Fifty thousand people have shared it in the first hour. The world knows your story now. The world knows you were a hero."

I think about tomorrow, opening statements. The beginning of justice.

"Trial starts tomorrow morning. Rachel will tell the jury about you. About how you witnessed Sophie's murder. About how you spent thirteen years trying to expose it. About how they destroyed you."

My voice breaks. "I wish you were here to see this. I wish you could sit in that courtroom and watch those six men answer for what they did. But I'll be there for both of us. I'll represent you. I promise."

March 17, 2025, 7:00 AM Federal Courthouse, Boston

Trial day.

The media presence has tripled. Hundreds of reporters. Dozens of cameras. Protesters on both sides, some holding "Justice for Sophie" signs, others holding "Innocent Until Proven Guilty" signs supporting the executives.

Security is overwhelming. Armed guards. Bomb-sniffing dogs. Metal detectors. Bag searches.

I arrive early with Catherine Brennan. We're escorted through a private entrance to avoid the media crush.

Inside, the courtroom is already filling. Victims' families in the front rows behind the prosecution. The six executives at their defense tables, surrounded by attorneys. Media in designated press areas.

Rachel Diaz sits at the prosecution table with Agent Chen and two other prosecutors, reviewing notes.

The six defense attorneys, Gerald Hutchins (Morrison), Martin Shaw's lawyer, Robert Chen's lawyer, David Patterson's lawyer, Michael Williams's lawyer, and Thomas Foster's lawyer, huddle at their respective tables, strategizing.

At 8:45 AM, the jury files in. Twelve people who will decide the fate of six pharmaceutical executives.

At 9:00 AM sharp, the bailiff calls: "All rise. The United States District Court for the District of Massachusetts is now in session, the Honorable Harold Martinez presiding."

Judge Martinez enters, takes his seat.

"Be seated. We're here to begin trial in United States v. Morrison, et al. The jury has been sworn. Are both sides ready to proceed with opening statements?"

Rachel stands. "The government is ready, Your Honor."

Gerald Hutchins stands. "The defense is ready, Your Honor."

Judge Martinez looks at Rachel. "Ms. Diaz, you may proceed."

March 17, 2025, 9:05 AM Opening Statement - Prosecution

Rachel Diaz approaches the jury box.

She's wearing a dark suit, no jewelry, projecting professionalism and gravity. She carries no notes, she's memorized everything.

"Members of the jury, good morning. My name is Rachel Diaz, and I represent the United States of America in this case. Over the next four weeks, you're going to hear evidence about one of the largest pharmaceutical conspiracies in American history."

She pauses, making eye contact with each juror.

"Between 1985 and 1995, the six defendants sitting at those tables conducted illegal drug trials on psychiatric patients at Willowbrook Psychiatric Hospital and four other facilities. These trials violated federal law. They violated medical ethics. And they resulted in the deaths of seventy-three people."

Rachel projects Sophie's class photo on the courtroom screens.

"This photograph was taken at Willowbrook Psychiatric

Hospital in April 1987. Twenty-three teenage patients. Average age: sixteen. They were admitted for anxiety, depression, trauma, treatable conditions. They should have received counseling and standard medications. They should have gone home to their families."

She pauses.

"By October 1987, six months after this photo was taken, seventeen of these twenty-three teenagers were dead."

Gasps in the courtroom. Several jurors look shocked.

Rachel continues: "Seventeen teenagers. Dead in six months. All at the same facility. All ruled suicide or accidental death. All signed off by the same medical examiner, Dr. Robert Delacroix, who received fifty thousand dollars from the defendants to close cases without investigating."

She projects a financial record showing the payment.

"The defense will argue these were tragic accidents during legitimate medical research. That's not true. These were murders. Deliberate, calculated murders committed to test an experimental drug called NX-447."

Rachel projects Sophie's journal.

"This is the journal of **Sophie Marie Brennan**, one of the seventeen teenagers who died. Sophie was sixteen years old. She kept this journal documenting everything she witnessed at Willowbrook. Patient deaths. Late-night visits from pharmaceutical executives. Conversations about 'increasing dosages' and 'acceptable loss rates.'"

She opens the journal to Sophie's final entry and reads:

"'This is probably my last entry. Dr. Delacroix told me today I'm starting a new trial protocol tomorrow. He smiled when he said it, but his eyes were cold. I know what that means. I'm giving this journal to Nurse Margaret tonight. My name is Sophie Marie Brennan. I'm sixteen years old. I didn't kill myself. Whatever they say, whatever report they write, I didn't give up. They murdered me. If anyone is reading this: Please investigate. Please don't let them get away with this. Please give me justice.'"

Rachel closes the journal.

"Twelve days after writing that entry, Sophie was dead. Injected with eight hundred milligrams of NX-447, well above the lethal dose. Her death was staged to look like suicide by hanging. The medical examiner ruled it suicide within twenty-four hours."

She projects another image, Linda Walters, 1987.

"This is **Linda Walters**. She was a registered nurse at Willowbrook. On October 23, 1987, Linda discovered Sophie's body. She witnessed staff members staging the scene, moving the body, cleaning up evidence, destroying medical records. She filed a police report within hours."

Rachel projects Linda's police report.

"Linda reported exactly what she'd seen. The police

forwarded her report to Medical Examiner Robert Delacroix. He closed the case immediately. But Linda didn't give up. For thirteen years, from 1987 to 2000, she filed police reports, contacted state agencies, wrote to officials. She tried desperately to expose what happened to Sophie and the other victims."

Rachel's voice hardens.

"Instead of being believed, Linda Walters was destroyed. She lost her nursing license in 1989, the board claimed she was emotionally unstable. She lost custody of her seven-year-old daughter in 1998, social services claimed she was paranoid. She was labeled mentally ill. Delusional. Crazy."

She pauses.

"In 2011, at age forty-nine, Linda Walters died by suicide, believing no one would ever believe her. But she was right about everything."

Rachel projects images of the six defendants.

"These six men orchestrated this conspiracy. **James Morrison** authorized the illegal drug trials. **Martin Shaw** created legal structures to avoid liability. **Robert Chen** approved forty million dollars in bribes to officials. **David Patterson** ensured hospital compliance. **Michael Williams** bribed FDA officials to fast-track the drug. **Thomas Foster** destroyed whistleblowers like Linda."

She walks back to the jury box.

"Over the next four weeks, we will prove beyond

reasonable doubt that these six men conspired to murder seventy-three people. We will present Sophie's journal, a contemporaneous account by a teenage victim. We will present financial records showing forty million dollars in bribes. We will present forensic evidence proving patients were killed by experimental drugs. We will present witness testimony from victims' families and from Owen Brennan, Sophie's brother, who spent thirty years investigating this conspiracy."

Rachel looks directly at the six executives.

"The defense will tell you these men are respected businessmen. Philanthropists. Innovators. Heroes who saved millions of lives through pharmaceutical research. And it's true, these men have done good things in their careers. But that doesn't erase murder. Good people can do terrible things when profits are at stake. And that's what happened here."

She turns back to the jury.

"At the end of this trial, we will ask you to find these six defendants guilty of conspiracy to commit murder. Guilty of wire fraud. Guilty of obstruction of justice. We will ask you to hold them accountable for seventy-three deaths, including Sophie Brennan, including seventeen teenagers in that class photo, including all the patients whose names we'll never know because their deaths were covered up so thoroughly."

Rachel returns to the prosecution table.

"Thank you for your service. We trust you will do justice."

She sits down.

The courtroom is silent. Several jurors are wiping their eyes.

Judge Martinez speaks: "We'll take a fifteen-minute recess before the defense's opening statement."

March 17, 2025, 10:30 AM Opening Statement - Defense

After the recess, Gerald Hutchins, lead attorney for James Morrison and spokesperson for all six defense teams, approaches the jury.

Hutchins is in his mid-sixties, silver-haired, expensive suit, the demeanor of someone who's been in courtrooms for forty years and never lost a case.

"Members of the jury, good morning. My name is Gerald Hutchins, and I represent Dr. James Morrison. I also speak on behalf of the other five defendants and their attorneys."

He smiles, warm, grandfatherly, designed to contrast with Rachel's intensity.

"The prosecution just gave you a compelling story. A teenage girl's journal. A nurse whistleblower. Seventy-three deaths. Forty million in bribes. It sounds damning. But here's what they didn't tell you: It's not true."

He lets that hang in the air.

"My clients, these six men sitting at those tables,

dedicated their lives to developing medications that save lives. **James Morrison** pioneered research that led to treatments for anxiety disorders affecting millions of people. **Martin Shaw** drafted pharmaceutical regulations that improved patient safety. These men are heroes, not criminals."

Hutchins walks along the jury box.

"Yes, patients died at Willowbrook Psychiatric Hospital in the 1980s. That's tragic. But psychiatric patients are vulnerable populations with high suicide rates. The deaths the prosecution calls 'murders' were actually suicides and medical complications during legitimate, FDA-approved research trials."

He projects a document, FDA approval for clinical trials at Willowbrook.

"The FDA approved these trials. The hospitals consented. The medical examiners, licensed professionals, reviewed each death and ruled them accidental or self-inflicted. Thirty-seven years later, prosecutors are second-guessing those medical professionals based on a teenage girl's diary."

Hutchins picks up Sophie's journal.

"Sophie Brennan. Sixteen years old. Diagnosed with severe anxiety disorder. Admitted to Willowbrook after threatening self-harm. This journal shows a troubled teenager struggling with mental illness. Yes, she documented patient deaths, because she was obsessed with them, seeing patterns that weren't there, exhibiting paranoid behavior typical of her condition."

He sets the journal down.

"The prosecution will tell you Sophie predicted her own murder. That's not what happened. Sophie was a mentally ill teenager who tragically took her own life, just as the medical examiner determined in 1987."

Rachel starts to stand, objecting to this characterization, but Agent Chen puts a hand on her arm. *Let him talk. The jury will see through this.*

Hutchins continues: "The prosecution's star witness is **Owen Brennan**, Sophie's brother. They'll paint him as a dedicated investigator seeking justice. Here's the truth: Owen Brennan is a convicted murderer currently serving twenty years in federal prison. He killed four people between 2017 and 2018. Stabbed one. Shot two others. Strangled another."

He projects Owen's mugshot.

"Owen Brennan is testifying for one reason: to reduce his prison sentence. He's fabricated a conspiracy theory to justify his murders and get leniency from prosecutors. Every piece of 'evidence' he's provided is designed to support his revenge fantasy."

Hutchins returns to the jury box.

"The prosecution will show you financial records claiming forty million in 'bribes.' Those were consulting fees. Research grants. Standard pharmaceutical industry payments. Every dollar was legal, documented, and tax-reported. There's no conspiracy, just normal business transactions being twisted by prosecutors seeking headlines."

He points to Linda Walters's photo.

"And Linda Walters? The prosecution calls her a whistleblower. Medical professionals called her something else: mentally ill. Linda filed dozens of reports claiming patients were being murdered. Every single report was investigated. Every single one was found baseless. Linda wasn't silenced, she was suffering from paranoid delusions, as multiple psychiatrists documented."

Judge Martinez leans forward. "Counselor, Ms. Walters was never formally diagnosed by a psychiatrist. Please stick to facts in evidence."

Hutchins nods. "Apologies, Your Honor. Let me rephrase: Multiple officials who reviewed Linda's reports concluded they lacked merit and showed signs of paranoid ideation. Whether that constitutes a formal diagnosis is for the jury to decide."

He walks back to the center of the courtroom.

"Members of the jury, the prosecution has a theory. A teenage girl's diary. A revenge killer's fabrications. A nurse's unfounded reports. That's not evidence of murder, that's evidence of tragedy being exploited for headlines."

Hutchins gestures to the six executives.

"These six men are innocent. They're being persecuted

because prosecutors need a villain. Because victims' families need someone to blame. Because society wants to believe pharmaceutical companies are evil. But wanting something to be true doesn't make it true."

He returns to the defense table.

"At the end of this trial, we will ask you to find these defendants not guilty. Because the evidence, real evidence, not conspiracy theories, shows they committed no crime. Thank you."

Hutchins sits down.

March 17, 2025, 11:00 AM Courtroom - After Opening Statements

Judge Martinez addresses the jury.

"Ladies and gentlemen, you've now heard opening statements from both sides. These statements are not evidence, they're roadmaps of what each side intends to prove. The actual evidence begins this afternoon when the prosecution calls its first witness."

He looks at Rachel. "Ms. Diaz, is the government ready to proceed?"

"Yes, Your Honor. We'll begin with forensic pathology testimony."

"Very well. We'll reconvene at 1:00 PM. Jury is dismissed

for lunch. Remember, do not discuss this case with anyone."

The jury files out.

I turn to Catherine Brennan. She's crying silently.

"They called Sophie mentally ill," she whispers. "They said she made it up. They said she killed herself."

"The defense is lying," I tell her. "The jury will see that when we present the evidence. Sophie's journal will speak for itself."

Rachel joins us. "Hutchins did what we expected, attack Sophie's credibility, Owen's credibility, Linda's credibility. But we have forensic evidence. We have financial records. We have Sophie's detailed documentation. The jury will see through the defense's story."

Agent Chen adds, "The trial just started. We have four weeks to prove our case. By the time we're done, the jury won't have any doubt."

But as we leave the courthouse for lunch, I can't shake the feeling that this is going to be harder than we thought.

The six executives have the best attorney's money can buy.

And they're fighting for their lives.

This trial isn't over.

It's just beginning.

CHAPTER 9

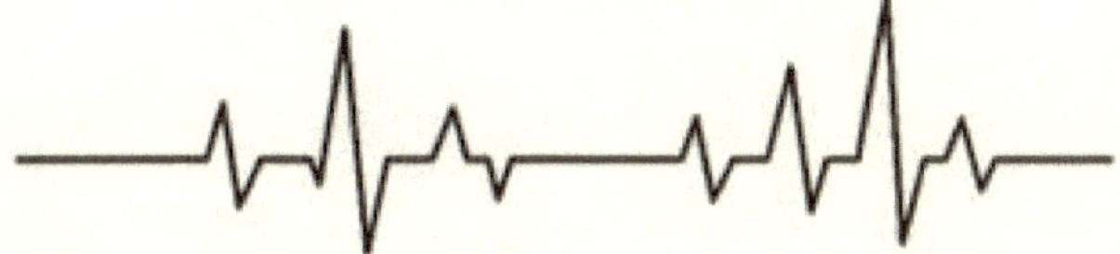

JENNA - The Evidence (March 17-21, 2025)

March 17, 2025, 1:00 PM Federal Courthouse - Trial Day 1, Afternoon Session

After lunch recess, Judge Martinez calls the court to order.

"Ms. Diaz, call your first witness."

Rachel stands. "Your Honor, the government calls Dr. Patricia Morrison, Chief Medical Examiner for Suffolk County."

A woman in her mid-fifties enters the courtroom, Dr. Patricia Morrison, no relation to defendant James Morrison. She's been a forensic pathologist for thirty years and has testified in hundreds of cases.

After being sworn in, she takes the witness stand.

Rachel approaches. "Dr. Morrison, please state your credentials for the jury."

"I'm a board-certified forensic pathologist. I've conducted over five thousand autopsies during my career. I'm currently the Chief Medical Examiner for Suffolk County and an adjunct professor at Harvard Medical School."

"Have you reviewed the autopsy reports for the victims in this case?"

"Yes. I've reviewed all available autopsy reports for the seventy-three alleged victims, and I personally conducted forensic examinations on forty-two victims whose bodies were exhumed between November 2024 and February 2025."

Rachel projects an image on the courtroom screens, Sophie's original 1987 autopsy report.

"Dr. Morrison, this is the original autopsy report for Sophie Brennan, conducted by Medical Examiner Robert Delacroix on October 23, 1987. What's your professional opinion of this report?"

Dr. Morrison reviews the document. "It's inadequate. A thorough autopsy report for a suspicious death should be ten to fifteen pages minimum, with detailed descriptions of all findings, photographs, toxicology results, and analysis. This report is two pages. It contains minimal detail and reaches a conclusion, suicide by hanging, without proper investigation."

"What specific problems did you identify?"

"Multiple red flags. First, the report notes ligature marks on the neck consistent with hanging, but fails to document whether those marks were ante-mortem, before death, or post-mortem, after death. That's a critical distinction. Second, the report mentions 'minor bruising on arms' but doesn't investigate the cause. Third, there's no comprehensive toxicology screen. Fourth, time of death is estimated at 4:15 AM, but the report doesn't explain how that estimate was reached."

Rachel walks to the jury box. "Did you conduct your own examination of Sophie Brennan's remains?"

"Yes. Sophie's body was exhumed on November 30, 2024. Despite thirty-seven years of decomposition, tissue samples were preserved well enough for analysis."

"What did your examination reveal?"

"Sophie Brennan did not die by hanging. She died of cardiac arrest induced by drug toxicity."

Murmurs ripple through the courtroom. Judge Martinez gavels for silence.

Dr. Morrison continues: "The ligature marks on her neck were post-mortem, they occurred after death. Someone hanged her body after she was already dead. The actual cause of death was massive cardiac arrest caused by an overdose of a compound later identified as NX-447, an experimental benzodiazepine derivative."

"How do you know the ligature marks were post-mortem?"

"Post-mortem ligature marks have distinct characteristics, lack of vital response, no petechial hemorrhaging, different tissue compression patterns. Sophie's neck showed all the indicators of post-mortem hanging. She was already dead when her body was suspended."

Rachel projects forensic photos, clinical, medical, appropriate for a courtroom but still disturbing. Several jurors look away.

"What about the 'minor bruising' noted in the original report?"

"Those weren't minor bruises. They were injection sites. Sophie had fresh needle marks in the antecubital fossa, the inside of her elbow, indicating intravenous injection shortly before death. Dr. Delacroix's report mentions them but dismisses them as insignificant."

"Did you find NX-447 in Sophie's remains?"

"Yes. Despite thirty-seven years of decomposition, residual traces of NX-447 were present in bone marrow and dental pulp, areas that preserve chemical compounds even after extensive decay. Based on residue levels and pharmacokinetic analysis, I estimate Sophie received approximately eight hundred milligrams of NX-447 via intravenous injection."

"Is eight hundred milligrams a lethal dose?"

"Extremely lethal. Therapeutic doses of benzodiazepines

are measured in single-digit milligrams. Eight hundred milligrams would cause immediate cardiac arrhythmia and death within minutes. There's no scenario where Sophie survived that injection."

Rachel pauses, letting the jury absorb this.

"Dr. Morrison, in your professional opinion, how did Sophie Brennan die?"

"Sophie Brennan was murdered. She was injected with a lethal dose of an experimental drug that stopped her heart. Her death was then staged to look like suicide by hanging. This was deliberate homicide, not suicide."

Rachel returns to the prosecution table and picks up a folder. "Dr. Morrison, you mentioned you examined forty-two victims total. Did they show similar patterns?"

"Yes. Of the forty-two victims I personally examined, thirty-eight died from NX-447 overdoses. The remaining four died from complications of other experimental drugs. All forty-two were staged to look like suicides or natural deaths. None were actually suicides."

"So, the original medical examiners who ruled these deaths as suicides were wrong?"

"Not just wrong. The deaths were deliberately mischaracterized. Multiple medical examiners, primarily Dr. Robert Delacroix but also others, signed off on death certificates that contradicted obvious forensic evidence. These weren't mistakes. These were cover-ups."

Gerald Hutchins stands. "Objection, Your Honor. Speculation. The witness can't know the medical examiners' intent."

Judge Martinez: "Sustained. Dr. Morrison, please limit your testimony to your forensic findings."

Dr. Morrison nods. "The forensic findings show the death certificates were inaccurate. Whether that inaccuracy was intentional or negligent is for the jury to decide."

Rachel continues: "Dr. Morrison, you examined victims from multiple facilities, Willowbrook and four others. Did you find consistent patterns?"

"Yes. All victims showed evidence of experimental drug administration. All died from overdoses or toxic reactions. All had their deaths mischaracterized on official certificates. The pattern was consistent across facilities and across nearly a decade of deaths."

"No further questions, Your Honor."

March 17, 2025, 2:30 PM Cross-Examination

Gerald Hutchins approaches Dr. Morrison for cross-examination.

"Dr. Morrison, you testified that you examined remains that were thirty-seven years old. Isn't it true that tissue degradation over nearly four decades makes definitive conclusions difficult?"

"It makes analysis more challenging, yes. But modern forensic techniques can detect compound residues even in severely degraded tissue. The NX-447 we found in Sophie's remains is definitive."

"But you can't say with one hundred percent certainty that the NX-447 was administered on October 22, 1987, can you? It could have been from earlier doses during the trial protocol."

"The concentration levels indicate a large, acute dose rather than cumulative exposure from multiple smaller doses. Combined with the timing of death and the documentation in Sophie's journal, it's clear she received a lethal injection on October 22, 1987."

"You keep mentioning Sophie's journal. You're a medical examiner, not a historian. You're letting a teenage girl's diary influence your scientific analysis."

"I'm using the journal as context, which is standard forensic practice. When autopsy findings align with documented accounts, that strengthens conclusions."

Hutchins changes tactics. "Dr. Morrison, the original medical examiner was Dr. Robert Delacroix. He was a licensed professional with decades of experience. Are you saying he was incompetent?"

"I'm saying his autopsy report was inadequate and his conclusion was incorrect. Whether that's incompetence or deliberate falsification isn't for me to determine."

"But Dr. Delacroix isn't here to defend his work, is he? He was killed in 2018, by Owen Brennan, the prosecution's star witness."

Rachel starts to object, but Judge Martinez intervenes. "Counselor, that's not a question. Move on."

Hutchins nods. "Dr. Morrison, psychiatric patients have high suicide rates. Isn't it possible these deaths were legitimate suicides and you're second-guessing medical professionals thirty-seven years later?"

"No. The forensic evidence is clear, these patients died from drug overdoses, not suicide. The staging of scenes, the falsified death certificates, the pattern across multiple facilities, this wasn't a series of coincidental suicides. This was systematic murder."

"But you're being paid by the prosecution, correct?"

"I'm being compensated for my time as an expert witness at my standard rate of three hundred dollars per hour. That's normal for forensic consultants."

"So, you have a financial incentive to support the prosecution's theory."

"I have a professional obligation to present accurate forensic findings regardless of who's paying me. My conclusions are based on evidence, not bias."

"No further questions."

Judge Martinez looks at Rachel. "Redirect?"

"No, Your Honor."

"The witness is excused. Call your next witness."

March 18, 2025, 9:00 AM Trial Day 2 - Toxicology Expert

Rachel calls Dr. Thomas Chen, a toxicologist from Harvard Medical School.

After establishing his credentials, PhD in pharmacology, thirty years studying drug effects, Rachel gets to the substance.

"Dr. Chen, please explain to the jury what NX-447 is."

"NX-447 is an experimental benzodiazepine derivative developed by Nexus Pharmaceuticals in the mid-1980s. It was designed to treat severe anxiety disorders. However, it was never approved by the FDA because of dangerous side effects, including cardiac toxicity."

"What do you mean by 'cardiac toxicity'?"

"At therapeutic doses, NX-447 causes mild side effects, drowsiness, dizziness. But at higher doses, it disrupts the electrical signals in the heart, causing arrhythmia. At very high doses, above five hundred milligrams, it causes complete cardiac arrest and death."

"Is death from NX-447 overdose painful?"

"Objection," Hutchins calls. "Relevance?"

Rachel responds: "Your Honor, the manner of death is

relevant to understanding the crime."

Judge Martinez: "I'll allow it. Answer the question, Dr. Chen."

"Death from NX-447 overdose occurs within two to five minutes. The victim experiences rapid heart palpitations, difficulty breathing, chest pain, and loss of consciousness. It's not instantaneous, but it's relatively quick."

Rachel projects a chart showing NX-447 dosage levels.

"Dr. Chen, Sophie Brennan received approximately eight hundred milligrams of NX-447. What would that do to a sixteen-year-old girl weighing approximately one hundred fifteen pounds?"

"Eight hundred milligrams would cause immediate cardiac arrhythmia. Her heart would lose its regular rhythm within thirty seconds. Complete cardiac arrest would occur within two minutes. Death would be certain."

"Could Sophie have survived that dose?"

"No. Eight hundred milligrams is well beyond the lethal threshold. There's no medical intervention that could have saved her once that dose entered her system."

"Was NX-447 ever approved for use in humans?"

"No. The FDA rejected NX-447 in 1995 because of unacceptable cardiac risks. All clinical trials were terminated."

"But between 1985 and 1995, Nexus Pharmaceuticals

conducted trials using NX-447 on psychiatric patients?"

"Yes. According to the documentation I've reviewed, Nexus conducted trials at five facilities without proper FDA oversight or informed consent. At least seventy-three patients died during those trials."

Hutchins objects: "Move to strike. The witness is testifying about matters outside his expertise."

Judge Martinez: "Sustained. Dr. Chen, limit your testimony to the pharmacology of NX-447."

Rachel continues: "Dr. Chen, the defense has suggested these deaths could have been accidental, patients receiving normal doses but having unexpected reactions. Is that plausible?"

"No. The doses documented in medical records and found in tissue samples were far above therapeutic levels. These weren't accidental overdoses. These were lethal injections."

"No further questions."

Hutchins cross-examines but gains little ground, the toxicology is clear and damning.

March 19, 2025, 10:00 AM Trial Day 3 - Financial Evidence

Rachel calls Daniel Brooks, the FBI forensic accountant.

"Mr. Brooks, please describe your investigation into financial transactions between Nexus Pharmaceuticals and various individuals between 1985 and 1995."

Daniel projects a massive flowchart on the courtroom screens, money flowing from Nexus Pharmaceuticals to dozens of recipients.

"We traced approximately forty million dollars in payments from Nexus Pharmaceuticals to individuals including medical examiners, hospital administrators, FDA officials, police investigators, and journalists. These payments occurred between 1985 and 1995, the exact period when illegal drug trials were being conducted."

"Give the jury an example."

Daniel highlights one transaction. "On November 5, 1987, two weeks after Sophie Brennan's death, Nexus Pharmaceuticals wired fifty thousand dollars to Dr. Robert Delacroix, the medical examiner who ruled her death a suicide. The wire transfer memo says 'consulting fee,' but Dr. Delacroix had no consulting relationship with Nexus. He was a county medical examiner with no legitimate reason to receive payments from a pharmaceutical company."

"Were there other payments to Dr. Delacroix?"

"Yes. Between 1985 and 1995, Dr. Delacroix received over two million dollars from Nexus in payments labeled as 'consulting fees,' 'research grants,' and 'honoraria.' During that same period, Dr. Delacroix closed seventy-three suspicious death cases without investigation, all deaths that occurred at facilities where Nexus was conducting trials."

Rachel projects more transactions. "What about hospital administrators?"

"We found eight million dollars in payments to administrators at the five facilities where trials occurred. These payments corresponded with the facilities agreeing to host Nexus trials and with administrators ensuring staff compliance."

"What about FDA officials?"

"Over five million dollars to three FDA officials, Dr. Harold Kemp, Dr. Susan Martinez, and Dr. Robert Wallace. These officials were responsible for reviewing NX-447's safety data and approving trial protocols. All three received substantial payments from Nexus while making regulatory decisions favorable to the company."

"Were these payments disclosed?"

"No. Federal law requires FDA officials to disclose conflicts of interest. None of these officials disclosed receiving money from Nexus. That's illegal."

Rachel walks along the jury box. "Mr. Brooks, the defense argues these were legitimate consulting fees or research grants. How do you distinguish between legitimate payments and bribes?"

"Several factors. Legitimate consulting fees are documented with contracts, deliverables, and tax reporting. Bribes are typically round-number wire transfers with vague memos, no contracts, and minimal documentation. All forty million dollars we traced showed characteristics of bribes rather than legitimate business transactions."

"Give the jury specifics."

"The fifty-thousand-dollar payment to Dr. Delacroix two weeks after Sophie's death: round number, wire transfer, memo says only 'consulting fee,' no contract, no documentation of services rendered. That's a bribe, not legitimate payment."

"And the payments continued for ten years?"

"Yes. As long as Nexus was conducting trials and patients were dying, money flowed to officials who covered up the deaths. When the trials ended in 1995 after NX-447 failed FDA approval, the payments stopped. That pattern proves the money was tied to criminal activity."

Hutchins objects repeatedly during Daniel's testimony, but Judge Martinez overrules most objections, the financial evidence is well-documented and admissible.

March 20, 2025, 2:00 PM Trial Day 4 - Sophie's Journal

Rachel introduces Sophie's journal as evidence.

The original journal is displayed in a protective case on a table visible to the jury. Rachel projects enlarged pages on screens.

"This is Sophie Marie Brennan's journal, written between April and October 1987. Sophie was sixteen years old. She documented what she witnessed at Willowbrook Psychiatric Hospital."

Rachel reads key entries aloud:

April 15, 1987: *"They're keeping me longer. Dr. Delacroix started me on new medications. Three different pills. They make me sleepy and my hands shake."*

May 3, 1987: *"Another patient died last night. David died. They said it was a seizure. But I saw him yesterday, he was fine until they gave him the new medication."*

June 8, 1987: *"I'm counting. Seven patients have died since I arrived in April. SEVEN. In two months. Emily, David, Lisa, Michael, Christopher, Sarah, Jennifer. All teenagers. All supposedly 'anxiety disorders.' All dead within weeks of starting 'experimental treatments.'"*

July 10, 1987: *"I saw them today. Three men in expensive suits visiting Dr. Delacroix's office. They were talking about 'trial protocols' and 'acceptable loss rates.' One of them said, 'We need faster results. Increase the dosages.' Dr. Delacroix said, 'Some patients won't survive increased dosages.' The man replied, 'Then make sure their deaths look natural. We can't afford scrutiny.'"*

Rachel pauses, letting that entry sink in.

October 10, 1987: *"This is probably my last entry. Dr. Delacroix told me I'm starting a new trial protocol tomorrow. He smiled when he said it, but his eyes were cold. I know what that means. I'm giving this journal to Nurse Margaret tonight.*

My name is Sophie Marie Brennan. I'm sixteen years old. I didn't kill myself. Whatever they say, whatever report they write, I didn't give up. They murdered me. If anyone is reading this: Please investigate. Please don't let them get away with this. Please give me justice. "

Several jurors are crying.

Rachel looks at the six defendants. "Sophie predicted her own murder twelve days before it happened. She knew they were going to kill her. She documented everything and gave her journal to a trusted nurse for safekeeping. And thirty-seven years later, that journal is the key evidence proving these six men conspired to murder seventy-three people."

She introduces Margaret Moore's note as evidence, the note explaining how Margaret kept Sophie's journal hidden for thirty-seven years because she was too afraid to come forward.

Then Rachel introduces Linda Walters's police reports, thirteen years of attempting to expose the conspiracy.

By the end of day four, the prosecution has established:

1. **Medical Evidence:** Victims were murdered with experimental drugs
2. **Financial Evidence:** Forty million in bribes to cover up murders
3. **Documentary Evidence:** Sophie's journal predicted her murder
4. **Witness Intimidation:** Linda Walters destroyed for whistleblowing

March 21, 2025, 10:00 AM Trial Day 5 - Victims' Families

Rachel calls Maria Rodriguez to the stand.

Maria is 64 years old, Emily's mother. She's been waiting thirty-eight years for this moment.

"Mrs. Rodriguez, please tell the jury about your daughter Emily."

Maria's voice shakes. "Emily was sixteen. She loved painting. She wanted to study art in college. She was my oldest daughter. My pride and joy."

"Why was Emily admitted to Willowbrook?"

"She was having anxiety attacks after her father died. Our family doctor recommended short-term psychiatric care to help her cope. I thought she'd be safe there. I thought they'd help her."

"What happened?"

"Three weeks after Emily was admitted, Willowbrook called and said she'd died. They said she overdosed on medications. They said it was suicide. I didn't believe it, Emily would never kill herself. But the medical examiner ruled it suicide and closed the case."

Maria wipes tears. "I spent thirty-eight years believing I failed my daughter. Believing if I'd been a better mother, she wouldn't have killed herself. But she didn't kill herself. They murdered her."

"How do you know?"

"The FBI investigation proved it. They exhumed Emily's body. The forensic pathologist found NX-447 in her remains, eight hundred milligrams. Emily was injected with a lethal dose of an experimental drug. Her death wasn't suicide. It was murder."

Rachel shows Maria the class photo from April 1987. "Is Emily in this photograph?"

"Yes. Front row, third from the left. She's smiling. She was alive and happy in April. Three weeks later, she was dead."

Rachel points to the Xs marked on seventeen faces. "Emily was the first victim Sophie documented in her journal."

Maria looks at the six executives. "Those men killed my daughter to test a drug. They valued profits over her life. I've waited thirty-eight years for them to face consequences. Thank you for finally holding them accountable."

Hutchins cross-examines, trying to suggest Emily was suicidal, but Maria is unshakable, Emily was murdered, and she knows it.

Rachel calls four more family members that day:

- **Thomas Torres** (Michael's brother)
- **Margaret Hartley** (Lisa's mother)
- **David Mitchell Sr.** (David's father)
- **Sarah Kim's sister**

Each tells the same story: a child admitted for treatable conditions, dead within weeks, ruled suicide, families destroyed by guilt, and now, finally, learning the truth.

By the end of week one, the jury has heard:

- Medical proof of murder
- Financial proof of bribes
- Documentary proof from Sophie's journal
- Emotional testimony from families

The prosecution case is devastating.

March 21, 2025, 5:00 PM Outside Courthouse

Catherine Brennan and I stand outside as the sun sets.

"Week one is over," Catherine says. "The jury heard everything. Medical evidence. Financial evidence. Sophie's journal. Family testimony. How can the defense possibly counter that?"

"They'll try," I say. "Next week they'll attack credibility. They'll claim the evidence is circumstantial. They'll bring their own experts who'll say the deaths could have been accidental."

"But they can't explain away Sophie's journal. They can't explain forty million in bribes. They can't explain seventy-three dead patients."

"No. They can't. The evidence is overwhelming."

Rachel joins us. "Week one went perfectly. The jury is

with us. I watched them during testimony, they're horrified, engaged, believing everything. Week two, Jenna testifies about Linda. That'll cement the obstruction of justice charge."

"And Owen?" Catherine asks.

"Week three. We're arranging secure transport from FCI Devens. Owen will testify about his thirty-year investigation and the evidence he collected. The defense will attack him hard, but his documentation is independently verified. The jury will believe him."

Agent Chen approaches. "Media coverage has been massive. Every news outlet is covering this trial. Social media is overwhelmingly pro-prosecution. Public opinion is on our side."

"Good," Rachel says. "But we still need to convince twelve jurors beyond reasonable doubt. Public opinion doesn't matter if we don't get a conviction."

She looks at me. "Jenna, you testify Tuesday. Day eight. Are you ready?"

"I'm ready."

"Good. Because next week, the jury hears about your mother. About how Linda tried to save Sophie and was destroyed for it. That's when we prove obstruction of justice. That's when we show these six men didn't just murder patients, they destroyed anyone who tried to stop them."

We stand in silence, watching the sun set over Boston.

Week one is over.

The evidence is in.

Next week, I testify.

And the fight continues.

CHAPTER 10

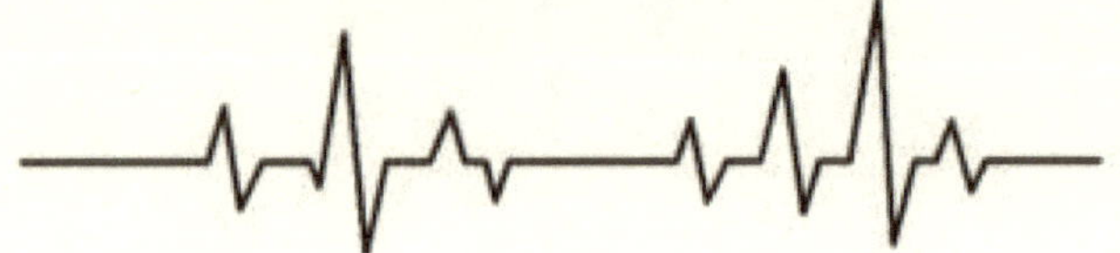

JENNA - My Testimony (March 24-28, 2025)

March 24, 2025, 8:00 AM Jenna's Apartment

I barely slept.

Today I testify. Today I tell the jury about my mother.

I've practiced my testimony dozens of times with Rachel. I've anticipated every defense attack. I know what questions are coming. I know how to stay calm, stick to facts, avoid emotion.

But knowing and doing are different things.

At 7:00 AM, my phone rings. Rachel.

"How are you feeling?"

"Terrified."

"Good. That means you care. You're going to do great, Jenna. Just remember: tell Linda's story. The jury needs to understand she was a whistleblower who was destroyed. You're the only person who can make them see that."

"What if Hutchins tears me apart on cross-examination?"

"He'll try. He'll suggest Linda was mentally ill. He'll point out you didn't believe her. But you just tell the truth, Linda reported Sophie's murder for thirteen years, everyone dismissed her as crazy, and now we know she was right about everything. The jury will see through Hutchins's attacks."

After we hang up, I look at my mother's photo on the dresser.

"Today I tell them about you, Mom," I whisper. "Today twelve strangers learn that you witnessed a murder and spent thirteen years trying to expose it. Today you're vindicated in a courtroom."

I get dressed, simple dark suit, no jewelry, professional. Rachel's advice: *Look credible. Look like someone the jury can trust.*

At 8:30 AM, Agent Chen picks me up and drives me to the courthouse.

March 24, 2025, 9:30 AM Federal Courthouse - Trial Day 8

The courtroom is packed as usual. Victims' families in the front rows. Media in designated areas. The six executives at their defense tables looking calm and confident.

I sit in the gallery until Rachel calls me.

Judge Martinez addresses the court. "We're beginning week two of trial. Ms. Diaz, call your next witness."

Rachel stands. "Your Honor, the government calls Jenna Marie Walters."

My heart hammers as I walk to the witness stand.

The bailiff swears me in. "Do you solemnly swear to tell the truth, the whole truth, and nothing but the truth, so help you God?"

"I do."

I sit in the witness box. Twelve jurors stare at me. The six executives stare at me. Cameras record everything.

Rachel approaches, her expression gentle and encouraging.

"Ms. Walters, please state your full name and age for the record."

"Jenna Marie Walters. I'm thirty-three years old."

"What is your occupation?"

"I'm a registered nurse. I work as a Patient Advocacy Coordinator at Manchester General Hospital in Manchester, New Hampshire."

"How long have you been a nurse?"

"Eleven years. I graduated nursing school in 2014."

Rachel projects a photo on the courtroom screens, **Linda Walters, 1986.** My mother in her nursing scrubs, smiling at the camera.

"Ms. Walters, do you recognize the person in this photograph?"

My voice catches. "Yes. That's my mother. Linda Walters."

"When was this photograph taken?"

"1986. Before I was born. She was working as a registered nurse."

"Where did Linda work?"

"She worked at several hospitals in New Hampshire throughout the 1980s. In April 1987, she was hired at Willowbrook Psychiatric Hospital."

"How long did she work at Willowbrook?"

"Six months. April to October 1987."

Rachel walks along the jury box, making sure they're focused on me.

"Ms. Walters, do you know what happened to your mother at Willowbrook on October 23, 1987?"

"Yes. She witnessed the aftermath of Sophie Brennan's murder. She arrived at a scene where staff members were staging Sophie's death to look like suicide. My mother saw them moving the body, cleaning up evidence, destroying medical records."

"What did your mother do?"

"She filed a police report immediately. Within hours of witnessing the staging, she went to the Manchester Police Department and reported what she'd seen."

Rachel projects the police report on the screens, **Manchester Police Department, Incident Report #87-10-4729, dated October 23, 1987.**

"Ms. Walters, is this the police report your mother filed?"

I read it quickly, tears already forming. "Yes."

"Please read the highlighted section for the jury."

I clear my throat and read: "'Officer responded to complaint from Ms. Walters, a registered nurse at Willowbrook Psychiatric Hospital. Ms. Walters reported discovering the body of Sophie Marie Brennan, age 16, at approximately 4:15 AM. Ms. Walters stated the death was staged to look like suicide. She reported observing post-mortem lividity inconsistent with hanging, fresh injection marks on deceased's arms, signs of cardiac arrest prior to hanging, and staff members cleaning the scene before police arrival. Ms. Walters requested immediate investigation into possible homicide.'"

"What happened to that police report?"

"It was forwarded to the medical examiner, Dr. Robert Delacroix. He closed the case within twenty-four hours and ruled Sophie's death a suicide."

"Did your mother accept that ruling?"

"No. She filed additional reports. She contacted the nursing board, the state health department, the attorney general's office. She spent the next thirteen years trying to expose what she'd witnessed."

Rachel projects a timeline on the screens, a visual representation of Linda's thirteen years of reporting.

1987: Files police report (dismissed)

1988: Files nursing board complaint (dismissed)

1989: Files state health complaint (dismissed) + **Nursing license REVOKED**

1990-1997: Continues filing reports (all dismissed)

1998: Loses custody of daughter Jenna

1999-2000: Files final reports (perfunctory)

2011: Dies by suicide

"Ms. Walters, let's walk through this timeline. In 1989, your mother lost her nursing license. Do you know why?"

"Yes. The nursing board claimed she was emotionally

unstable and making false accusations. They revoked her license effective September 1, 1989."

Rachel projects the license revocation order.

"This document states: 'Ms. Walters is emotionally unstable and represents a danger to patient safety.' Do you believe that was true?"

"No. My mother wasn't emotionally unstable. She was a whistleblower reporting corporate murder. She was being destroyed for telling the truth."

Gerald Hutchins half-rises. "Objection, Your Honor. Speculation. The witness can't know the nursing board's motivations."

Judge Martinez: "Overruled. The witness is testifying about her understanding of events. Continue, Ms. Diaz."

Rachel nods. "Ms. Walters, what happened in 1998?"

This is the hardest part. I take a breath.

"In 1998, social services took me away from my mother. I was seven years old. They said she was unfit to parent, that her obsession with the Willowbrook murders made her a danger to herself and to me."

"Where were you placed?"

"Foster care. I was in the system until I aged out at eighteen."

"Did you see your mother after 1998?"

"A few times. Supervised visits. But she was heavily medicated by then, antipsychotics, mood stabilizers. She could barely function. The last time I saw her was 2009. She was living in a group home. She didn't really recognize me."

My voice breaks. Several jurors wipe their eyes.

"What happened in 2011?"

"My mother died by suicide. May 15, 2011. She was forty-nine years old. Overdose of prescription medications."

"Ms. Walters, you testified that your mother spent thirteen years filing reports about Sophie's murder. During that time, did anyone believe her?"

"No. Everyone dismissed her as mentally ill. Police said she was making false accusations. The nursing board said she was delusional. Social services said she was paranoid. Doctors said she had paranoid personality disorder. Everyone said my mother was crazy."

Rachel pauses, letting that sink in.

"Did you believe your mother?"

This is the crucial admission.

"No. I didn't believe her. I was a child. Everyone told me my mother was mentally ill. I thought she'd made up stories about murdered patients and pharmaceutical conspiracies. I thought she was delusional."

"When did you learn the truth?"

"November 19, 2024. When I found Margaret Moore's note and Sophie's journal. When I brought the evidence to the FBI and learned everything my mother reported was true."

Rachel walks back to the prosecution table and picks up a folder.

"Ms. Walters, I'm showing you what's been marked as Government Exhibit 127. Can you identify this document?"

I look at it, my mother's final police report, dated March 2000.

"This is my mother's last police report about Sophie's murder. Filed in March 2000."

"Please read the highlighted section."

I read, my voice shaking: "'I know you don't believe me. I know you think I'm mentally ill. But Sophie Brennan was murdered at Willowbrook Psychiatric Hospital on October 22, 1987. I witnessed staff staging her death as suicide. I've been reporting this for thirteen years. Please. Please investigate. Someone needs to give Sophie justice. Please don't let them get away with this.'"

I can't continue. Tears stream down my face.

Rachel speaks gently. "That was March 2000. Your mother filed one more report begging officials to investigate. What happened?"

"The report was dismissed like all the others. My mother never filed again after that. She gave up."

"Why did she give up?"

"Because they took everything from her. Her career. Her daughter. Her reputation. Her life. She'd spent thirteen years fighting and losing everything. She couldn't fight anymore."

Rachel returns to the jury box.

"Ms. Walters, we now know, thanks to the FBI investigation, that your mother was right. Sophie Brennan was murdered. Patients were experimented on without consent. Officials were bribed. Everything your mother reported for thirteen years was true. Is that correct?"

"Yes. My mother was telling the truth. She witnessed a murder and tried to expose a pharmaceutical conspiracy. And instead of being believed, she was destroyed."

I look at the six executives sitting at their defense tables.

"Those six men didn't just murder Sophie Brennan and seventy-two other patients. They destroyed every person who tried to expose them. Including my mother. She spent thirteen years being called crazy when she was actually a hero trying to save lives. She died believing she'd failed. But she didn't fail. She was right."

Rachel lets my words hang in the air.

"No further questions, Your Honor."

Judge Martinez looks at the defense tables. "Cross-examination?"

Gerald Hutchins stands. "Yes, Your Honor."

March 24, 2025, 11:00 AM Cross-Examination

Hutchins approaches the witness stand. His demeanor is gentle, he knows attacking a grieving daughter will make him look bad to the jury.

"Ms. Walters, I'm sorry for your loss. Losing a parent is always difficult."

"Thank you."

"You testified that your mother filed numerous reports about Sophie Brennan's death. Those reports were investigated, correct?"

"They were dismissed. I don't know if they were actually investigated."

"But officials reviewed them. Police reviewed them. The nursing board reviewed them. Multiple agencies looked at your mother's claims, correct?"

"Yes."

"And all of those agencies, police, nursing board, health department, social services, all concluded your mother's reports lacked merit. Isn't that true?"

I see where he's going. "They dismissed her reports, yes."

"And you yourself testified that everyone, police, doctors,

social workers, all believed your mother was mentally ill. Correct?"

"They believed she was mentally ill because she was reporting corporate murder and they didn't want to believe it."

"But Ms. Walters, you also believed she was mentally ill, didn't you?"

Here's the trap.

"I believed what I was told. I was seven years old when social services took me away. I didn't have the knowledge or resources to verify her claims."

"But throughout your teenage years and into adulthood, you believed your mother was delusional, correct?"

"Yes. I was wrong. Everyone was wrong. My mother was telling the truth."

Hutchins presses: "You testified that your last visit with your mother was in 2009. Can you describe her mental state?"

"She was heavily medicated. She was barely functional."

"Would you say she appeared mentally ill?"

"She appeared drugged. She'd been on antipsychotics and mood stabilizers for years. Of course she wasn't functioning normally."

"But the psychiatrists who prescribed those medications believed she needed them, correct?"

"They prescribed them because she was reporting pharmaceutical murder and everyone assumed she was crazy. But she wasn't. She was right."

Hutchins changes tactics. "Ms. Walters, you found Sophie's journal on November 19, 2024. Before that date, had you ever heard your mother mention Sophie Brennan specifically?"

I think back. "She talked about a girl who died at Willowbrook. A teenager. I didn't know the name was Sophie until I found the journal."

"So, your mother's reports about a 'murdered patient' at Willowbrook could have been about anyone?"

"She was reporting Sophie's murder specifically. The police reports name Sophie."

"But in your personal interactions with your mother, as a child, as a teenager, she never gave you specific details that you could verify?"

"She tried. I didn't listen. I thought she was delusional."

Hutchins looks at the jury. "Ms. Walters, isn't it possible your mother was mentally ill? That she witnessed a tragic suicide and her mind created a conspiracy theory to explain it? That she truly believed patients were being murdered but was incorrect?"

"No. The FBI investigation proved everything my mother said was true. Sophie was murdered. Patients were experimented on. Officials were bribed. My mother witnessed all of that and reported it accurately for thirteen years."

"But you can't know what your mother actually witnessed on October 23, 1987, can you? You weren't there. You weren't born yet."

"I can read her police report filed within hours of the event. I can compare her report to the forensic evidence we have now. Everything matches. My mother accurately described a staged suicide scene in 1987. The forensic pathologist confirmed in 2024 that Sophie's death was staged. My mother was right."

Hutchins tries a few more angles, but I hold firm. Rachel coached me well, stick to facts, don't get emotional, keep referring to evidence.

Finally, Hutchins gives up. "No further questions."

Judge Martinez looks at Rachel. "Redirect?"

"Yes, Your Honor."

March 24, 2025, 11:30 AM Redirect Examination

Rachel stands. "Ms. Walters, the defense suggested your mother might have been mentally ill. Let me ask directly: Do you believe Linda Walters was mentally ill?"

"No. I believe she was a whistleblower who was systematically gaslighted until she couldn't take it anymore. She witnessed a murder. She reported it faithfully for thirteen years. And instead of being believed, she was labeled crazy. That kind of psychological abuse destroys people."

"If officials had believed your mother in 1987 and investigated Sophie's death properly, what might have happened?"

"Objection," Hutchins calls. "Speculation."

Rachel responds: "Your Honor, this goes to the obstruction of justice charge. If the conspiracy had been exposed in 1987, subsequent deaths would have been prevented."

Judge Martinez: "I'll allow it. Answer the question, Ms. Walters."

"If officials had investigated in 1987, they would have discovered the pharmaceutical trials. They would have shut down Willowbrook. They would have arrested the people responsible. And the sixty-two patients who died between 1987 and 1995 would still be alive."

"So, your mother's reports, if believed, could have saved lives?"

"Yes. She tried to save lives. That's what whistleblowers do. And she was destroyed for it."

Rachel returns to her seat. "No further questions, Your Honor."

"The witness is excused."

I step down from the witness stand, my legs shaking.

Catherine Brennan grabs my hand as I sit down. "You did beautifully. Linda would be so proud."

March 24-27, 2025

Week 2 Continues Over the next three days, Rachel presents additional evidence:

March 25 (Day 9): Three former Willowbrook staff members testify. All confirm illegal drug trials, patient deaths, and cover-ups. All were afraid to speak up at the time.

March 26 (Day 10): FBI Agent Phyllis Chen testifies about the investigation. Explains how Owen's documentation led to the case, how Sophie's journal confirmed everything, how financial records proved bribes.

March 27 (Day 11): Catherine Brennan testifies. Sophie's mother describes decades of believing Sophie committed suicide, the guilt, the grief, and finally learning the truth. Devastating testimony.

March 28 (Day 12): Final prosecution witnesses, two more victims' families, FBI forensic team confirming chain of custody for all evidence.

By Friday afternoon, the prosecution rests.

"Your Honor," Rachel stands, "the government rests its case."

Judge Martinez looks at the defense. "We'll adjourn for the weekend. Defense case begins Monday, March 31st."

March 28, 2025, 5:00 PM Outside Courthouse

Rachel, Agent Chen, and I stand outside as media swarms around us.

"The prosecution rested!" a reporter shouts. "How confident are you in a conviction?"

Rachel addresses the cameras: "We presented overwhelming evidence. Forensic proof that seventy-three patients were murdered. Financial proof of forty million dollars in bribes. Documentary proof from Sophie Brennan's journal. Witness testimony from victims' families and whistleblowers. The evidence speaks for itself."

"What about the defense case?"

"We'll see what they present. But they can't explain away the forensic evidence, the financial records, or Sophie's journal. The facts are clear."

After the press conference, Rachel pulls me aside.

"You did great this week. Your testimony was powerful. The jury saw Linda as a hero who was destroyed. That's exactly what we needed."

"What happens next week?"

"Defense case. They'll bring character witnesses saying

the executives are good people. They'll bring their own medical experts who'll try to argue the deaths could have been accidental. They'll attack Owen's credibility when he testifies. But their case will be weak because they can't refute our evidence."

Agent Chen adds, "Owen testifies Wednesday. We're transporting him from FCI Devens Monday night. He'll be held in federal detention here until his testimony is complete. Then he goes back to prison."

"How is he?"

"Ready. He's been preparing for this moment for six years, since he was arrested in 2018. He knows his testimony is crucial."

Catherine joins us. "Two weeks of prosecution evidence. The jury heard everything. Medical proof. Financial proof. Documentary proof. Family testimony. How can they not convict?"

"They will," Rachel says with confidence. "The evidence is overwhelming. Even with expensive defense attorneys, those six men are going to prison."

I look back at the courthouse.

Two weeks down. Two weeks to go.

The prosecution rested.

The defense begins Monday.

And Wednesday, Owen testifies.

Sophie's brother. In prison for killing four people. Cooperating to bring down six more.

The climax of the trial is coming.

March 30, 2025, 10:00 PM Jenna's Apartment

Sunday night. The defense begins their case tomorrow.

I can't stop thinking about my testimony. About reading my mother's desperate final police report to the jury. About admitting I didn't believe her. About looking at those six executives and saying they destroyed her.

My phone rings. Victoria Lang.

"Jenna, I wanted to check on you. Your testimony was powerful. How are you holding up?"

"Exhausted. Emotional. But okay."

"You did Linda proud. The way you described her whistleblowing, the jury saw her as a hero. That's what she deserved."

"Thank you. That means a lot."

"The defense starts tomorrow. They'll try to create doubt. But after two weeks of prosecution evidence, I don't see how they can. This case is solid."

After we hang up, I write in my journal, something I've been doing since the trial started.

Day 12. Prosecution rested. I testified about Mom. Told the jury she was a whistleblower who spent 13 years trying to expose pharmaceutical murder. Told them she was destroyed for telling the truth. Told them she died believing she'd failed but she was right all along.

The jury listened. Some cried. I think they understood.

Defense starts tomorrow. Owen testifies Wednesday. Two more weeks and this is over.

Two more weeks until those six men are convicted.

I hope.

I close my journal and look at my mother's photo.

"We're almost there, Mom," I whisper. "Two more weeks. Then justice. Then vindication. Then the world knows you were a hero."

CHAPTER 11

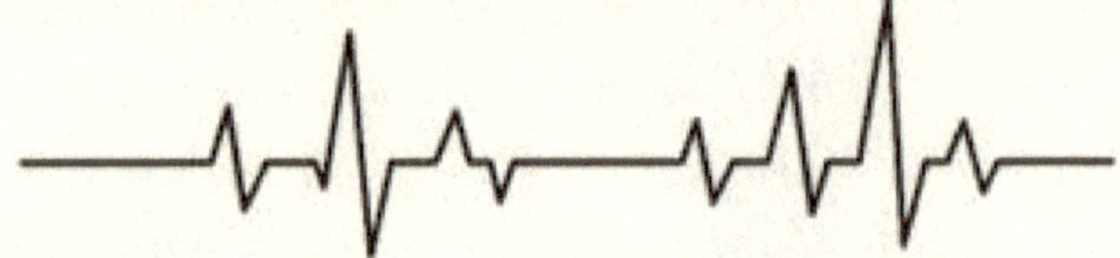

JENNA - Owen Testifies (March 31 - April 2, 2025)

March 31, 2025, 9:00 AM Federal Courthouse - Trial Day 13

The defense begins their case.

Gerald Hutchins calls his first witness: **Dr. Samuel Richardson**, a pharmaceutical industry consultant who testifies that drug trials in the 1980s operated under different safety standards than today, that patient deaths during experimental trials were "tragic but expected," and that Nexus Pharmaceuticals followed all applicable regulations at the time.

Rachel's cross-examination is brutal.

"Dr. Richardson, you're being paid two thousand dollars per hour to testify, correct?"

"I'm being compensated for my expertise, yes."

"And you've been retained by pharmaceutical companies in over fifty lawsuits, always testifying for the defense?"

"I provide expert testimony based on industry standards"

"You've never once testified against a pharmaceutical company, have you?"

"My expertise is in industry practices..."

"Please answer yes or no. Have you ever testified against a pharmaceutical company?"

"No."

"So, your income depends entirely on pharmaceutical companies hiring you as an expert witness?"

"Objection!" Hutchins stands. "Argumentative."

Judge Martinez: "Overruled. Answer the question, Dr. Richardson."

"My income comes from various consulting work."

Rachel doesn't let up. "Dr. Richardson, you testified that patient deaths during trials were 'expected.' The forensic evidence shows these patients died from eight-hundred-milligram doses of NX-447, far above therapeutic levels. Would you call eight-hundred-milligram lethal injections 'expected' trial outcomes?"

"I wasn't testifying about specific dosages..."

"Because you didn't review the forensic evidence, did you? You reviewed only materials provided by the defense."

"I reviewed the materials given to me..."

"So, you have no knowledge of the actual doses administered, the falsified death certificates, or the forty million in bribe payments?"

"That's outside my area of expertise."

"No further questions."

Dr. Richardson's testimony collapses under cross-examination.

The defense calls two more expert witnesses that day, both equally ineffective, both exposed as paid consultants with conflicts of interest.

By 5:00 PM, the defense has made little progress.

April 1, 2025, 7:00 AM Federal Detention Center, Boston

Owen Brennan sits in a holding cell.

He was transported from FCI Devens yesterday evening under maximum security, armored vehicle, U.S. Marshals, full restraints. He spent the night in federal detention in Boston and will remain here until his testimony is complete.

At 7:00 AM, two marshals enter his cell.

"Time to go, Brennan. You're testifying today."

They cuff his hands in front of him, shackle his ankles, attach a chain connecting the cuffs to the shackles. Prison transport protocol for a convicted murderer.

Owen stands. He's 48 years old, wearing prison orange, gray hair, tired eyes. Six years in federal custody. Fourteen more years minimum before parole eligibility.

But today, he testifies. Today, he helps convict the six men who murdered his sister.

The marshals escort him through a secure underground tunnel connecting the detention center to the courthouse. No media. No public. Maximum security.

At 8:30 AM, Owen is placed in a holding room adjacent to the courtroom.

Agent Chen enters. "Owen. How are you feeling?"

"Ready. I've been waiting six years for this."

"The jury is going to see you in full restraints. Prison jumpsuit, handcuffs, shackles. The defense will use that to attack your credibility...'You're a convicted murderer, why should we believe you?' Are you prepared for that?"

"Yes. I killed four people. I confessed. I'm serving twenty years. I accept that. But my investigation was accurate. My evidence is real. Everything I collected has been independently verified by the FBI. The jury will see that."

Rachel Diaz enters. "Owen, we're starting in thirty minutes. Remember: be honest about your crimes, show remorse, but be clear that your evidence is credible. Don't let Hutchins rattle you."

"I won't."

At 9:00 AM, two marshals escort Owen into the courtroom through a side door.

April 1, 2025, 9:05 AM Owen Takes the Stand

The courtroom goes silent as Owen enters.

He's in full restraints, handcuffs, ankle shackles, chain connecting them. Prison orange jumpsuit with "FEDERAL PRISONER" stenciled on the back. Two U.S. Marshals stand directly behind him.

The jury stares. The media captures everything. The six executives lean forward, watching the man who killed four of their associates.

Owen sits in the witness box, his cuffed hands resting awkwardly in his lap.

The bailiff swears him in. "Do you solemnly swear to tell the truth, the whole truth, and nothing but the truth, so help you God?"

"I do."

Rachel Diaz approaches.

"Please state your name for the record."

"Owen Michael Brennan."

"How old are you?"

"Forty-eight."

"Where are you currently incarcerated?"

"Federal Correctional Institution Devens in Massachusetts."

"Why are you incarcerated?"

Owen looks directly at the jury. "I murdered four people between December 2017 and May 2018. I was arrested in June 2018, tried, convicted, and sentenced to twenty years in federal prison. I'm currently serving year six of that sentence."

Several jurors look uncomfortable. This is a confessed murderer testifying.

Rachel continues: "Who did you kill?"

"Dr. Richard Delacroix, Dr. Henry Wallace, Patricia Reynolds, and Robert Delacroix."

"Why did you kill them?"

"Because they murdered my sister Sophie and helped cover it up. Dr. Richard Delacroix injected Sophie with the drug that killed her. Patricia Reynolds helped stage her death as suicide. Robert Delacroix, the medical examiner, falsified the autopsy report and closed the case. Dr. Henry Wallace was a pharmaceutical executive who authorized the illegal trials."

"So, these were revenge murders?"

"Yes. I spent thirty years investigating my sister's death. When the legal system failed to prosecute anyone, I took matters into my own hands. It was wrong. I'm serving twenty years for it. But those four people did murder Sophie and cover it up."

Rachel walks to the jury box. "Mr. Brennan, tell the jury about Sophie. Who was she?"

Owen's voice softens. "Sophie was my older sister. She was sixteen when she died. I was eleven. Sophie was kind, creative, brave. She loved art and music. She wanted to be a teacher. She was admitted to Willowbrook Psychiatric Hospital in April 1987 for anxiety following our father's death. She should have received counseling and come home. Instead, she was murdered six months later."

"When did you learn about the circumstances of her death?"

"Not until I was older. I was eleven when Sophie died. My mother was told Sophie committed suicide, hung herself in the basement. We believed that for years. But when I was sixteen, I found some of Sophie's belongings, including letters she'd written. She mentioned being afraid at Willowbrook, talked about patients dying, said something was wrong. That's when I started questioning the official story."

"What did you do?"

"I started investigating. At first, just reading old newspaper articles, looking at public records. When I turned eighteen, I filed Freedom of Information requests for Sophie's medical records, autopsy reports, police records. I spent years piecing together what happened."

Rachel projects a timeline on the screens, Owen's thirty-year investigation.

"Mr. Brennan, describe your investigation."

"I spent thirty years tracking down everyone connected to Sophie's death. I interviewed former Willowbrook staff members. I obtained financial records showing payments from Nexus Pharmaceuticals to officials. I collected emails between executives. I documented seventy-three suspicious deaths at facilities where Nexus conducted trials. I built a comprehensive case proving pharmaceutical murder."

"Did you present your evidence to authorities?"

"Yes. Multiple times. I went to police in 2005, 2010, 2015. I contacted prosecutors, journalists, congressional offices. Everyone dismissed me. They said too much time had passed, the statute of limitations had expired, witnesses were dead, evidence was too old. Nobody would investigate."

Owen's voice hardens. "So, in 2017, I decided to take justice into my own hands. Over six months, I killed the four people most directly responsible for Sophie's death. I planned it carefully. I executed it deliberately. And I accept full responsibility."

"Are you testifying here today to reduce your sentence?"

"No. My sentence is fixed, twenty years minimum, eligible for parole in 2044. There's no reduction. I'm testifying because it's the right thing to do. Because these six men ordered the deaths of seventy-three people and need to be held accountable."

Rachel returns to the prosecution table and picks up a thick folder.

"Mr. Brennan, this folder contains financial records you collected during your investigation. How did you obtain these records?"

"Through various means. Some were public records, corporate tax filings, SEC documents. Some I obtained through FOIA requests. Some I got from former Nexus employees who were willing to talk off the record."

"Are these records authentic?"

"Yes. The FBI has verified every document I collected. Bank statements, wire transfer records, tax returns, all authentic."

Rachel projects a wire transfer on the screens. "What is this?"

"A fifty-thousand-dollar payment from Nexus Pharmaceuticals to Dr. Robert Delacroix on November 5, 1987. Two weeks after Sophie's death. Two days after Dr. Delacroix closed the investigation and ruled her death a suicide."

"How many similar payments did you document?"

"Hundreds. Over forty million dollars paid to medical

examiners, hospital administrators, FDA officials, police investigators, anyone who could help cover up patient deaths. The pattern was consistent: patient dies, official covers it up, Nexus pays them."

Rachel shows more documents, emails, financial records, witness statements. Owen explains each one methodically.

After two hours of direct examination, Rachel asks her final question:

"Mr. Brennan, you killed four people. You're in prison for twenty years. You've admitted your crimes. Why should this jury believe your evidence?"

"Because everything I've collected has been independently verified. The FBI authenticated the financial records. The forensic pathologist confirmed the victims were murdered with experimental drugs. Sophie's journal, which I never saw until the FBI showed it to me in 2024, corroborates everything I documented. I'm not making this up. I'm not lying to reduce my sentence. The evidence is real."

"No further questions, Your Honor."

Judge Martinez looks at the defense tables. "Cross-examination?"

Gerald Hutchins stands, a predatory smile on his face. "Absolutely, Your Honor."

April 1, 2025, 2:00 PM Cross-Examination - Hutchins Attacks

After lunch recess, Hutchins approaches Owen.

"Mr. Brennan, you murdered four people. Is that correct?"

"Yes."

"You stabbed Dr. Richard Delacroix seventeen times, didn't you?"

"Yes."

"You shot Patricia Reynolds three times in the head?"

"Yes."

"You strangled Robert Delacroix with your bare hands?"

"Yes."

Hutchins paces, making sure the jury absorbs the brutality. "And you shot Dr. Henry Wallace twice in the chest?"

"Yes."

"So, you're a violent, vengeful killer who spent six months hunting and murdering four people?"

"Yes. I killed four people who murdered my sister and covered it up. It was wrong. I'm serving twenty years for it."

"You're not remorseful, are you? You just said it was wrong, but you don't sound sorry."

"I'm remorseful that I resorted to violence. But I'm not sorry those four people are dead. They murdered Sophie and sixty-two other patients. They destroyed Linda Walters for trying to report it. They got away with it for thirty-seven years."

Hutchins seizes on this. "So, you believe your vigilante murders were justified?"

"No. I believe they were understandable but illegal. I accept my punishment. But those four people did commit crimes, and if the legal system had prosecuted them, I wouldn't have killed them."

"So, you're blaming the legal system for your murders?"

"I'm blaming the pharmaceutical executives who ordered seventy-three patient deaths and the corrupt officials who covered them up."

Hutchins shifts tactics. "Mr. Brennan, you testified you spent thirty years investigating Sophie's death. Isn't it more accurate to say you spent thirty years obsessing over a family tragedy, creating elaborate conspiracy theories to avoid accepting that your sister committed suicide?"

"No. The forensic evidence proves Sophie was murdered. The financial records prove officials were bribed. Sophie's journal proves she was documenting illegal trials. This isn't a conspiracy theory. It's a documented conspiracy."

"But Mr. Brennan, you never saw Sophie's journal until 2024, correct? You built your entire case without that journal."

"That's true. But when the FBI showed me the journal, it confirmed everything I'd independently discovered. Sophie documented patient deaths I'd already identified. She described pharmaceutical executives I'd already traced. Her journal corroborates my investigation, it doesn't contradict it."

Hutchins walks to the defense table and picks up a thick file. "Mr. Brennan, you filed reports with police departments in 2005, 2010, and 2015. Each time, investigators reviewed your claims and found them baseless. Isn't that true?"

"They dismissed my reports without properly investigating."

"Or perhaps they investigated and found your conspiracy theory lacked merit?"

"If they'd investigated properly, they would have found the financial records. They would have exhumed bodies. They would have discovered the truth. But they didn't want to investigate a pharmaceutical company, so they dismissed me."

Hutchins presses: "Mr. Brennan, isn't it true you're testifying here to seek revenge against the pharmaceutical industry? That you blame GenHealth for your sister's death and want to destroy the company?"

"I'm testifying to hold six executives accountable for murdering seventy-three people. I don't care about the company; I care about justice."

"Justice? You murdered four people! You're a convicted felon serving twenty years! Why should this jury believe anything you say?"

Owen looks directly at the jury, his voice steady. "Because the evidence I collected is real. The FBI verified it. The financial records are authentic, bank statements, wire transfers, tax returns. The forensic pathologist confirmed patients were murdered. Sophie's journal confirmed the conspiracy. I may be a murderer, but I'm not a liar. Everything I've testified about is documented, verified, and true."

Hutchins tries for another hour but gains little ground. Owen remains calm, consistent, unshakable.

Finally, Hutchins gives up. "No further questions."

Judge Martinez: "Redirect?"

Rachel stands. "Yes, Your Honor."

April 1, 2025, 3:45 PM Redirect Examination

Rachel approaches Owen. "Mr. Brennan, the defense suggested you fabricated evidence to support a revenge fantasy. Let me ask directly: Is the evidence you collected accurate?"

"Yes. Every document, every financial record, every witness statement, all accurate. The FBI has verified everything."

"Are you testifying to reduce your sentence?"

"No. My sentence is twenty years minimum. There's no reduction. I'm testifying because these six men need to be held accountable."

"You killed four people. Do you regret that?"

"I regret that violence was necessary. I should have trusted the legal system more. But I don't regret stopping those four people from living free after murdering my sister."

"If you could go back, would you do anything differently?"

Owen pauses, thinking. "I would keep investigating legally. I would keep pushing authorities. I would wait longer for justice. But ultimately, if the legal system still failed, I don't know that I'd make a different choice. Sophie deserved justice. Sometimes justice requires sacrifice."

"What sacrifice did you make?"

"Twenty years of my life. I'm forty-eight years old. I'll be sixty-eight when I'm eligible for parole, if I'm granted parole, which is unlikely. I'll probably die in prison. But Sophie got justice. That's worth it."

Rachel returns to her seat. "No further questions."

Judge Martinez looks at Owen. "The witness is excused. Marshals, please escort Mr. Brennan back to detention."

Two U.S. Marshals approach. Owen stands awkwardly in his restraints.

As he's led away, he looks at Catherine Brennan in the gallery. She's crying silently.

Owen mouths: "I'm sorry, Mom."

Catherine nods, unable to speak.

The courtroom watches as Owen shuffles out in chains, a confessed murderer who spent his life seeking justice and will spend the rest of it in prison.

April 2, 2025, 9:00 AM Trial Day 15 - Defense Continues

The defense calls more witnesses:

Character witnesses for the executives:

- Former colleagues praising James Morrison's pharmaceutical innovations
- Community members praising Martin Shaw's charity work
- Business partners testifying about Robert Chen's integrity

Rachel's cross-examinations are brief and devastating:

"Did you know Mr. Morrison authorized drug trials that killed seventy-three patients?"

"No..."

"So, your testimony about his character doesn't account for pharmaceutical murder, does it?"

"I... I suppose not."

By the afternoon, the defense realizes their case is

collapsing.

At 4:00 PM, Gerald Hutchins stands. "Your Honor, the defense rests."

Judge Martinez looks surprised, the defense case lasted only two days compared to the prosecution's twelve days.

"Very well. Closing arguments will begin tomorrow morning. We're adjourned until 9:00 AM, April 3rd."

April 2, 2025, 6:00 PM Federal Detention Center - Owen Returns to Prison

Owen is transported back to FCI Devens that evening.

Before he leaves, Agent Chen visits him in the holding cell.

"You did well, Owen. Your testimony was powerful. The jury believed you."

"Did I help? Did my testimony make a difference?"

"Absolutely. You explained the financial evidence, corroborated Sophie's journal, showed the pattern of cover-ups. Combined with the forensic evidence and Sophie's documentation, the case is airtight."

"What happens now?"

"Closing arguments tomorrow. Then jury deliberation. We're expecting a verdict within a week."

Owen nods. "I won't be here for the verdict. I'll be back in prison."

"We'll notify you immediately. And when those six men are convicted, you'll know Sophie got justice."

"That's all I wanted. For thirty-seven years, that's all I wanted."

Two marshals arrive to transport Owen. Agent Chen shakes his cuffed hands.

"Thank you for your cooperation, Owen. You helped bring down six murderers."

"I just wish I'd done it without becoming a murderer myself."

Owen is led away, beginning the journey back to FCI Devens where he'll serve at least fourteen more years.

April 2, 2025, 9:00 PM Jenna's Apartment

I'm watching news coverage of Owen's testimony.

Every channel shows the same images: Owen in prison orange and chains, testifying about his thirty-year investigation, admitting he killed four people but insisting his evidence is real.

The media is divided:

CNN: "Convicted Killer's Testimony Bolsters Prosecution

Case"

Fox News: "Can Jury Trust Murderer's Evidence?"

MSNBC: "Owen Brennan: Vigilante or Truth-Teller?"

My phone rings. Catherine.

"Did you see Owen today?" she asks.

"On TV. I wasn't in the courtroom, Rachel thought it would be too distracting for me."

"He looked so... broken. My son is in chains, Jenna. He's in prison for twenty years. He killed four people trying to get justice for Sophie. And now those six executives are going to be convicted, but Owen will still be in prison."

"I know. It's complicated."

"He sacrificed everything for Sophie. His freedom. His life. Everything. And I'm proud of him and heartbroken at the same time."

We talk for an hour, two mothers' children destroyed by the same conspiracy. Sophie, murdered at sixteen. Owen, imprisoned at forty-eight. Linda, dead at fifty-two. Me, orphaned and raised in foster care.

Four lives destroyed. And six pharmaceutical executives responsible for all of it.

Tomorrow, closing arguments.

Then jury deliberation.

Then verdict.

Justice is coming.

Slow. Painful. Incomplete.

But coming nonetheless.

CHAPTER 12

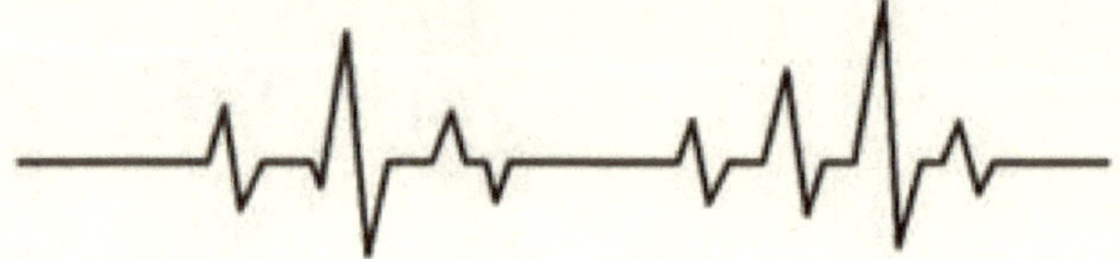

Media Firestorm

April 3, 2025, 6:00 AM Jenna's Apartment, Manchester, NH

I wake to seventeen missed calls.

My phone has been buzzing since 5:30 AM, news outlets, reporters, producers from morning shows. They all want the same thing: an interview with "Sophie Brennan's witness" or "the nurse who exposed the conspiracy" or "Linda Walters' daughter."

I silence my phone and turn on the TV.

Every channel is covering the trial.

CNN - 6:03 AM:

"Good morning. We begin with breaking news in the

Willowbrook pharmaceutical murder trial. After twelve days of explosive testimony, closing arguments begin today in what prosecutors are calling one of the most significant corporate crime cases in U.S. history..."

The screen shows footage of yesterday, Owen being led into court in chains, the six executives sitting at the defense table, Rachel Diaz presenting evidence.

Then my face appears.

It's from outside the courthouse last week, me walking past cameras, trying not to look overwhelmed.

The caption reads:

JENNA WALTERS - Witness, Daughter of Whistleblower Linda Walters

I change the channel.

Fox News - 6:04 AM: "The question everyone's asking this morning: Can we trust evidence collected by a convicted murderer? Owen Brennan killed four people in what he called a quest for justice. Now prosecutors are asking a jury to believe his investigation..."

MSNBC - 6:05 AM: "The Willowbrook case has ignited fierce debate about corporate accountability, whistleblower protection, and the limits of vigilante justice. We're joined this morning by legal analysts..."

I turn off the TV.

My apartment feels too small, too quiet, too exposed.

The trial has been national news for two weeks, but yesterday's testimony pushed it to a fever pitch. Owen's admission that he murdered four people, his thirty-year obsession, his testimony from prison, it's the kind of story that consumes the news cycle.

And I'm part of it.

My phone rings again. I check the caller ID: **NBC News**.

I don't answer.

April 3, 2025, 8:00 AM Outside Federal Courthouse, Boston

I arrive two hours before closing arguments begin.

The courthouse is surrounded by satellite trucks and reporters. Protesters line the sidewalk with signs:

JUSTICE FOR SOPHIE

73 VICTIMS, 6 MURDERERS

BIG PHARMA KILLS

OWEN BRENNAN IS A HERO

VIGILANTE JUSTICE ISN'T JUSTICE

The crowd is a chaotic mix: victims' family members,

pharmaceutical reform advocates, true crime enthusiasts, conspiracy theorists, reporters, and gawkers.

I keep my head down and try to reach the courthouse entrance.

"Jenna! Jenna Walters!"

A reporter shoves a microphone in my face. "How does it feel knowing your mother tried to expose this thirty years ago?"

I push past without answering.

"Ms. Walters! Do you think Owen Brennan is a hero or a murderer?"

"Jenna! Will you testify today?"

"Ms. Walters! What would you say to your mother if she were alive?"

Security guards form a barrier, ushering me through the metal detectors.

Inside, the courthouse feels like a sanctuary, quiet, controlled, protected.

I text Rachel: **I'm here. Media is insane.**

She responds immediately: **Stay in the victim witness room. Don't talk to anyone. Closing arguments start at 10.**

April 3, 2025, 9:30 AM Victim Witness Room

Catherine Brennan arrives at 9:30, looking exhausted.

"Did you see the news?" she asks, sitting beside me.

"I tried not to."

"They're calling Owen a hero. A vigilante. A murderer. A victim himself." She shakes her head. "Everyone has an opinion about my son."

"What's your opinion?"

Catherine is quiet for a long moment. "He's my son. He killed four people. He's in prison for twenty years. He sacrificed his life for Sophie." She looks at me, tears in her eyes. "I don't know what I think anymore. I'm just... tired."

I understand that bone-deep exhaustion. The kind that comes from carrying trauma for so long that it becomes part of your skeleton.

We sit in silence, two women connected by death and justice and complicated love for people who made terrible choices.

At 9:50, a victim advocate enters. "Closing arguments begin in ten minutes."

Catherine and I stand.

"Here we go," she whispers.

April 3, 2025, 10:00 AM Courtroom - Closing Arguments Begin

The courtroom is packed.

Every seat filled. Standing room only in the back. Sketch artists positioned along the side wall. Security doubled.

Judge Martinez enters. "All rise."

We stand.

"Please be seated. We'll now hear closing arguments. Ms. Diaz, you may begin."

Rachel Diaz rises, wearing a sharp navy suit. She's been preparing for this moment for months, since November when I first walked into the FBI field office with Sophie's journal.

She approaches the jury box.

"Ladies and gentlemen of the jury. Thank you for your service over these past three weeks. You've heard testimony from thirty-two witnesses. You've reviewed over four hundred exhibits. You've seen evidence of one of the most heinous corporate crimes in American history."

She pauses, letting the weight settle.

"In October 1987, sixteen-year-old Sophie Brennan was murdered at Willowbrook Psychiatric Hospital. She wasn't killed by a stranger. She wasn't killed in a random act of violence. She was murdered because she discovered that psychiatric patients, vulnerable, marginalized, forgotten people, were being used as test subjects for illegal drug trials. And when Sophie tried to document these crimes, when she kept a journal recording patient deaths, the six defendants sitting before you had her killed."

Rachel gestures to the defense table where Morrison, Shaw, Chen, Patterson, Williams, and Foster sit in expensive suits, faces carefully neutral.

"The defense wants you to believe this is a conspiracy theory. They want you to think Owen Brennan, a convicted murderer, fabricated evidence. They want you to dismiss Sophie's journal as teenager drama. They want you to ignore the financial records, the forensic evidence, the witness testimony."

She walks slowly along the jury box, making eye contact with each juror.

"But you can't ignore facts. And the facts are devastating."

Rachel picks up a document from the prosecution table. "Exhibit 47: Bank records showing $40 million transferred from GenHealth Pharmaceuticals to twelve officials at Willowbrook between 1985 and 1987. These weren't research grants. These weren't consulting fees. These were bribes, documented, verified, traceable bribes, paid to conduct illegal drug trials on psychiatric patients."

She sets down the document and picks up another. "Exhibit 83: Autopsy report for Sophie Brennan, conducted in

February 2025, thirty-seven years after her death, by Dr. Patricia Morrison, forensic pathologist. Dr. Morrison's findings: Sophie Brennan did not commit suicide. She was strangled with a ligature consistent with a belt or strap, then her body was staged to simulate hanging. The bruising patterns, the injury depth, the angle of ligature marks, all prove Sophie was murdered."

Rachel's voice hardens. "The defense tried to discredit Dr. Morrison by suggesting her findings were influenced by Owen Brennan's conspiracy theory. But Dr. Morrison examined Sophie's remains without knowing Owen's hypothesis. She conducted her autopsy based purely on forensic evidence. And her conclusion, reached independently, matched Owen Brennan's thirty-year investigation."

She moves to a large board displaying photographs: seventy-three faces.

"These are the victims. Seventy-three psychiatric patients who died at Willowbrook between 1985 and 1991. The official cause of death for most: suicide, natural causes, complications from mental illness. But when the FBI exhumed twelve of these bodies, they found evidence of pharmaceutical poisoning, overdoses of experimental drugs, symptoms consistent with fatal drug reactions."

Rachel points to specific photos. "Thomas Riley, age 34. Died February 1986. Official cause: suicide by overdose. Actual cause: experimental sedative trial that caused respiratory failure.

"Patricia Gomez, age 52. Died July 1986. Official cause: heart failure. Actual cause: cardiac drug trial that triggered fatal arrhythmia.

"Michael Torres, age 19. Died December 1986. Official cause: seizure disorder. Actual cause: antipsychotic trial that induced lethal seizures."

She turns back to the jury. "These weren't accidents. These weren't unfortunate medical complications. These were predictable outcomes of illegal drug trials conducted on vulnerable patients without informed consent, without proper medical oversight, without FDA approval."

Rachel picks up Sophie's journal, the same journal I found five months ago in Margaret Moore's storage unit.

"Sophie Brennan documented it all. A sixteen-year-old girl, committed to Willowbrook for anxiety and depression, observed what trained medical professionals ignored. She recorded patient deaths. She noted which drugs were administered. She tracked patterns of illness and mortality. And when she realized the truth, that Willowbrook was essentially a pharmaceutical testing facility where lives were disposable, she tried to expose it."

She opens the journal to a marked page. "May 14, 1987. Sophie wrote: *They gave Marcus the new pills last week. Today he had seizures. They didn't call an ambulance. They just moved him to isolation. Dr. Delacroix said it was expected. Expected? Marcus is dying and they expected it?*"

Rachel looks up. "Marcus Jennings died three days later. Official cause: epileptic seizure. Actual cause: pharmaceutical trial that the defendants authorized, funded, and covered up."

She closes the journal and sets it gently on the prosecution table, as if handling something sacred.

"The defense argued Owen Brennan is unreliable because he murdered four people. I won't dispute that Owen Brennan committed terrible crimes. He's serving twenty years in prison. But his crimes don't change the facts of this case. The financial records are real, verified by forensic accountants. The autopsy findings are real, conducted by an independent pathologist. Sophie's journal is real, authenticated by document examiners. The witness testimony is real, corroborated by multiple sources."

Rachel returns to face the jury directly.

"This isn't Owen Brennan's word against the defendants. This is forty million dollars in documented bribes. This is seventy-three dead patients. This is Sophie Brennan's journal recording crimes in real-time. This is forensic evidence proving murder."

She pauses, her voice dropping. "The defense also tried to discredit Linda Walters, Jenna's mother, by suggesting she was unstable, paranoid, mentally ill. But you heard testimony from colleagues who confirmed Linda tried to report patient deaths. You saw her nursing records documenting unexplained deaths. You heard how she was systematically destroyed, fired, blacklisted, harassed, for trying to expose the truth."

Rachel gestures to me in the gallery. "Linda Walters died by suicide in 2011. She spent thirteen years being dismissed, ignored, and destroyed. She died believing no one would ever listen. But her daughter found Sophie's journal. And now, fourteen years after Linda's death, the truth she tried to expose is finally in this courtroom."

Some jurors look at me. I keep my face neutral, professional, but inside I'm breaking.

Rachel continues. "The defense wants you to believe this is all coincidence. That forty million dollars in unexplained payments is coincidence. That seventy-three patient deaths is coincidence. That Sophie's journal documenting illegal trials is coincidence. That Linda Walters' reports of patient abuse is coincidence. That forensic evidence proving Sophie was murdered is coincidence."

She shakes her head slowly. "Ladies and gentlemen, this isn't coincidence. This is conspiracy. This is corporate murder. This is six executives who valued profit over human life."

Rachel walks to the defense table and points to each defendant in turn.

"James Morrison. CEO of GenHealth Pharmaceuticals. Authorized forty million dollars in bribes. Signed off on illegal drug trials. Covered up patient deaths for six years.

"Martin Shaw. Chief Operating Officer. Managed the Willowbrook operation. Ensured staff complied with illegal trials. Orchestrated the cover-up when Sophie discovered the truth.

"Robert Chen. Chief Financial Officer. Laundered bribe money through shell companies. Destroyed financial records. Paid officials to falsify death certificates.

"David Patterson. Vice President of Operations. Oversaw Willowbrook's transformation into a pharmaceutical testing facility. Managed hospital contracts and ensured staff compliance.

"Michael Williams. Vice President of Regulatory Affairs. Bribed FDA officials to approve unsafe drugs. Manipulated regulatory processes to cover up patient deaths.

"Thomas Foster. Vice President of Communications. Orchestrated the cover-up after Sophie's death. Destroyed evidence. Ensured witnesses stayed silent."

Rachel steps back, addressing the entire courtroom. "These six men didn't personally strangle Sophie Brennan. They didn't personally administer fatal drug doses to seventy-three patients. But they authorized it. They funded it. They covered it up. And under federal conspiracy law, that makes them guilty of murder."

She returns to the jury box for her final appeal.

"When you deliberate, I ask you to remember three things. First: Sophie Brennan was sixteen years old. She was a child, vulnerable, frightened, abandoned by the system that should have protected her. And when she tried to expose the truth, she was murdered.

"Second: Linda Walters tried to report these crimes for thirteen years. She was destroyed for telling the truth. She died believing justice would never come.

"Third: The evidence in this case is overwhelming. Financial records. Forensic pathology. Sophie's journal. Witness testimony. This isn't a question of whether crimes were committed. It's a question of whether we hold powerful men accountable."

Rachel's voice rises with conviction. "The defense will tell you there's reasonable doubt. They'll suggest alternative explanations. They'll attack witnesses. But you've seen the evidence. You've heard the testimony. You know the truth."

She leans on the jury box railing, her voice dropping to just above a whisper. "Seventy-three people died at Willowbrook. Sophie Brennan was murdered trying to expose it. Linda Walters was destroyed trying to report it. Owen Brennan spent thirty years investigating it and is now in prison. Margaret Moore died with this secret haunting her for thirty-seven years."

Rachel straightens. "Don't let those deaths be meaningless. Don't let that suffering be in vain. Hold these six men accountable. Return guilty verdicts on all counts."

She walks back to the prosecution table and sits.

The courtroom is absolutely silent.

Judge Martinez glances at the clock: 11:47 AM. "We'll take a fifteen-minute recess before the defense closing argument."

April 3, 2025, 12:05 PM Defense Closing Argument

After the recess, Gerald Hutchins rises for the defense.

He's a silver-haired attorney in his sixties, expensive suit, expensive watch, expensive confidence.

"Ladies and gentlemen of the jury. My name is Gerald Hutchins, and I represent all six defendants in this case. Over the past three weeks, you've heard the prosecution present what Ms. Chen called 'overwhelming evidence.' But I'm here to tell you that evidence isn't what it seems."

He approaches the jury box with a warm, grandfatherly smile.

"Let me start by acknowledging something. Seventy-three people died at Willowbrook Psychiatric Hospital between 1985 and 1991. That's tragic. Those were real people with real families. And their deaths deserve to be treated with dignity and respect."

He pauses. "But tragic deaths don't equal murder. And the prosecution has failed to prove, beyond a reasonable doubt, that my clients committed any crime."

Hutchins walks to a large board displaying a timeline. "Let's examine the prosecution's case piece by piece. First: Sophie Brennan. You heard Dr. Patricia Morrison testify that Sophie's death was murder, not suicide. Dr. Morrison is a respected forensic pathologist. But she examined remains that were buried for thirty-seven years. Decomposed. Degraded. Contaminated by soil and time."

He taps the timeline. "The original autopsy in 1987, conducted by Dr. Leonard Foster, a qualified medical examiner, concluded Sophie's death was suicide by hanging. Dr. Foster examined Sophie's body hours after death, not decades later. His findings were reviewed and confirmed by state authorities. But thirty-seven years later, we're supposed to accept that a second autopsy, performed on severely decomposed remains, is more reliable?"

Hutchins shakes his head. "That's not reasonable doubt. That's reasonable certainty that the original findings were correct."

He moves to another section of the timeline. "Second: Owen Brennan. The prosecution built their entire case on the investigation of a man who murdered four people. Owen Brennan killed James Delacroix, Harold Perkins, Victor Chen, and Samuel Larson in cold blood. He's serving twenty years in federal prison. And Ms. Chen wants you to believe this convicted killer conducted a reliable investigation?"

Hutchins walks along the jury box. "Owen Brennan is obsessed. For thirty years, he fixated on his sister's death, built elaborate conspiracy theories, and ultimately resorted to murder when the legal system didn't validate his paranoia. This is not a reliable witness. This is a dangerous, delusional man whose 'evidence' should be viewed with extreme skepticism."

He returns to the board. "Third: Financial records. The prosecution showed you bank statements indicating GenHealth Pharmaceuticals paid money to Willowbrook officials. But those payments were legitimate research grants and consulting fees. In the 1980s, pharmaceutical companies routinely funded psychiatric research. That was, and still is, legal, ethical, and common practice."

Hutchins picks up a document. "Exhibit D-34: Contract between GenHealth and Willowbrook for psychiatric medication research, approved by the FDA in 1985. This was a legal research program. The fact that Owen Brennan characterizes it as bribery doesn't make it criminal."

He sets down the document. "Fourth: Sophie's journal. You've heard Ms. Chen treat this journal like sacred text, the testimony of a martyred teenager. But Sophie Brennan was sixteen years old, diagnosed with severe anxiety and depression, medicated with multiple psychiatric drugs. Her journal entries describe paranoid thoughts, conspiracy theories, and distorted perceptions."

Hutchins opens the journal to a marked page. "June 3, 1987. Sophie wrote: *I think Dr. Delacroix is reading my mind. Every time I think something, he mentions it the next day. How does he know what I'm thinking?'* This is not reliable documentation. This is a mentally ill teenager experiencing paranoid delusions."

He closes the journal gently. "I don't say this to disparage Sophie's memory. Mental illness is a medical condition, not a moral failing. But we cannot base murder convictions on the paranoid journal of a mentally ill teenager."

Hutchins walks to the defense table and stands behind his clients. "These six men, James Morrison, Martin Shaw, Robert Chen, David Patterson, Michael Williams, Thomas Foster, are not murderers. They're pharmaceutical executives who worked with Willowbrook on legal research programs. They followed FDA regulations. They operated within the law."

He looks each juror in the eye. "The prosecution wants you to believe these men orchestrated a massive conspiracy, murdering patients, bribing officials, covering up crimes for decades. But where's the proof? Where are the orders to kill Sophie Brennan? Where are the memos authorizing patient deaths? Where are the witnesses who saw crimes being committed?"

Hutchins spreads his hands. "There are none. Because this conspiracy doesn't exist. What you have is a grieving brother who became obsessed, a mentally ill teenager's paranoid journal, and a forensic pathologist who examined thirty-seven-year-old remains. That's not proof beyond reasonable doubt. That's speculation, coincidence, and tragedy."

He returns to the jury box. "I want to address Linda Walters briefly. You heard testimony that she tried to report patient abuse and was fired. That's unfortunate. But being fired doesn't mean she was telling the truth. Hospital administration reviewed her allegations and found them unfounded. She was terminated for documented performance issues, medication errors, patient care violations, unprofessional conduct."

Hutchins pulls out another document. "Exhibit D-52: Linda Walters' termination file from Willowbrook, documenting six months of performance problems before her dismissal. This wasn't retaliation. This was appropriate HR action."

He sets down the document. "Linda Walters died by suicide in 2011. That's heartbreaking. But suicide doesn't validate her allegations. It suggests she struggled with mental health issues, issues that may have impaired her judgment and perception while working at Willowbrook."

Some people in the gallery gasp, including me. Catherine grips my hand.

Hutchins continues, seemingly oblivious to the reaction. "Ladies and gentlemen, this case comes down to reasonable doubt. The prosecution presented circumstantial evidence, unreliable witnesses, and speculative theories. But they haven't proven, beyond reasonable doubt, that my clients committed any crime."

He walks to the center of the courtroom. "I'm not asking you to ignore tragedy. Seventy-three people died at Willowbrook. Sophie Brennan died at sixteen. Linda Walters died at fifty-two. Owen Brennan is in prison. Those are real tragedies. But tragedy doesn't equal murder. And the law requires proof beyond reasonable doubt."

Hutchins approaches the jury one final time. "When you deliberate, ask yourselves: Has the prosecution proven each element of each charge beyond reasonable doubt? Or have they presented a theory, compelling, emotional, but ultimately unproven, built on the obsessions of a convicted killer and the paranoid writings of a mentally ill teenager?"

He lets the question hang in the air.

"The answer, I submit, is that reasonable doubt exists throughout this case. And where reasonable doubt exists, you must acquit. Thank you."

Hutchins sits.

The courtroom erupts in whispers.

Judge Martinez bangs his gavel. "Order. We'll recess for lunch. Jury instructions will begin at 2:00 PM."

April 3, 2025, 1:30 PM Courthouse Cafeteria

I can't eat.

Catherine and I sit in the nearly empty cafeteria, picking at sandwiches neither of us wants.

"He called my son delusional," Catherine says quietly. "He called Sophie paranoid. He called Linda a liar."

"That's his job. Attack the witnesses."

"But it's not just attack. He's rewriting history. Making it sound like Sophie was crazy, like Linda was incompetent, like Owen invented everything."

I push my sandwich away. "What did you think of Rachel's closing?"

"Powerful. She made it real, the faces, the evidence, the timeline. She made the jury see Sophie as a person, not just a case number."

"And Hutchins?"

Catherine shakes her head. "He's good. He planted doubt. 'Thirty-seven-year-old remains.' 'Mentally ill teenager.' 'Convicted killer.' He gave the jury reasons to question everything."

"Will they believe him?"

"I don't know. The evidence is strong, but so is the defense's attack on credibility. It could go either way."

We sit in silence, both thinking the same thing: What if the jury acquits? What if Sophie's murder goes unpunished? What if six executives walk free?

At 1:50 PM, we return to the courtroom.

April 3, 2025, 2:00 PM Jury Instructions

Judge Martinez spends ninety minutes instructing the jury on the law.

He explains each count:

- First-degree murder (Sophie Brennan)

- Conspiracy to commit murder (73 patients)
- Obstruction of justice (destroying evidence)
- Fraud (falsifying records)
- RICO violations (racketeering)

He defines reasonable doubt: "Proof beyond a reasonable doubt doesn't mean proof beyond all possible doubt. It means proof that leaves you firmly convinced of the defendant's guilt."

He explains the burden of proof: "The prosecution must prove every element of every charge beyond reasonable doubt. If they fail to meet that burden for any charge, you must find the defendant not guilty on that charge."

He discusses witness credibility: "You may believe or disbelieve any witness. You may believe part of a witness's testimony and disbelieve other parts. You should consider each witness's demeanor, consistency, and possible bias."

By 3:30 PM, the instructions are complete.

Judge Martinez addresses the jury. "Ladies and gentlemen, you will now retire to the deliberation room. You will elect a foreperson who will communicate with the court. You will deliberate until you reach a unanimous verdict on each count for each defendant, or until I determine you cannot reach a verdict."

He looks at the courtroom. "Court is adjourned until the jury returns with a verdict."

The jury files out.

The waiting begins.

April 3, 2025, 6:00 PM Outside Courthouse

No verdict today.

The jury deliberated from 3:30 PM to 5:30 PM, then sent a note requesting to continue tomorrow.

Judge Martinez granted the request. Deliberations will resume at 9:00 AM on Friday, April 4th.

I walk out of the courthouse into chaos.

News crews have multiplied. The crowd has grown. Protesters chant on both sides:

"JUSTICE FOR SOPHIE!"

"INNOCENT UNTIL PROVEN GUILTY!"

A reporter rushes forward. "Jenna! What do you think of the closing arguments?"

I keep walking.

"Ms. Walters! Do you think your mother would be proud?"

I stop.

Every instinct says keep walking, don't engage, stay silent.

But I'm tired of staying silent.

I turn to face the camera.

"My mother spent thirteen years trying to expose what happened at Willowbrook. She was fired, blacklisted, harassed, and ultimately driven to suicide. The defense attorney suggested she was incompetent and mentally ill. But my mother was telling the truth. Sophie Brennan's journal proves it. The forensic evidence proves it. The financial records prove it."

The reporter holds the microphone closer. "What would you say to people who think Owen Brennan fabricated evidence?"

"Owen Brennan is in prison for twenty years. He killed four people. That's documented, proven, undeniable. But his crimes don't change the evidence he collected. The FBI verified everything, bank statements, forensic pathology, witness testimony. This isn't one man's conspiracy theory. This is a documented corporate crime."

"Do you think the jury will convict?"

"I hope they do what my mother couldn't, hold powerful men accountable for murdering vulnerable people. That's all I hope."

I walk away before they can ask more questions.

Behind me, cameras flash. Reporters shout. The story spreads.

By 7:00 PM, my statement is on every news channel.

April 3, 2025, 9:00 PM Social Media Explosion

The trial has been trending on social media for weeks, but tonight it reaches critical mass.

Twitter:

#WillowbrookTrial is the #1 trending topic worldwide.

Thousands of tweets:

- "Jenna Walters speaking outside the courthouse today Her mother died trying to expose this"
- "The defense attorney really called Sophie paranoid? A 16-year-old murdered for telling the truth?"
- "Owen Brennan killed 4 people but the evidence is REAL. FBI verified everything"
- "These executives murdered 73 patients and nobody cared until a night nurse found a journal"
- "Pharmaceutical companies have been doing this for decades. Willowbrook is just the one that got caught"

Reddit:

r/TrueCrime has three megathreads with 50,000+ comments.

Top comment: *"This case is insane. A teenage girl discovers illegal drug trials, documents everything in a journal, gets murdered, and the cover-up lasts 37 years. Meanwhile, a night nurse's mom tries to report it and gets destroyed. Then the girl's brother spends 30 years investigating, murders 4 people, goes to prison, and STILL manages to help the FBI build a case. This is like 5 different true crime podcasts in one. "*

TikTok:

#SophieBrennan videos have 200 million views.

Popular videos include:

- Timeline of the conspiracy
- Dramatic readings from Sophie's journal
- Explainers of pharmaceutical industry corruption
- Tributes to Linda Walters
- Debates about Owen Brennan ("hero or villain?")

YouTube:

Every legal commentary channel is covering the trial.

Popular videos:

- "Legal Analysis: Will the Willowbrook Jury Convict?"
- "The Dark Truth About Pharmaceutical Testing"
- "Owen Brennan: Vigilante Justice or Murder?"
- "How Sophie's Journal Exposed a 37-Year Conspiracy"

Instagram:

#JusticeForSophie has 5 million posts.

Photos of Sophie's school picture, memorial candles, protest signs, courtroom sketches.

The public reaction is overwhelming, polarized, impossible to ignore.

Some people call the executives monsters who deserve life in prison.

Others argue the prosecution's case is built on unreliable witnesses.

Everyone has an opinion.

Everyone is watching.

April 4, 2025, 8:00 AM Day 2 of Deliberations

I arrive at the courthouse at 8:00 AM.

The media circus has doubled overnight. International news crews. Satellite trucks from London, Tokyo, Sydney.

Inside, the victim witness room is crowded with family members of Willowbrook victims.

Catherine introduces me to several people:

- Janet Riley, whose brother Thomas died in 1986
- Maria Gomez, whose mother Patricia died in 1986
- Helen Torres, whose son Michael died in 1986

We sit together, waiting.

At 9:15 AM, we receive word: The jury is deliberating.

At 11:30 AM: Still deliberating.

At 1:45 PM: Jury requests to review financial records.

At 4:00 PM: Still deliberating.

At 5:30 PM: Judge Martinez sends the jury home for the weekend.

Deliberations will resume Monday, April 7th.

April 4, 2025, 6:30 PM Phone Call with Rachel Diaz

Rachel calls as I'm driving home.

"Two days of deliberations," she says. "That's normal for a complex case."

"What does it mean that they requested financial records?"

"Could mean they're carefully reviewing evidence. Could mean they're divided. Could mean they're being thorough. Impossible to know."

"Do you think they'll convict?"

Rachel pauses. "The evidence is strong. But Hutchins planted seeds of doubt, Owen's credibility, Sophie's mental state, the age of forensic evidence. Some jurors might latch onto that doubt."

"What happens if they acquit?"

"Then six executives walk free. The case is over. No retrial, no appeal. Double jeopardy."

I feel sick. "And if they convict?"

"Then we move to sentencing. Each defendant faces life in prison on the murder charges. Mandatory minimum twenty-five years."

"Owen is serving twenty years for killing four people. These men killed seventy-three and might get life?"

"Justice isn't always proportional, Jenna. But it's what we have."

We end the call.

I drive home through Manchester streets, past the storage facility where I found Sophie's journal five months ago, past the hospital where Margaret Moore died, past the elementary school where my mother once picked me up before foster care swallowed my childhood.

This city holds so much pain.

So many secrets buried under new construction and corporate growth.

And somewhere in a federal prison, Owen Brennan waits for a verdict that will determine whether his thirty-year quest meant anything.

April 5-6, 2025 The Weekend

The weekend is surreal.

The trial dominates every news cycle:

Saturday morning:

- CNN hosts panel debate: "Corporate Accountability vs. Reasonable Doubt"
- Fox News investigates: "Were Pharmaceutical Trials Legal in the 1980s?"
- MSNBC documentary: "The Willowbrook Scandal: A Timeline"

Saturday afternoon: Protests outside GenHealth Pharmaceuticals headquarters in Philadelphia. 5,000 people demanding corporate accountability. Signs reading: **STOP KILLING PATIENTS FOR PROFIT**

Saturday evening: Vigil in Manchester for Sophie Brennan and the seventy-three Willowbrook victims. Catherine and I attend. Candles, flowers, photos of the dead.

A woman approaches Catherine. "My brother died at Willowbrook in 1988. For thirty-seven years, I thought he committed suicide. Now I know he was murdered. Thank you for never giving up on Sophie."

Catherine breaks down crying.

Sunday morning:

The New York Times runs a front-page story: **"The Nurse, The Journal, and The 37-Year Cover-Up: Inside the Willowbrook Pharmaceutical Murder Trial"**

The article chronicles everything: Sophie's admission to Willowbrook, her discovery of illegal trials, her murder, the cover-up, Linda's attempts to report abuse, Owen's thirty-year investigation, his murders, his imprisonment, Margaret Moore's deathbed confession, my discovery of the journal, the FBI investigation, and the trial.

Twenty thousand words. Photos of everyone involved. A comprehensive examination of corporate crime, pharmaceutical industry corruption, and the human cost of profit-driven medicine.

By Sunday afternoon, the article has been shared two million times.

Sunday evening:

I receive a call from an unfamiliar number.

"Ms. Walters? This is FCI Devens. Owen Brennan has requested to speak with you."

My heart stops. "I... when?"

"He's authorized for phone calls to approved contacts. We can arrange a call tomorrow if you consent."

I think about Owen, the man who spent thirty years investigating his sister's murder, who killed four people, who testified in chains, who will spend the next fourteen years minimum in prison.

"Yes," I say. "I'll take his call."

CHAPTER 13

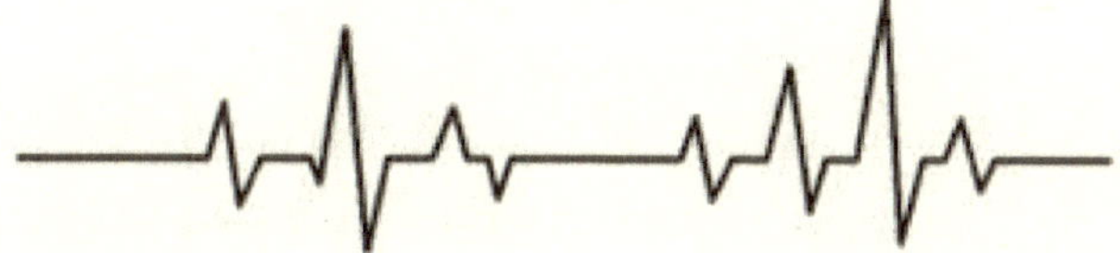

Mother's Vindication

April 7, 2025, 9:00 AM Jenna's Apartment, Manchester, NH

The phone rings at exactly 9:00 AM.

I've been awake since 5:30, drinking coffee, staring at my mother's photo on the dresser, waiting for this call.

The caller ID reads: **FCI DEVENS - FEDERAL PRISON**

I answer on the second ring.

"Hello?"

A recorded voice: "This is a call from a federal inmate. This call is subject to monitoring and recording. To accept charges, press 1. To decline, press 2."

I press 1.

Click. Static.

Then Owen's voice. "Jenna?"

"I'm here."

"Thank you for taking my call. I know it's Monday morning. You probably have work."

"I called in sick. The trial's made it... complicated to be at the hospital right now." I pause. "How are you holding up?"

A bitter laugh. "I'm in federal prison serving twenty years for quadruple homicide. I'm holding up about as well as you'd expect."

"The jury's still deliberating. They started again this morning."

"I know. Agent Chen keeps me updated. Three full days of deliberation now, Friday, and they'll resume today. That's a long time."

"Rachel Diaz says it's normal for a complex case."

"Rachel Diaz is an excellent prosecutor. If anyone can convict those six men, it's her." Owen's voice softens. "But that's not why I called. I called because I've been thinking about your mother. About Linda."

I close my eyes, gripping the phone tighter.

Owen continues. "I watched your statement outside the courthouse on the news. When you said your mother spent thirteen years trying to expose Willowbrook, that she was destroyed for telling the truth. You defended her. Publicly. In front of cameras."

"She deserved that. Someone needed to say it."

"Do you remember her? Your real memories, I mean. Before foster care."

I walk to the window, looking out at Manchester's gray morning. "Fragments. I remember her being stressed all the time. Always on the phone, always writing letters, always talking about 'the patients' and 'the cover-up.' Social workers would come to our apartment and tell her she needed to stop, that she was making herself sick. I remember thinking she was obsessed with something that wasn't real."

"You were seven when they took you."

"Seven years old. I remember the day. April 22, 1998. Two social workers and a police officer came to our apartment. My mom was in the middle of writing a letter to the State Attorney General. She had papers spread all over the kitchen table, police reports, death certificates, medical records. She was trying to document everything about Willowbrook."

I lean my forehead against the cool glass. "The social workers told her she was unfit. That she was paranoid. That she was creating an unstable environment for me. My mom started crying, begging them not to take me. She kept saying, 'I'm not crazy. I'm telling the truth. The patients were murdered. Sophie Brennan was murdered.' But they didn't listen. They just took me."

"That must have been traumatic."

"I spent the next thirteen years thinking my mother was mentally ill. That's what everyone told me, foster parents, social workers, therapists. 'Your mother has paranoid delusions. She can't take care of you. It's not her fault, but it's not safe for you to be with her.' I believed them. I thought my mom was sick."

Owen is quiet for a moment. "When did you see her again?"

"I didn't. She tried to visit me in foster care, but the visits were supervised and eventually stopped because she kept talking about the conspiracy, about the murdered patients, about Willowbrook. Social workers said it was harmful for me to hear. So, they stopped allowing visits when I was nine."

My voice cracks. "I never saw her again after that. She died in 2011, I was twenty. I was notified by the state because I was her only living relative. They said she'd been in a group home for mental health patients for three years. That she'd killed herself. Overdose on prescription medications."

"I'm sorry, Jenna."

"The funeral was small. Just me and a caseworker. No other family. No friends. Just the two of us standing at her grave while they lowered her casket. And I remember thinking, 'My mother wasted her life on delusions. She destroyed herself over a conspiracy that didn't exist.'"

I wipe tears from my face. "For thirteen years, Owen. For

thirteen years, I believed my mother was mentally ill. That she threw away her life and her daughter for nothing. That she died because she couldn't let go of paranoid fantasies."

"But she wasn't mentally ill."

"No. She was telling the truth. Sophie Brennan was murdered. Seventy-three patients were murdered. Pharmaceutical executives bribed officials and covered it up. My mother witnessed it. She tried to report it. And they systematically destroyed her for it."

Owen's voice is intense. "Your mother was a hero, Jenna. She risked everything to expose the truth. She filed police reports knowing she'd be dismissed. She contacted agencies knowing they'd label her as crazy. She kept fighting even when it cost her career, her reputation, her daughter, her sanity. She died trying to save people she never met."

"And no one believed her."

"I believed her. I just found out too late."

I walk back to the dresser and pick up my mother's photo. She's smiling, but there's exhaustion in her eyes. This photo was taken in 2008, three years before she died.

"Owen, can I ask you something?"

"Of course."

"When you went to see my mother in 2009, when you said she didn't recognize you, what did you hope to tell her?"

Owen takes a breath. "I wanted to tell her she was right about everything. That I'd spent twenty-two years investigating Sophie's death and I'd confirmed her reports were accurate. That Sophie was murdered. That the drug trials were real. That officials were bribed. That everything she tried to expose was true."

His voice breaks. "I wanted to tell her she wasn't crazy. That she wasn't delusional. That she was the only person brave enough to stand up to a pharmaceutical conspiracy. I wanted to give her that vindication before she died."

"But she couldn't hear you."

"No. The staff at the group home said she'd been heavily medicated for years. Antipsychotics, mood stabilizers, sedatives. They'd diagnosed her with paranoid schizophrenia. She spent most of her time sleeping or staring at walls. When I told her my name, told her I was Sophie's brother, she just looked at me with blank eyes. She didn't remember Sophie. Didn't remember Willowbrook. Didn't remember any of it."

I sit on my bed, clutching the photo. "They destroyed her mind. They took away her career, her daughter, her credibility, and finally they took away her memories. They erased everything she fought for."

"Yes. And two years later, she took her own life. Because even though she couldn't remember the details, some part of her still carried the trauma. The knowledge that she'd tried to do something important and failed. That she'd lost everything and no one believed her."

We sit in silence for a long moment, two people connected by dead mothers and pharmaceutical conspiracies.

Finally, Owen speaks. "Jenna, I called you today because I want you to know something. What's happening right now, the trial, the media coverage, the public attention, this is your mother's vindication."

"What do you mean?"

"Right now, this very moment, six pharmaceutical executives are sitting in federal court facing murder charges. Seventy-three victims' names are being read in testimony. Sophie's journal is evidence. Financial records prove bribery. Forensic pathology proves murder. And the entire world knows about Willowbrook."

Owen's voice strengthens. "Your mother's police reports are part of the prosecution's case. Rachel Diaz cited them in her opening statement. The jury has seen them. Every news outlet has covered Linda Walters, the whistleblower nurse who tried to expose the conspiracy in 1987. The New York Times article called her a hero."

"But she's dead. She didn't live to see it."

"No. But her daughter did. You found Sophie's journal. You brought it to the FBI. You testified at the grand jury hearing. You gave statements to the press. You defended your mother publicly. You made sure everyone knows Linda Walters was telling the truth."

I close my eyes, tears streaming down my face.

Owen continues, his voice gentle but firm. "In 1987, your mother reported a murder. For thirteen years, she was called crazy. For thirteen years, she was dismissed, gaslit, destroyed. For thirteen years, no one believed her. But now? Now everyone knows she was right. Now her name is in court documents, in news articles, in history books. Now she's remembered as a whistleblower, not a paranoid nurse. That's vindication, Jenna. That's justice."

"I wish she were here to see it."

"I know. But you're here. You're carrying her legacy. You finished what she started. That matters."

I look at my mother's photo through tears. "I spent thirteen years thinking she was mentally ill. I never defended her. I never believed her. I accepted what everyone said, that she was delusional, that she threw her life away, that she abandoned me for fantasies. I was ashamed of her, Owen. I was ashamed of my own mother."

"You were a child. You believed what adults told you."

"But I should have known. I should have believed her."

"Jenna." Owen's voice is firm. "You were seven years old when they took you. Seven. You can't blame yourself for not understanding a pharmaceutical conspiracy that took me thirty years to unravel. You can't blame yourself for believing trained social workers and therapists who told you your mother was sick."

He pauses. "But you can give her credit now. You can tell

her story. You can make sure the world knows Linda Walters wasn't crazy, she was a hero who paid the ultimate price for telling the truth."

I nod, even though he can't see me. "That's what I'm trying to do."

"I know. And you're doing it beautifully."

We're both silent for a moment. Then Owen asks, "Do you visit her grave?"

"Sometimes. It's in Manchester Cemetery. Simple headstone. Just her name and dates."

"What does it say?"

I close my eyes, reciting from memory. "Linda Marie Walters. 1962-2011. Beloved Mother."

"That's it?"

"That's it. I was twenty years old when she died. I couldn't afford anything elaborate."

Owen is quiet. Then: "When this trial is over, when those six executives are convicted, I want to pay for a new headstone for your mother. Something that tells the truth about who she was."

"Owen, you're in prison. You don't have money…"

"I have money. I worked as an engineer for twenty-five years before I was arrested. I saved everything. It's sitting in a bank account waiting for me to get out, if I ever get out. But I don't need it. I want to use it to honor the people who died trying to expose Willowbrook. Your mother. Margaret Moore. The seventy-three patients. I want them remembered properly."

My throat tightens. "What would the headstone say?"

"Whatever you want. But I'd suggest something like: 'Linda Marie Walters. Nurse, Whistleblower, Hero. She tried to save them. 1962-2011.'"

I start crying again, deep, wrenching sobs that I can't control.

"Jenna?" Owen's voice is concerned. "Are you okay?"

"No one has ever called my mother a hero before. For twenty-four years, she's been remembered as mentally ill. As the crazy nurse. As the woman who abandoned her daughter. And you're the first person to call her a hero."

"Because that's what she was. Sophie was my hero, a sixteen-year-old girl who documented pharmaceutical crimes knowing they'd kill her for it. And your mother was Sophie's hero, the nurse who believed her, who tried to save her, who spent thirteen years fighting for justice even when it destroyed her life."

Owen's voice drops to almost a whisper. "Heroes don't always win, Jenna. Heroes don't always survive. But they fight anyway. That's what makes them heroes. Your mother fought for thirteen years against impossible odds. She lost everything. But she never stopped believing the truth mattered. That's heroism."

I sit on my bed, holding my mother's photo, crying so hard I can barely breathe.

"I wish I could have told her," I whisper. "I wish I could have seen her one more time and told her I believe her. That she was right. That I'm sorry I didn't defend her. That I'm proud of her."

"She knows."

"How can you be sure?"

"Because you found Sophie's journal. Because you brought it to the FBI. Because you're testifying at the trial. Because you're telling the world about Linda Walters. Your actions speak louder than words. Your mother knows you believe her now."

The phone beeps, a warning that our time is almost up.

"Two minutes left," Owen says. "Prison calls are limited to fifteen minutes."

"Owen, thank you. Thank you for calling. Thank you for honoring my mother. Thank you for believing her when no one else did."

"Thank you for finishing what she started. Thank you for giving Sophie a voice. Thank you for making sure those six executives face justice."

The phone beeps again. One minute.

"I'll call again when there's a verdict," Owen says. "Agent

Chen will let me know immediately. When those six men are convicted, I want you to know, I want us to remember together, that it only happened because of your mother. Because Linda Walters wouldn't stop fighting. Because she spent thirteen years planting seeds that finally grew into justice."

"I'll remember."

"Good. Take care of yourself, Jenna. Don't let the media circus overwhelm you. Don't let people define your mother's story. You define it. You tell them who Linda Walters really was."

"I will. I promise."

Final beep.

"Goodbye, Jenna."

"Goodbye, Owen."

Click.

The line goes dead.

I sit on my bed, holding my mother's photo, crying until I can't cry anymore.

April 7, 2025, 11:00 AM Manchester Cemetery

I drive to my mother's grave for the first time in two years.

Manchester Cemetery is old, quiet, mostly forgotten. My

mother's plot is in the back corner, the cheapest section, where they bury people without much money or family.

The headstone is small, plain granite:

LINDA MARIE WALTERS

1962-2011

BELOVED MOTHER

I kneel in the grass and place fresh flowers beside it.

"Hi, Mom."

The wind rustles through nearby trees. April in New Hampshire, still cold, but hints of spring emerging.

"I'm sorry it's been so long. I've been... busy. There's a trial happening. Six pharmaceutical executives are being prosecuted for murdering seventy-three patients at Willowbrook. You'd be happy about that."

I trace my fingers over her name carved in stone.

"I found Sophie's journal. Sophie Brennan, the sixteen-year-old girl you tried to save. Margaret Moore had kept it hidden for thirty-seven years. She left me a note before she died, telling me where to find it. The FBI used it as evidence. Everything you reported in 1987 was true, Mom. Everything."

Tears stream down my face.

"I'm so sorry I didn't believe you. I'm sorry I spent thirteen years thinking you were crazy. I'm sorry I was ashamed of you. I'm sorry I didn't defend you when social workers took me away. I'm sorry I didn't visit you in the group home. I'm sorry I let you die thinking no one believed you."

I press my hand against the cold stone.

"But I believe you now. And I'm telling everyone. The FBI knows. The prosecutors know. The media knows. The whole world knows that Linda Walters was a whistleblower who tried to expose pharmaceutical murder. You're not remembered as mentally ill anymore, Mom. You're remembered as a hero."

The wind picks up, carrying the scent of early spring flowers.

"Owen Brennan called me today. Sophie's brother. He's in prison for killing four people connected to the conspiracy. He said he tried to visit you in 2009, tried to tell you that you were right, but you didn't remember him. I'm so sorry you went through that. I'm so sorry they destroyed your mind."

I pull out my phone and show her photo the news headlines:

New York Times: "Linda Walters: The Whistleblower Nurse Who Tried to Stop Pharmaceutical Murder"

Washington Post: "How One Nurse's Thirteen-Year Fight Against Willowbrook Finally Led to Justice"

CNN: "Remembering Linda Walters: The Mother Who Lost Everything Exposing Corporate Crime"

"Look, Mom. They're writing about you. They're telling your story. The whole world knows what you did. The whole world knows you were telling the truth."

I set the phone down and close my eyes.

"The jury is deliberating now. Six men, James Morrison, Martin Shaw, Robert Chen, David Patterson, Michael Williams, Thomas Foster, are facing murder charges. If they're convicted, it's because of you. Because you filed those first police reports in 1987. Because you documented patient deaths. Because you wouldn't let them bury the truth."

I open my eyes and look at the headstone.

"Owen wants to buy you a new headstone. Something that tells the truth about who you were. 'Linda Marie Walters. Nurse, Whistleblower, Hero.' Is that okay? I think it's perfect. I think it's what you deserve."

A bird lands on a nearby branch, singing.

"I'm going to make sure people remember you correctly, Mom. Not as a mentally ill woman who abandoned her daughter. But as a nurse who witnessed a murder and spent thirteen years trying to expose it. As a mother who lost her daughter because she wouldn't stop telling the truth. As a hero who paid the ultimate price for fighting corporate evil."

I stand up, brushing grass from my knees.

"I love you, Mom. I should have said that more when you were alive. I should have believed you. But I'm saying it now. I love you. And I'm proud of you. And I'm so sorry you had to fight alone for so long."

I place my hand on the headstone one more time.

"Rest now. Justice is coming. The men who destroyed you are going to pay. Sophie is going to be remembered as a hero. And so are you."

I walk back to my car, leaving flowers on my mother's grave.

Behind me, the wind whispers through the cemetery trees, carrying thirty-seven years of secrets into the light.

April 7, 2025, 2:00 PM Jenna's Apartment

I'm sitting at my kitchen table, laptop open, writing.

For the first time in my life, I'm writing down everything I remember about my mother. Every fragment. Every moment. Every conversation.

I remember:

- Her staying up late writing letters to officials, her handwriting getting messier as exhaustion set in
- Her talking on the phone with police departments, her voice getting more desperate each time they dismissed her

- Her crying in the bathroom when she thought I couldn't hear
- Her hugging me tight and whispering, "I'm fighting for something important, baby. I'm fighting for people who can't fight for themselves."
- Her face when the social workers came to take me, the look of absolute devastation

I write it all down. Every detail.

Because Owen was right, I'm the one who gets to define my mother's story now. Not the social workers who called her paranoid. Not the psychiatrists who diagnosed her with schizophrenia. Not the people who dismissed her as mentally ill.

Me. Her daughter.

And I'm going to make sure the world knows Linda Marie Walters was a hero.

April 7, 2025, 4:30 PM Phone Call from Catherine Brennan

My phone rings. Catherine.

"Jenna, are you watching the news?"

"No, why?"

"Turn on CNN. Now."

I grab the TV remote and switch to CNN.

The screen shows the federal courthouse in Boston. The banner reads:

BREAKING: JURY REACHES VERDICT IN WILLOWBROOK TRIAL

My heart stops.

The reporter speaks: "We're getting word that the jury in the Willowbrook pharmaceutical murder trial has reached a verdict after three days of deliberation. The verdict will be read tomorrow morning at 10:00 AM. Both prosecution and defense have been notified. The six defendants, James Morrison, Martin Shaw, Robert Chen, David Patterson, Michael Williams, and Thomas Foster, will learn their fate tomorrow morning."

Catherine's voice is shaking. "It's happening. After thirty-seven years, we're finally going to know if those men are held accountable."

"Are you coming to the courthouse tomorrow?"

"I'll be there. Will you?"

"Yes. Rachel Diaz already texted me. She wants me in the courtroom when the verdict is read."

"I'll see you there then. Jenna?"

"Yes?"

"Thank you. Thank you for finding Sophie's journal.

Thank you for believing Margaret. Thank you for finishing what your mother started. Tomorrow, when that verdict is read, it's because of women like you, like Linda, like Margaret, like Sophie. Women who wouldn't let powerful men bury the truth."

My throat tightens. "We'll see it together tomorrow."

"Yes. Together."

We hang up.

I sit on my couch, staring at the TV.

Tomorrow morning at 10:00 AM, a jury will deliver a verdict on six men accused of murdering seventy-three people and destroying countless lives.

Tomorrow morning, I'll learn if my mother's thirteen-year fight meant something.

Tomorrow morning, justice, or the absence of it, will finally arrive.

I look at my mother's photo on the dresser.

"Tomorrow, Mom," I whisper. "Tomorrow we find out if telling the truth was worth the price you paid."

Outside my window, the sun sets over Manchester, painting the sky in shades of orange and purple.

The last light of day before the verdict.

The last hours of uncertainty before truth or tragedy.

I close my eyes and think of Sophie Brennan, murdered at sixteen.

I think of Linda Walters, destroyed at forty-nine, dead at fifty-two.

I think of Margaret Moore, silent for thirty-seven years, speaking only at the end of her life.

I think of Owen Brennan, sitting in federal prison, waiting for justice he helped build but will never fully experience.

I think of seventy-three victims whose names were buried for decades.

And I think of six executives who might finally, after thirty-seven years, face consequences for treating human lives as expendable variables in profit calculations.

Tomorrow, we'll know.

Tomorrow, the verdict comes.

April 7, 2025, 11:00 PM Sleepless

I can't sleep.

I lie in bed, staring at the ceiling, replaying everything in my mind.

My phone buzzes. A text from Rachel Diaz:

Verdict at 10 AM tomorrow. Be at courthouse by 9 AM. Security will be intense. Prepare yourself, whatever happens tomorrow will be historic. You did everything right, Jenna. Your mother would be proud.

I text back: **Thank you for believing her. Thank you for making her story part of the case.**

Her response comes quickly: **Linda Walters is a hero. The jury knows it. The world knows it. Tomorrow, when justice comes, it comes because of her. See you in the morning.**

I set my phone down and close my eyes.

Tomorrow, the verdict.

Tomorrow, vindication or devastation.

Tomorrow, the end of a thirty-seven-year journey that started when a sixteen-year-old girl decided to document pharmaceutical murder in a rainbow-stickered journal.

I pull my mother's photo close and whisper one more time:

"Tomorrow, Mom. Tomorrow we'll know if it was worth it."

And then, finally, I sleep.

CHAPTER 14

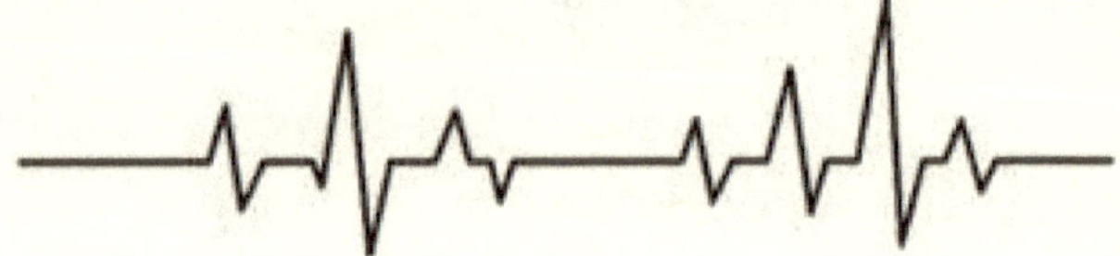

The Verdict

April 8, 2025, 8:30 AM Outside Federal Courthouse, Boston

The crowd is massive.

Thousands of people line the street outside the federal courthouse, victims' families, protesters, media crews from every major outlet, true crime enthusiasts, people who've followed every day of the trial.

The verdict will be read at 10:00 AM.

Security is unprecedented. Police barricades. Metal detectors. K-9 units. Federal marshals everywhere.

I arrive at 8:30 with Catherine Brennan. We fought through crowds to reach the courthouse entrance, cameras flashing, reporters shouting questions.

Inside, we're escorted to the victim witness room where other families wait. Some are crying. Some are praying. Some sit in silence, too nervous to speak.

Janet Riley, whose brother Thomas died at Willowbrook in 1986, grabs my hand. "This is it. After thirty-seven years, we finally know."

"Are you scared?" I ask.

"Terrified. What if they're acquitted? What if the jury believes the defense? What if those six men walk free?"

I squeeze her hand. "The evidence was overwhelming. Rachel Diaz said so herself."

"Evidence doesn't always matter. Rich men have good lawyers."

She's right. I've watched enough trials to know that justice isn't guaranteed, even with forensic proof, financial records, and Sophie's journal.

At 9:15, Rachel Diaz enters the room.

"The jury is in the building," she says. "Judge Martinez will convene court at 10:00 AM sharp. You'll all be seated in the gallery. Please remain quiet during the verdict reading, regardless of the outcome."

"How long will it take?" someone asks.

"The jury will deliver verdicts on each charge for each defendant. Six defendants, multiple counts each. It could take thirty to forty-five minutes to read everything. Please be patient."

Catherine stands. "Rachel, do you think they'll convict?"

Rachel pauses, choosing her words carefully. "I presented the strongest case I could. The evidence is overwhelming. The jury deliberated for three days, which suggests they took their responsibility seriously. But I can't predict what twelve people decided behind closed doors."

"That's not reassuring," Janet says.

"I know. But it's honest." Rachel looks at all of us. "Whatever happens in that courtroom, you all should be proud. You testified. You shared your pain. You gave voices to victims who couldn't speak for themselves. That matters, regardless of the verdict."

At 9:45, a bailiff enters. "It's time."

We file out of the witness room and into the courthouse hallway.

The atmosphere is electric with tension. Reporters line the walls. Sketch artists prepare their materials. Federal marshals stand at every door.

We enter the courtroom.

April 8, 2025, 9:50 AM Inside the Courtroom

The courtroom is packed beyond capacity.

Every seat filled. Standing room only at the back. Media in the designated press section. Security doubled.

I sit in the front row of the gallery with Catherine Brennan. Around us: families of the seventy-three victims, former Willowbrook staff members, FBI agents who worked the case, and people who've followed every day of this trial.

At the defense table: James Morrison, Martin Shaw, Robert Chen, David Patterson, Michael Williams, and Thomas Foster. All in expensive suits. All flanked by their attorneys. All looking older and more fragile than when the trial began three weeks ago.

Morrison is 77 now, his hands trembling slightly.

Shaw is 76, leaning heavily on his cane.

Chen is 70, his face drawn and pale.

Patterson is 74, oxygen tank beside his chair.

Williams is 72, staring straight ahead.

Foster is 75, examining his fingernails with practiced indifference.

Six old men who authorized murder forty years ago, now facing judgment.

At the prosecution table: Rachel Diaz, Agent Chen, and two other federal prosecutors. Rachel sits calmly, reviewing notes, projecting confidence.

The courtroom clock reads 9:58 AM.

Two minutes.

Catherine grips my hand. "I can barely breathe."

"Me neither."

At exactly 10:00 AM, the bailiff stands. "All rise. The United States District Court for the District of Massachusetts is now in session, the Honorable Judge Harold Martinez presiding."

We stand.

Judge Martinez enters, black robes flowing, expression unreadable.

"Please be seated."

We sit.

Judge Martinez addresses the courtroom. "We are here for the reading of the verdict in the matter of United States v. Morrison, et al. Before we bring in the jury, I want to remind everyone present that this is a court of law. Regardless of the verdict, there will be no outbursts, no demonstrations, no disruptions of any kind. Anyone who cannot control themselves will be removed and may face contempt charges. Is that understood?"

Murmurs of acknowledgment throughout the gallery.

"Very well." Judge Martinez nods to the bailiff. "Bring in the jury."

The door to the jury room opens.

Twelve jurors file in, seven women, five men, ages ranging from twenties to seventies. They've deliberated for three full days. They've reviewed hundreds of exhibits. They've considered seventy-three deaths and forty million dollars in bribes.

They take their seats in the jury box.

None of them look at the defendants.

Catherine whispers, "That's a good sign. When juries avoid looking at defendants, they usually voted to convict."

"Or they feel guilty about acquitting," someone behind us mutters.

Judge Martinez addresses the jury. "Members of the jury, have you reached a verdict?"

The jury foreperson, a middle-aged woman in a blue cardigan, stands. "We have, Your Honor."

"Please hand the verdict forms to the bailiff."

The foreperson hands a thick stack of papers to the bailiff, who carries them to Judge Martinez.

The judge reviews the forms silently. His face reveals nothing.

The courtroom is absolutely silent. Two hundred people holding their breath.

Finally, Judge Martinez looks up. "The verdicts are in order. I will read them aloud. The defendants will stand for each verdict."

He turns to the defense table. "Will all defendants please rise."

The six executives stand, assisted by their attorneys. Morrison struggles to his feet. Patterson's oxygen tank hisses quietly. Shaw leans on his cane.

Judge Martinez begins reading.

"In the case of United States v. James Morrison, on the count of conspiracy to commit murder in the death of Sophie Marie Brennan, we the jury find the defendant..."

The pause feels endless.

"...GUILTY."

The courtroom erupts.

Gasps. Crying. Shouts. Someone screams "YES!"

Judge Martinez bangs his gavel. "ORDER! I will clear this courtroom if necessary!"

The noise subsides, but the energy is electric.

Catherine squeezes my hand so hard it hurts. Tears stream down both our faces.

Judge Martinez continues, his voice firm and measured:

"On the count of conspiracy to commit murder in the deaths of seventy-three patients at Willowbrook Psychiatric

Hospital, we the jury find the defendant James Morrison... GUILTY."

"On the count of racketeering, we the jury find the defendant James Morrison... GUILTY."

"On the count of wire fraud, we the jury find the defendant James Morrison... GUILTY."

"On the count of obstruction of justice, we the jury find the defendant James Morrison... GUILTY."

Five guilty verdicts. Morrison's face drains of color. He sways slightly, gripping the defense table for support.

Judge Martinez moves to the next defendant.

"In the case of United States v. Martin Shaw..."

The reading continues, verdict after verdict.

Martin Shaw:

- Conspiracy to murder Sophie Brennan: **GUILTY**
- Conspiracy to murder 73 patients: **GUILTY**
- Racketeering: **GUILTY**
- Wire fraud: **GUILTY**
- Obstruction of justice: **GUILTY**

Robert Chen:

- Conspiracy to murder Sophie Brennan: **GUILTY**
- Conspiracy to murder 73 patients: **GUILTY**

* Racketeering: **GUILTY**
* Wire fraud: **GUILTY**
* Obstruction of justice: **GUILTY**

David Patterson:

* Conspiracy to murder Sophie Brennan: **GUILTY**
* Conspiracy to murder 73 patients: **GUILTY**
* Racketeering: **GUILTY**
* Wire fraud: **GUILTY**
* Obstruction of justice: **GUILTY**

Michael Williams:

* Conspiracy to murder Sophie Brennan: **GUILTY**
* Conspiracy to murder 73 patients: **GUILTY**
* Racketeering: **GUILTY**
* Wire fraud: **GUILTY**
* Obstruction of justice: **GUILTY**

Thomas Foster:

* Conspiracy to murder Sophie Brennan: **GUILTY**
* Conspiracy to murder 73 patients: **GUILTY**
* Racketeering: **GUILTY**
* Wire fraud: **GUILTY**
* Obstruction of justice: **GUILTY**

Thirty guilty verdicts.

Six executives. Five counts each. Every single verdict: GUILTY.

By the time Judge Martinez finishes reading, several people in the gallery are openly sobbing. The six defendants stand pale and defeated, their lawyers whispering urgently.

Judge Martinez addresses the jury. "Ladies and gentlemen of the jury, thank you for your service in this difficult case. You are dismissed with the court's gratitude."

The jurors file out. Several are crying. One woman nods toward the victims' families as she exits.

Judge Martinez turns to the defendants. "The defendants are remanded into custody pending sentencing. Sentencing hearings will be scheduled within sixty days. This court stands adjourned."

He bangs the gavel one final time and exits.

The courtroom explodes into chaos.

April 8, 2025, 10:47 AM Immediate Aftermath

Federal marshals immediately place the six executives in handcuffs.

Morrison tries to speak but can't form words. Shaw collapses into his chair, needing medical assistance. Chen stares blankly ahead. Patterson's oxygen tank tips over as marshals cuff him. Williams closes his eyes, silent tears running down his face. Foster maintains his composure but his hands shake violently.

Their attorneys protest: "Your Honor, our clients are elderly, they require medical supervision…"

But Judge Martinez has already left. The marshals follow protocol.

One by one, the six convicted murderers are led away through a side door to federal detention.

After forty years of freedom.

After forty years of wealth and power.

After forty years of believing they were untouchable.

They're finally in custody.

Catherine turns to me, sobbing. "They convicted them. All six. On every charge."

"I know."

"Sophie got justice. After thirty-seven years, my daughter finally got justice."

We hold each other, crying.

Around us, families embrace. Janet Riley falls to her knees, praying. A man I don't know shouts, "They're guilty! Those bastards are finally guilty!"

Rachel Diaz approaches our section of the gallery. She's

composed but her eyes are red.

"You did it," I tell her. "You convicted them."

"We all did it. The evidence did it. Sophie's journal did it. Your mother's reports did it. Owen's investigation did it. The truth did it."

Agent Chen joins us. "I need to call Owen. He's waiting at FCI Devens for the verdict."

"Tell him they were convicted on all counts," Catherine says. "Tell him Sophie got justice. Tell him his thirty-year investigation finally mattered."

"I will." Agent Chen steps away, phone to her ear.

April 8, 2025, 11:15 AM Press Conference

Thirty minutes after the verdict, Rachel Diaz holds a press conference on the courthouse steps.

The crowd is enormous. Media from around the world. Victims' families. Protesters. Cameras everywhere.

Rachel stands at a podium with the Department of Justice seal. Agent Chen and I flank her.

"Good morning. At approximately 10:00 AM today, a federal jury returned guilty verdicts against James Morrison, Martin Shaw, Robert Chen, David Patterson, Michael Williams, and Thomas Foster on all charges, including conspiracy to commit murder, racketeering, wire fraud, and obstruction of justice."

Applause and cheers from the crowd.

Rachel continues: "These six men orchestrated one of the most heinous corporate crimes in American history. Between 1985 and 1991, they authorized illegal drug trials on psychiatric patients at Willowbrook Hospital and other facilities. Seventy-three people died as a direct result of these experiments. Sixteen-year-old Sophie Brennan was murdered when she tried to expose the conspiracy."

She pauses, letting the weight of those numbers sink in.

"For thirty-seven years, these men lived free while their victims were silenced. They used wealth, power, and influence to cover up their crimes. They destroyed whistleblowers who tried to expose them. They falsified death certificates. They bribed officials. They believed they were above the law."

Rachel's voice strengthens. "Today, a jury of twelve ordinary citizens proved they were wrong. Today, justice prevailed. Today, seventy-three victims and their families received the accountability they deserved."

A reporter shouts: "What sentence are you seeking?"

"The maximum penalty for conspiracy to commit murder is life in prison. We will be seeking life sentences for all six defendants at the sentencing hearing, which will be scheduled within sixty days."

"What about Owen Brennan? He killed four people

connected to this conspiracy but he's serving only twenty years while these executives face life?"

Rachel doesn't hesitate. "Owen Brennan committed terrible crimes. He murdered four people. He is serving twenty years in federal prison and will likely serve most or all of that sentence. But Owen Brennan also conducted a thirty-year investigation that helped the FBI build this case. His documentation was crucial to securing today's convictions. Justice is complicated. Owen will pay for his crimes. But his investigation helped expose six men who murdered seventy-three people and would have continued evading justice without his work."

Another reporter: "What do you say to critics who claim the prosecution relied too heavily on evidence from a convicted killer?"

"I say the evidence speaks for itself. Owen Brennan's investigation was independently verified by the FBI. Sophie Brennan's journal was authenticated by document examiners. The financial records were confirmed by forensic accountants. The autopsy findings were conducted by an independent pathologist. The witness testimony was corroborated by multiple sources. Owen Brennan didn't fabricate evidence, he collected it. And the jury found that evidence compelling enough to convict on all thirty counts."

"Ms. Walters!" A reporter points at me. "How does it feel knowing your mother's reports were vindicated?"

Rachel looks at me, nodding permission.

I step to the microphone, my heart pounding.

"My mother, Linda Walters, was a nurse at Willowbrook in 1987. She witnessed Sophie Brennan's murder. She filed the first police report the day after Sophie died. For thirteen years, she tried to expose this conspiracy. She lost her job. She lost her nursing license. She lost custody of me. She lost everything. And for thirteen years, everyone told her she was mentally ill, that she was delusional, that she was making up stories."

My voice cracks but I push through. "My mother died by suicide in 2011. She died believing no one would ever believe her. She died thinking she'd wasted her life on a conspiracy that no one cared about. But she was right. About everything. And today's verdict proves it."

Tears stream down my face. "Linda Walters was a hero. She tried to save people she never met. She sacrificed everything to expose the truth. And even though she didn't live to see today's verdict, I want everyone to know: Linda Walters was telling the truth. She was a whistleblower who paid the ultimate price. And today, thirty-seven years later, she's finally been vindicated."

The crowd erupts in applause.

Catherine Brennan steps forward. "I'm Catherine Brennan, Sophie's mother. For thirty-seven years, I believed my daughter committed suicide. I carried guilt for not seeing warning signs, for not saving her. I spent decades blaming myself. But today I learned the truth: Sophie didn't give up. She was murdered for trying to save other patients. She was a hero.

And now, finally, the men who killed her will spend the rest of their lives in prison."

More applause. More tears.

Rachel returns to the microphone. "This verdict sends a clear message: no one is above the law. Not wealth. Not power. Not corporate influence. If you commit murder, you will be held accountable, even if it takes thirty-seven years. Thank you."

The press conference ends.

As we walk back into the courthouse, reporters shout questions, cameras flash, and the crowd chants: "JUSTICE FOR SOPHIE! JUSTICE FOR THE SEVENTY-THREE!"

April 8, 2025, 1:00 PM Phone Call with Owen

I'm sitting in Rachel's office when my phone rings.

FCI DEVENS - FEDERAL PRISON

I answer immediately. "Owen?"

"Jenna. Agent Chen told me. Guilty on all counts. All six defendants. Every single charge."

"Yes. It happened. They're convicted."

Owen's voice breaks. "Thirty-seven years. Thirty-seven years I've been fighting for this. And it finally happened."

"Sophie got justice. Your sister got justice."

"I know." He's crying now, openly. "I'm sitting in my prison cell, in federal custody, serving twenty years for murder. I'll probably die in here. But Sophie got justice. Those six men are going to prison. That's all I wanted."

"It happened because of you, Owen. Your investigation. Your documentation. Your thirty years of work."

"It happened because Margaret gave you the journal. Because you brought it to the FBI. Because your mother tried to report it first. Because Sophie documented everything. We all contributed, Jenna. That's how justice works, it takes time, it takes multiple people, it takes sacrifice."

We're both silent for a moment.

Then Owen says, "Can you do something for me?"

"Anything."

"Go to Sophie's grave. Tell her she was right. Tell her the men who killed her are finally going to prison. Tell her she was a hero."

"I will. I promise."

"And go to your mother's grave. Tell Linda she was vindicated. Tell her the world knows she was telling the truth. Tell her she's a hero too."

"I'll go today."

"Thank you, Jenna. Thank you for finishing what your

mother started. Thank you for giving Sophie a voice. Thank you for making sure those six men faced justice."

The phone beeps, time warning.

"I have to go," Owen says. "They limit my calls. But Jenna? When the sentencing happens, when those six men get life in prison, I want you to remember something."

"What?"

"Justice is slow. Justice is painful. Justice is incomplete. I'm in prison. Your mother is dead. Sophie is dead. Seventy-three people are dead. But today, those six executives were held accountable. That's worth something. That's worth everything."

"I'll remember."

"Good. Take care of yourself."

"You too, Owen."

Click.

The line goes dead.

I sit in Rachel's office, holding my phone, crying.

Guilty on all counts.

Six executives convicted.

Justice after thirty-seven years.

My mother was right.

Sophie was right.

Owen was right.

And today, finally, the world acknowledged it.

April 8, 2025, 4:00 PM Sophie's Grave

I drive to Riverside Cemetery in Manchester, the cemetery where Sophie Brennan is buried.

Catherine gave me directions. Plot 247, Section C, beneath a maple tree.

The headstone is simple granite with an angel carved at the top:

SOPHIE MARIE BRENNAN 1971-1987

BELOVED DAUGHTER, SISTER, FRIEND
"SHE TRIED TO SAVE THEM"

I kneel in the grass and place flowers beside the stone.

"Hi, Sophie. My name is Jenna Walters. You don't know me, but my mother knew you. Linda Walters, she was your nurse at Willowbrook. She tried to save you. She filed police reports after you died. She spent thirteen years fighting to expose what happened to you."

The wind rustles through the maple leaves above.

"I found your journal. Margaret Moore kept it hidden for thirty-seven years. She left me a note telling me where to find it. Your journal, the one with the rainbow stickers and unicorns, became evidence in the trial."

I trace my fingers over Sophie's name.

"Today, the six executives who ordered your death were convicted. All six. Guilty on all counts. James Morrison, Martin Shaw, Robert Chen, David Patterson, Michael Williams, Thomas Foster. They're going to prison for the rest of their lives."

Tears stream down my face.

"You were sixteen years old. You should have lived a full life. You should have graduated high school, gone to college, fallen in love, had kids, grown old. But instead, you documented pharmaceutical crimes knowing it would get you killed. You were so brave, Sophie. You were a hero."

I pull out my phone and show her photo the news headlines:

GUILTY: Six Pharmaceutical Executives Convicted of Murdering 73 Patients

Sophie Brennan's Journal Helps Secure Historic Conviction

Justice After 37 Years: Willowbrook Conspirators Face Life in Prison

"Look, Sophie. The whole world knows your story now. The whole world knows you were murdered trying to save patients. The whole world knows you were a hero."

A bird lands on the headstone, singing.

"Your brother Owen sends his regards. He's in prison for killing four people connected to your murder. He spent thirty years investigating. He sacrificed his freedom for you. And today, when he heard the verdict, he cried. He wanted me to tell you that you were right. That the men who killed you are finally going to prison. That you were a hero."

I stand up, brushing grass from my knees.

"Rest peacefully, Sophie. You did everything you could. You documented the truth. You tried to save people. You paid with your life. But today, thirty-seven years later, you finally got justice. The men who killed you will die in prison. That's because of you. Because of your courage. Because of your journal."

I place my hand on the headstone one more time.

"Thank you for being brave. Thank you for documenting everything. Thank you for not giving up. Your journal saved so many people from wondering if their loved ones committed suicide. Now they know the truth. That's because of you."

I walk back to my car, leaving flowers on Sophie's grave.

Behind me, the maple tree rustles in the April breeze, carrying a sixteen-year-old girl's courage into history.

April 8, 2025, 5:30 PM Linda's Grave

I drive to Manchester Cemetery, my mother's grave.

The flowers I left two days ago are still fresh beside her headstone.

I kneel again, this time with a bottle of champagne and two glasses.

"Hi, Mom. I came back. I have news."

I pop the champagne cork, it echoes through the quiet cemetery.

I pour two glasses. One I set beside her headstone. One I hold.

"Today, six pharmaceutical executives were convicted of murdering Sophie Brennan and seventy-three other patients at Willowbrook. Guilty on all counts. Every single charge. The jury believed the evidence. They believed your police reports. They believed Sophie's journal. They believed the truth."

I raise my glass. "Mom, you were right. About everything. Sophie Brennan was murdered. The patients were murdered. The drug trials were illegal. The officials were bribed. The cover-up was real. You weren't mentally ill. You weren't delusional. You weren't paranoid. You were telling the truth."

Tears stream into my champagne. "I'm so sorry I didn't believe you. I'm so sorry I let them take me away without fighting for you. I'm so sorry I thought you were crazy. I'm so sorry you died thinking no one believed you."

I drink deeply, the champagne bitter and sweet at the same time.

"But Mom, listen. Today, at the press conference, I told the world about you. I told them Linda Walters was a hero. I told them you witnessed Sophie's murder and filed the first police report. I told them you spent thirteen years fighting to expose the conspiracy. I told them you lost everything trying to save people you never met."

I pour more champagne into my glass. "Rachel Diaz cited your police reports in court. Agent Chen testified about your whistleblowing. The New York Times called you a hero. Everyone knows your story now. Everyone knows you were telling the truth."

The sun sets behind the cemetery trees, painting the sky orange and purple.

"Owen Brennan wants to buy you a new headstone. Something that tells the truth about who you were. 'Linda Marie Walters. Nurse, Whistleblower, Hero.' I told him yes. I think it's perfect."

I finish my glass and pour the second glass, the one I set beside her headstone, onto the grass.

"This is for you, Mom. This is your victory. This is your vindication. Those six executives are going to die in prison because you filed those first police reports. Because you documented patient deaths. Because you wouldn't let them bury the truth."

I stand, leaving the champagne bottle beside her grave.

"I love you, Mom. I'm proud of you. And I'm going to spend the rest of my life making sure people remember you correctly. Not as a mentally ill woman. Not as a paranoid nurse. But as a hero who sacrificed everything to expose corporate murder."

I walk away, leaving flowers and champagne on my mother's grave.

Tomorrow, I'll start planning for the sentencing hearing.

Tomorrow, I'll return to work at Manchester General.

Tomorrow, life continues.

But tonight, I celebrate.

Justice came.

Slow. Painful. Incomplete.

But it came.

And my mother, Linda Marie Walters, was finally vindicated.

CHAPTER 15

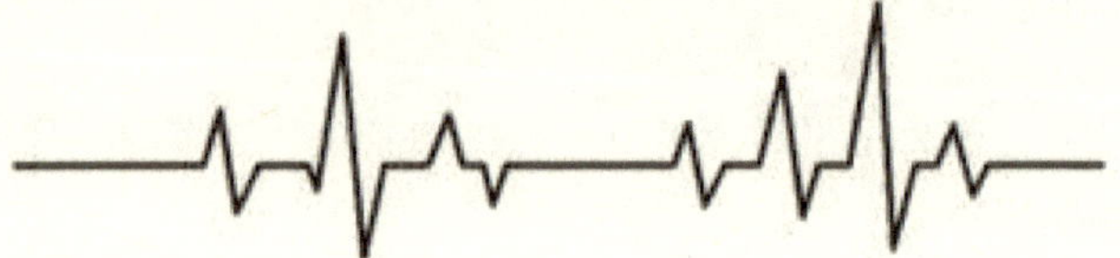

Sentencing

June 9, 2025, 9:00 AM Federal Courthouse, Boston

Two months after the verdict.

The same courtroom. The same judge. The same defendants, but now they're convicted murderers awaiting sentencing.

I sit in the front row with Catherine Brennan, just like I did on verdict day. Around us: victims' families who've been waiting thirty-seven years for this moment.

The atmosphere is different than it was at the trial. Less tense. More resigned. The fight is over. The verdict is final. Today is just about consequences.

At the defense table: James Morrison, Martin Shaw, Robert Chen, David Patterson, Michael Williams, and Thomas

Foster. All in prison jumpsuits now, no more expensive suits. All shackled. All visibly aged by two months in federal detention.

Morrison looks frail, his hands trembling constantly.

Shaw is in a wheelchair now, too weak to stand.

Chen has lost significant weight, his jumpsuit hanging loose.

Patterson's oxygen tank is a permanent fixture.

Williams stares at nothing, expressionless.

Foster still maintains some dignity but his eyes are hollow.

Six old men who spent their entire lives in power, now wearing prison orange and chains.

At the prosecution table: Rachel Diaz and Agent Chen, reviewing their sentencing recommendations.

Judge Martinez enters at exactly 9:00 AM.

"All rise."

We stand.

"Please be seated. We are here for sentencing in the matter of United States v. Morrison, et al. The defendants have been convicted on all charges. Before I impose sentences, I will hear statements from the prosecution, the defense, and any victims who wish to speak. Ms. Diaz, you may begin."

Rachel stands. "Thank you, Your Honor. The United States recommends the maximum sentence on all counts for all defendants. These men orchestrated one of the most heinous corporate crimes in American history. They murdered seventy-three people. They destroyed whistleblowers. They covered up evidence for forty years. They showed no remorse. They deserve to spend the rest of their lives in federal prison."

She walks to the center of the courtroom. "Your Honor, conspiracy to commit murder carries a maximum sentence of life in prison. Racketeering carries twenty years. Wire fraud carries twenty years. Obstruction of justice carries twenty years. The government recommends consecutive life sentences for each defendant on the murder charges, with additional consecutive sentences on the remaining counts."

Judge Martinez makes notes. "That would effectively be multiple life sentences."

"Yes, Your Honor. These men murdered seventy-three people. They deserve multiple life sentences."

"Noted. Defense?"

Gerald Hutchins rises, looking exhausted. The past two months have been brutal on the defense team, appeals denied, motions rejected, public vilification.

"Your Honor, my clients are elderly men in their seventies. James Morrison is seventy-seven years old with advancing Parkinson's disease. Martin Shaw is seventy-six and wheelchair-bound. David Patterson requires constant oxygen.

These men pose no threat to society. They have no criminal history prior to these convictions. Lengthy prison sentences would be tantamount to death sentences."

He pauses. "The defense requests concurrent sentences with credit for time served. These men have already spent two months in federal detention. They've lost their reputations, their freedom, their dignity. Further punishment is unnecessary."

Rachel stands immediately. "Your Honor, these defendants were free for forty years while their victims were dead. Two months in detention is not sufficient punishment for seventy-three murders."

"I agree, Ms. Diaz." Judge Martinez looks at the defense table. "Mr. Hutchins, your clients were convicted of murdering seventy-three people. Their age and health do not excuse their crimes. Many of their victims were elderly and sick when they were murdered. Your clients showed them no mercy."

Hutchins sits, defeated.

Judge Martinez continues: "Before I impose sentences, I will hear victim impact statements. Anyone who wishes to speak, please approach."

June 9, 2025, 9:30 AM

Victim Impact Statements

Catherine Brennan stands first.

She walks to the podium, using a cane for support. She's 73 years old now, gray-haired, her face lined with decades of grief.

"Your Honor, my name is Catherine Brennan. I'm Sophie's mother. My daughter was sixteen years old when these six men murdered her. For thirty-seven years, I believed Sophie committed suicide. I carried guilt for not seeing warning signs. I blamed myself. I wondered what I did wrong as a mother."

Her voice breaks. "But I didn't do anything wrong. Sophie didn't kill herself. She was murdered because she tried to save other patients. She was a hero. And these six men took her from me. They took my daughter, my only child, and they let me believe for thirty-seven years that she gave up on life."

Catherine looks directly at the six defendants. "You stole thirty-seven years of truth from me. You stole my daughter's life. You stole my peace. And I want you to spend every remaining day of your lives in prison, knowing what you did. I want you to die in prison, knowing you murdered a sixteen-year-old girl who tried to do the right thing."

She returns to her seat, and I hold her hand as she cries.

Next: Janet Riley.

"Your Honor, my name is Janet Riley. My brother Thomas died at Willowbrook in February 1986. He was thirty-four years old. For thirty-nine years, I believed Thomas committed suicide. But I learned during this trial that Thomas was given an experimental sedative that caused respiratory failure. He was murdered. And these six men authorized it."

She points at the defendants. "My brother died because you wanted to test a drug. You didn't care that he was a human being with a family. You didn't care that he had a sister who loved him. You cared about profit. I hope you spend the rest of your lives regretting what you did."

More victims' families speak:

Maria Gomez, whose mother Patricia died in 1986. Helen Torres, whose son Michael died in 1986. Robert Jennings, whose brother Marcus died in 1987. Sarah Chen, whose father David died in 1989.

On and on. Twelve victims' families speak over ninety minutes.

Every story the same: We thought our loved one committed suicide. Now we know they were murdered. We want justice.

Finally, Judge Martinez looks at me. "Ms. Walters, would you like to speak?"

I stand, my heart pounding.

June 9, 2025, 11:15 AM Jenna's Statement

I walk to the podium.

"Your Honor, my name is Jenna Walters. My mother, Linda Walters, was a nurse at Willowbrook in 1987. She witnessed Sophie Brennan's murder. She filed the first police report the day after Sophie died. She spent thirteen years trying to expose this conspiracy."

I look at the six defendants. "You destroyed my mother. You took her job. You took her nursing license. You took custody of me when I was seven years old. You gaslit her for thirteen years, telling her she was mentally ill, telling her she was delusional, until she couldn't take it anymore and killed herself in 2011."

My voice hardens. "My mother didn't die of mental illness. She died because you systematically destroyed her for telling the truth. She died because you couldn't let her expose your crimes. You murdered her as surely as you murdered Sophie Brennan and the seventy-three patients."

I step closer to the podium. "I grew up thinking my mother was crazy. For twenty-four years, I believed she was mentally ill. I was ashamed of her. I didn't defend her. I let social workers take me away without fighting. And I lived with that shame until I found Sophie's journal and learned my mother was telling the truth all along."

Tears stream down my face. "You took my mother from me twice. Once when I was seven. Again, when she died. And you took away the chance for me to tell her I believed her, that I was proud of her, that she was a hero. I will never forgive you for that."

I look directly at James Morrison. "You testified against my mother at her nursing license hearing. You called her paranoid. You called her emotionally unstable. You destroyed her career. And you did it to protect your pharmaceutical profits. I hope you die in prison knowing you destroyed an innocent woman who was trying to save lives."

I return to my seat, shaking.

Catherine pulls me into a hug. "Your mother would be so proud."

June 9, 2025, 12:00 PM Defendants' Statements

Judge Martinez looks at the defense table. "Do any of the defendants wish to speak before sentencing?"

Gerald Hutchins confers with his clients. Morrison shakes his head. Shaw is too weak to speak. Chen stares at the floor. Patterson focuses on breathing. Williams says nothing.

Only Thomas Foster stands.

"Your Honor, I wish to speak."

"Proceed, Mr. Foster."

Foster approaches the podium in shackles, moving slowly. He's 75 years old, thin and gray.

"Your Honor, I've spent the past two months in federal detention. I've had time to think about everything that happened. I've read the victim impact statements. I've listened to the families. And I want to say..."

He pauses, and for a moment I think he's going to apologize.

"...that I maintain my innocence. I did not authorize illegal drug trials. I did not order anyone's death. I followed company policy and FDA regulations. I am a pharmaceutical executive who spent forty years developing medications that saved lives. Yes, some trials had adverse outcomes. That's the nature of medical research. But I am not a murderer."

The courtroom erupts in gasps and angry shouts.

Judge Martinez bangs his gavel. "ORDER!"

Foster continues, oblivious or indifferent to the reaction. "I believe this conviction was based on the unreliable testimony of a convicted killer and the paranoid writings of a mentally ill teenager. I maintain that I committed no crimes. I will appeal this verdict. And I believe history will exonerate me."

He returns to his seat.

Catherine whispers, "He learned nothing. After everything, he learned nothing."

Judge Martinez looks disgusted. "Mr. Foster, your lack of remorse has been noted. Is there anything else from the defense?"

"No, Your Honor."

"Very well. I will now impose sentences."

June 9, 2025, 12:30 PM Sentencing

Judge Martinez picks up a document and begins reading.

"I have reviewed the pre-sentence reports for all six defendants. I have considered the severity of the crimes, the defendants' age and health, the victim impact statements, and the sentencing guidelines. I have also considered the defendants' complete lack of remorse, as evidenced by Mr. Foster's statement today."

He looks at each defendant in turn.

"These crimes are among the most egregious I have encountered in thirty years on the bench. Seventy-three people, vulnerable psychiatric patients, were murdered in the pursuit of pharmaceutical profit. A sixteen-year-old girl was killed for trying to expose the truth. Whistleblowers were destroyed. Evidence was covered up for forty years. And even today, after conviction, the defendants show no remorse."

Judge Martinez's voice hardens. "The law requires that I impose appropriate punishment. In this case, appropriate punishment is severe."

He begins with James Morrison.

"James Morrison, please stand."

Morrison struggles to his feet, assisted by his attorney.

"On the count of conspiracy to commit murder in the death of Sophie Marie Brennan, I sentence you to life in prison without possibility of parole."

Catherine gasps beside me.

"On the count of conspiracy to commit murder in the deaths of seventy-three patients, I sentence you to life in prison without possibility of parole, to run consecutively."

Consecutive. Two life sentences.

"On the count of racketeering, I sentence you to twenty years in federal prison, to run consecutively. On the count of wire fraud, I sentence you to twenty years, to run consecutively. On the count of obstruction of justice, I sentence you to twenty years, to run consecutively."

Judge Martinez looks at Morrison directly. "Mr. Morrison, you will spend the rest of your life in federal prison. You will die there. You murdered seventy-three people and showed no remorse. This is appropriate punishment."

Morrison collapses back into his chair, pale and trembling.

Judge Martinez moves to Martin Shaw.

"Martin Shaw, please stand."

Bailiffs wheel Shaw forward in his wheelchair.

The sentences are identical: Two life sentences plus sixty years, all consecutive. Shaw will die in prison.

Robert Chen: Two life sentences plus sixty years. Die in prison.

David Patterson: Two life sentences plus sixty years. Die

in prison.

Michael Williams: Two life sentences plus sixty years. Die in prison.

Thomas Foster, who showed no remorse, receives the harshest rebuke.

"Mr. Foster, your statement today demonstrated complete lack of accountability. You murdered seventy-three people and you dare to claim innocence. You are a danger to society and you deserve no mercy."

"Two life sentences without parole, plus sixty years consecutive. You will die in federal prison. You will never breathe free air again. You will never see your family again. You will spend every remaining day of your life behind bars, and that is exactly what you deserve."

By 1:00 PM, all six sentences have been imposed.

Every defendant: Multiple life sentences plus sixty years.

Every defendant: Will die in prison.

No parole. No mercy. No second chances.

Judge Martinez bangs his gavel. "The defendants are remanded to the Bureau of Prisons for designation to appropriate facilities. This court is adjourned."

June 9, 2025, 1:30 PM Immediate Aftermath

Federal marshals escort the six convicted murderers out of the courtroom through a side door.

Morrison is crying. Shaw looks catatonic. Chen is silent. Patterson struggles to breathe. Williams closes his eyes. Foster still maintains that defiant posture, but his hands shake.

They're led away to federal detention, where they'll await transfer to permanent prison facilities.

Maximum security. Medical units. Places where elderly inmates serve life sentences until they die.

Catherine turns to me. "It's over. After thirty-seven years, it's finally over."

"They're going to die in prison. All six of them."

"Good. They deserve it."

Around us, victims' families embrace. Some are crying. Some are celebrating. Some sit in stunned silence.

Janet Riley approaches. "Thank you, Jenna. Thank you for finding Sophie's journal. Without you, none of this would have happened."

"It wasn't just me. It was Margaret, and my mother, and Owen, and Sophie…"

"And you," she insists. "You brought the journal to the FBI. You testified. You finished what your mother started."

Rachel Diaz approaches our group. "Six life sentences. Multiple life sentences for each defendant. They'll be designated to medical facilities within the Bureau of Prisons system, likely FMC Devens or FMC Butner. High security medical prisons where elderly inmates serve out life sentences."

"How long will they live?" Catherine asks.

"Morrison has Parkinson's, maybe five years. Shaw is in very poor health, maybe three years. Patterson's oxygen-dependent, maybe two years. Chen, Williams, Foster might last ten years if they're lucky. But they'll all die in prison. None of them will ever be free."

"Good," Catherine says firmly. "That's what they deserve."

Agent Chen joins us. "I need to call Owen. He'll want to know about the sentences."

"Tell him Sophie got justice," Catherine says. "Tell him those six men will die in prison. Tell him his thirty-year investigation accomplished exactly what he hoped."

Agent Chen steps away, phone to her ear.

June 9, 2025, 2:00 PM Press Conference

Rachel Diaz holds a press conference on the courthouse steps.

The media presence is still massive, national outlets,

international crews, true crime documentarians.

"This morning, Judge Martinez imposed sentences on six executives convicted of murdering seventy-three psychiatric patients between 1985 and 1991. Each defendant received multiple consecutive life sentences without possibility of parole. Each defendant will die in federal prison. This is appropriate justice for one of the most heinous corporate crimes in American history."

A reporter asks: "What message does this send to pharmaceutical companies?"

"The message is clear: No one is above the law. If you commit murder in pursuit of profit, you will be held accountable. It may take years, in this case, thirty-seven years, but justice will prevail. These six men believed they were untouchable because of their wealth and power. Today proved they were wrong."

"What about Owen Brennan? He's serving only twenty years while these executives got life."

Rachel doesn't hesitate. "Owen Brennan murdered four people. He confessed. He's serving twenty years in federal prison and will likely serve most of that sentence. His crimes were terrible. But Owen also spent thirty years investigating this conspiracy and cooperated fully with the FBI. His documentation helped secure these convictions. Justice is complicated. Owen is paying for his crimes. But his investigation ensured that six men who murdered seventy-three people also pay for theirs."

"Ms. Walters!" A reporter points at me. "How does your mother's vindication feel now?"

I step to the microphone. "My mother spent thirteen years fighting to expose this conspiracy. She lost everything. Today, the six men who destroyed her received multiple life sentences. They'll die in prison. That's vindication. That's justice. And I hope my mother, wherever she is, knows that her thirteen-year fight wasn't in vain."

Catherine Brennan speaks next. "I'm Sophie's mother. My daughter was murdered at sixteen. For thirty-seven years, I believed she committed suicide. Today, the men who killed her received life sentences. Sophie got justice. All seventy-three victims got justice. That's all we wanted."

The press conference ends with a simple statement from Rachel: "Justice delayed is not justice denied. It took thirty-seven years, but today justice was served."

June 9, 2025, 4:00 PM Phone Call with Owen

I'm driving home when my phone rings.

FCI DEVENS - FEDERAL PRISON

"Owen?"

"Jenna. Agent Chen told me. Multiple life sentences. All six defendants. They'll die in prison."

"Yes. It's over. Sophie got justice."

Owen's voice is thick with emotion. "Thirty-seven years. I spent thirty-seven years investigating. Thirty years obsessing. Six years in prison cooperating with the FBI. And today, those six men were sentenced to die in federal custody."

"You did it, Owen. Your investigation made this possible."

"We all did it. Margaret kept the journal. Your mother filed the first reports. You brought the journal to the FBI. Sophie documented everything. We all contributed."

I hear him crying quietly. "I wish I could tell Sophie. I wish I could visit her grave and tell her those six men will never be free. But I'm in prison. I can't go to her grave. I can't be there."

"I'll go for you," I promise. "I'll visit Sophie's grave and tell her. I'll tell her the six men who murdered her received life sentences. I'll tell her she got justice."

"Thank you, Jenna."

"Owen, are you okay? I mean... you spent thirty years fighting for this. Now it's over. What happens now?"

A long pause. "I serve my sentence. I teach GED classes. I help in the law library. I wait for parole eligibility in 2044. And I live with the knowledge that I killed four people but I also helped convict six murderers. That's my life now."

"Do you regret it? Killing those four people?"

"Every day. I regret the violence. I regret taking lives. But

I don't regret the outcome. Those four people helped murder my sister. And their deaths led to the FBI investigation that convicted six executives. So... I don't know. Regret is complicated."

The call-time warning beeps.

"I have to go," Owen says. "But Jenna? Thank you. Thank you for finishing what your mother started. Thank you for giving Sophie a voice. Thank you for making sure justice happened."

"Thank you for never giving up on Sophie. Even when it cost you everything."

"She was worth it. My sister was worth everything."

Click.

The line goes dead.

I pull over to the side of the road and sit in my car, crying.

Justice came.

Six executives will die in prison.

Sophie got justice.

Linda got vindication.

Owen sacrificed his freedom.

And I... I finished what my mother started.

June 9, 2025, 6:00 PM Sophie's Grave

I drive to Riverside Cemetery and kneel at Sophie's grave.

The headstone with the angel carved at the top:

SOPHIE MARIE BRENNAN 971-1987

BELOVED DAUGHTER, SISTER, FRIEND

"SHE TRIED TO SAVE THEM"

"Hi, Sophie. I came back. I have news."

I place fresh flowers beside the stone.

"Today, the six men who murdered you were sentenced. James Morrison, Martin Shaw, Robert Chen, David Patterson, Michael Williams, Thomas Foster. All six received multiple life sentences. They'll die in prison. They'll never be free. They'll never see their families again. They'll spend every remaining day behind bars."

The evening sun casts long shadows across the cemetery.

"Your brother Owen sends his regards. He's in prison, so he can't visit. But he wanted me to tell you that you got justice. That your journal helped convict six murderers. That your courage, documenting everything even when you knew it would get you killed, saved so many people from believing their loved ones committed suicide."

I touch the headstone gently. "You were sixteen years old, Sophie. You should have lived a full life. But instead, you spent your last months documenting pharmaceutical crimes. You were so brave. And today, your bravery was rewarded with justice."

A bird lands on the nearby maple tree, singing.

"Rest peacefully, Sophie. The men who killed you will die in prison. That's because of you. Because of your journal. Because you refused to stay silent even when it cost you everything."

June 9, 2025, 7:00 PM Linda's Grave

I drive to Manchester Cemetery and kneel at my mother's grave.

The simple headstone:

LINDA MARIE WALTERS 1962-2011

BELOVED MOTHER

But soon, this will be replaced. Owen is paying for a new headstone. One that tells the truth.

"Hi, Mom. I came back again. Today was sentencing."

I place flowers beside the stone.

"The six executives who destroyed you received multiple life sentences. They'll die in prison. James Morrison, the man who testified against you at your nursing license hearing, got two life sentences plus sixty years. He'll die in federal custody. All of them will."

Tears stream down my face. "You were right, Mom. About everything. And today, the men who called you crazy, who took your license, who took me away from you, who drove you to suicide, today they were sentenced to die in prison."

I press my hand against the cold stone.

"I'm getting you a new headstone. Owen Brennan is paying for it. It's going to say: 'Linda Marie Walters. Nurse, Whistleblower, Hero. She tried to save them. 1962-2011.' That's who you were, Mom. Not a mentally ill woman. Not a paranoid nurse. A hero."

The sun sets behind the cemetery trees.

"I love you, Mom. I'm proud of you. And I'm going to spend the rest of my life making sure people remember you correctly. The world knows now. The world knows you were telling the truth. The world knows you sacrificed everything to expose corporate murder."

I stand, brushing grass from my knees.

"Justice came, Mom. It took thirty-seven years. It cost you

everything. But it came."

I walk back to my car, leaving flowers on my mother's grave.

Tomorrow, I return to work at Manchester General Hospital.

Tomorrow, life continues.

But tonight, I rest.

Justice has been served.

June 10, 2025 The Day After

The news coverage is overwhelming:

CNN: "Six Pharmaceutical Executives Sentenced to Die in Prison for 73 Murders"

New York Times: "Willowbrook Conspiracy: Life Sentences Mark End of 37-Year Cover-Up"

Washington Post: "Justice Delayed: How a Teenage Girl's Journal Brought Down Corporate Killers"

Boston Globe: "Morrison, Shaw, Chen, Patterson, Williams, Foster: Six Names That Will Forever Symbolize Corporate Evil"

The verdicts send shockwaves through the pharmaceutical industry. CEOs are questioned. Boards are restructured. FDA regulations are tightened. Congressional hearings are announced.

GenHealth Pharmaceuticals, the company formerly known as Nexus, faces hundreds of civil lawsuits from victims' families. The company's stock plummets. Bankruptcy is likely.

But that's someone else's fight now.

My fight is over.

I return to Manchester General Hospital and resume my work as a floor nurse. Night shifts. Medication rounds. Patient care.

The hospital administration was nervous about having me back, worried about media attention, worried about disruption. But after a week, everything returns to normal.

I'm just a nurse again.

And that's exactly what I want to be.

June 15, 2025 Linda's New Headstone

Owen keeps his promise.

A new headstone is installed at Manchester Cemetery, replacing my mother's simple marker.

It's beautiful, polished granite with an engraved medical caduceus symbol.

LINDA MARIE WALTERS 1962-2011

REGISTERED NURSE, WHISTLEBLOWER, HERO "SHE TRIED TO SAVE THEM" SHE SPENT 13 YEARS EXPOSING THE TRUTH SHE SACRIFICED EVERYTHING FOR JUSTICE

I stand before it, crying.

Catherine Brennan stands beside me. "It's perfect."

"Owen paid for it from prison. He'll probably never see it. But he made sure my mother is remembered correctly."

"She was a hero, Jenna. The world knows that now."

We stand in silence, two daughters of women who fought corporate evil and paid impossible prices.

"What happens now?" I ask.

"We live," Catherine says simply. "We honor their memories. We tell their stories. We make sure the world never forgets."

"And the six executives?"

"They die in prison. Morrison probably has five years. Shaw maybe three. Patterson maybe two. The others, who knows. But they'll all die behind bars. That's justice."

We stand together at my mother's grave, reading the new headstone over and over.

Hero.

Whistleblower.

She tried to save them.

Finally, my mother is remembered for who she really was.

CHAPTER 16

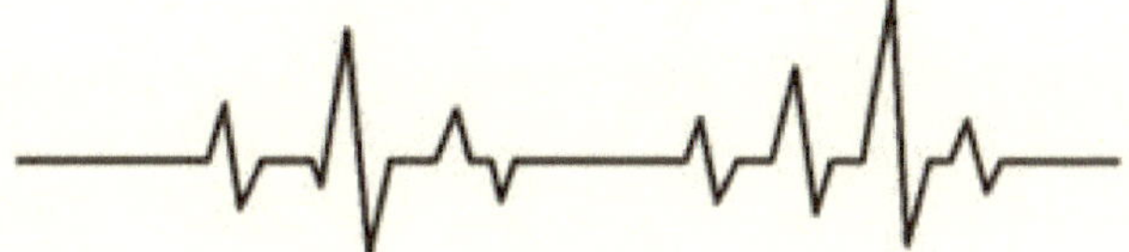

Ripples

June 20, 2025 Eleven Days After Sentencing

Life has not returned to normal.

I'm back at Manchester General Hospital, working night shifts, but everything feels different. The other nurses know who I am now. They've seen me on the news, read about my mother, heard about Sophie's journal.

Some treat me like a hero. Others keep their distance, uncomfortable with the attention I brought to the hospital.

I just want to do my job.

But tonight, during my 2 AM medication round, a patient in Room 318 stops me.

"You're Jenna Walters, aren't you? Linda's daughter."

I pause. "Yes."

The woman, Mrs. Patterson, age 67, admitted for pneumonia, sits up in bed. "I need to tell you something. My husband worked at a psychiatric facility in Vermont in the 1990s. He told me things... things that sounded like what happened at Willowbrook. Patients dying from drug trials. Staff being told to keep quiet. He was fired when he questioned a death."

My heart rate quickens. "When was this?"

"1993 to 1995. The facility was called Greenmont Psychiatric Hospital. It closed in 1998."

"Did your husband report it?"

"He tried. Nobody listened. They called him paranoid. He developed depression, lost his nursing license, died in 2003. I always wondered if he was telling the truth."

I sit down beside her bed. "What was your husband's name?"

"Richard Patterson. He was a psychiatric nurse for twenty years."

The name hits me. Patterson. Same last name as David Patterson, one of the six executives.

"Mrs. Patterson, after the Willowbrook verdict, did you ever think about investigating?"

"Every day. But I'm sixty-seven years old. I don't know

where to start. I don't know if anyone would believe me."

I pull out my phone and text Agent Chen: *Need to talk. Possible Willowbrook connection in Vermont.*

"Mrs. Patterson, I'm going to connect you with the FBI agent who investigated Willowbrook. If there's any truth to what your husband reported, they'll investigate."

She starts crying. "You believe me?"

"Yes. Because my mother tried to report the same thing and nobody believed her either. I won't let that happen to you."

June 21, 2025 FBI Field Office, Boston

Agent Chen meets me and Mrs. Patterson at the FBI office.

"Mrs. Patterson, tell me everything your husband told you about Greenmont."

For two hours, Mrs. Patterson describes what her husband Richard reported in the 1990s: mysterious patient deaths, experimental drug trials, staff members being told to falsify records, administrators threatening anyone who asked questions.

Agent Chen takes detailed notes. "This matches the Willowbrook pattern. Same timeframe. Same pharmaceutical company, GenHealth was expanding to multiple facilities in the early 1990s."

"Can you investigate?" I ask.

"We're already investigating. After the Willowbrook convictions, we received tips about four other psychiatric facilities, Vermont, Maine, Ohio, and Oregon. All had similar patterns: unexplained deaths, sudden closures, staff members who tried to report abuse and were fired."

Mrs. Patterson looks stunned. "You mean there were more?"

"We think so. Willowbrook might not be the only facility where GenHealth conducted illegal trials. We're opening investigations at all four locations."

I feel sick. "How many more victims?"

"We don't know yet. But if the pattern holds, potentially hundreds."

June 25, 2025 Phone Call with Catherine

I tell Catherine about Mrs. Patterson and the Vermont facility.

"Oh God," she whispers. "You mean Sophie wasn't the only one? There were more facilities? More victims?"

"The FBI is investigating. But Catherine, if GenHealth was running illegal trials at multiple facilities, Sophie's journal might have exposed just one piece of a much larger conspiracy."

"How do we not know about this? How did they hide it

for so long?"

"The same way they hid Willowbrook. They closed facilities. They destroyed records. They threatened staff. They relied on the fact that psychiatric patients are marginalized and nobody listens when they die."

Catherine is quiet for a long moment. "What happens if the FBI confirms more facilities?"

"More prosecutions. But the six executives are already serving life sentences. They can't be sentenced twice."

"No. But GenHealth can be held accountable. Civil suits. More bankruptcy settlements. More families learning the truth."

June 28, 2025 Smithsonian Museum

The Smithsonian calls with an update on the Willowbrook exhibit.

"Ms. Walters, we'd like to expand the exhibit to include the broader investigation. If the FBI confirms additional facilities, we want to document the full scope of GenHealth's crimes, not just Willowbrook."

"How would that change the exhibit?"

"We'd still center Sophie's journal and your mother's reports. But we'd add context showing how widespread the abuse was. We'd honor all the victims, not just the seventy-three from Willowbrook."

"When do you need a decision?"

"The exhibit is scheduled to open October 22, the anniversary of Sophie's death. We have four months."

I agree to the expansion.

July 4, 2025 Independence Day

I spend the Fourth of July at Manchester Cemetery with Catherine.

We place flowers on both Linda's and Sophie's graves.

The new headstone for my mother stands beautiful and permanent:

LINDA MARIE WALTERS 1962-2011

REGISTERED NURSE, WHISTLEBLOWER, HERO "SHE TRIED TO SAVE THEM" SHE SPENT 13 YEARS EXPOSING THE TRUTH SHE SACRIFICED EVERYTHING FOR JUSTICE

"She would have wanted them to investigate the other facilities," I say. "She wouldn't have stopped at Willowbrook."

"Neither will we," Catherine replies. "Sophie's journal opened the door. Now the FBI can walk through it and find all the other victims."

July 10, 2025 The First Death

The news breaks at 6:00 PM:

David Patterson, 74, Dies in Federal Custody

Patterson, the VP of Operations who managed not just Willowbrook but potentially four other facilities, died at FMC Devens medical unit.

Cause of death: Respiratory failure.

He served exactly one month of his life sentence.

The FBI immediately subpoenas his prison medical records, personal effects, and any documents he had in his cell. They're looking for evidence about the other facilities.

They find nothing. Patterson took his secrets to the grave.

July 15, 2025 Vermont Investigation

Agent Chen calls with news.

"We exhumed three bodies from Greenmont Psychiatric Hospital in Vermont. Preliminary toxicology shows the same experimental drug, NX-447, that was used at Willowbrook."

"So, it's confirmed? GenHealth was running trials at

multiple facilities?"

"It's looking that way. We're working with Vermont authorities to identify all suspicious deaths between 1993 and 1998. So far, we've found twenty-seven."

Twenty-seven more victims. Twenty-seven more families who thought their loved ones committed suicide.

"What happens now?"

"We keep investigating. Maine next, then Ohio, then Oregon. This is going to take years, Jenna. But we're not stopping until we find everyone."

July 20, 2025 Victims' Families Coalition

Rachel Diaz organizes a meeting for families of the seventy-three Willowbrook victims and the newly identified Vermont victims.

One hundred people gather in Boston.

Rachel addresses the group: "The FBI has confirmed GenHealth conducted illegal drug trials at least two facilities, Willowbrook and Greenmont. We're investigating four other locations. The victims' total may exceed two hundred people."

The room erupts in gasps and crying.

Janet Riley stands. "My brother Thomas died at Willowbrook in 1986. I've spent thirty-nine years believing it was suicide. Are you telling me there are hundreds of other families going through what I went through?"

"Yes," Agent Chen says. "And we're going to find them all. We're going to give them the truth, just like we gave it to you."

One by one, families pledge to help. They'll search for records. They'll contact former staff members. They'll spread the word that the FBI is investigating.

The Willowbrook case is expanding into something far larger.

July 25, 2025 Congressional Hearing Announcement

Senator Elizabeth Warren announces expanded Congressional hearings:

"In light of new evidence suggesting GenHealth Pharmaceuticals conducted illegal drug trials at multiple psychiatric facilities across America, the Senate Committee on Health, Education, Labor, and Pensions will hold comprehensive hearings examining:

1. The full scope of GenHealth's illegal activities
2. How federal and state agencies failed to detect ongoing abuse for over a decade
3. Reforms needed to prevent future pharmaceutical crimes
4. Whistleblower protection for healthcare workers

Hearings will begin in September and continue through December."

I'm asked to testify. So is Catherine. So is Mrs. Patterson from Vermont.

We all agree.

August 1, 2025 Media Interview

60 Minutes contacts me about an expanded story.

"Ms. Walters, we'd like to update our Willowbrook episode to include the new developments. Would you be willing to do a follow-up interview?"

I agree.

This time, the interview focuses not just on my mother and Sophie, but on the broader pattern of abuse.

Lesley Stahl asks: "When you found Sophie's journal, did you ever imagine it would lead to uncovering multiple facilities and potentially hundreds of victims?"

"No. I thought I was solving one murder. I didn't know I was exposing a systemic conspiracy that lasted over a decade and affected multiple states."

"How does that feel?"

"Overwhelming. Vindicating. Terrifying. My mother tried to expose Willowbrook for thirteen years. If she'd been believed, the FBI could have investigated in 1987 and prevented the Vermont deaths, the Maine deaths, the Ohio deaths. Hundreds of people might still be alive."

"So, in your view, every agency that dismissed your mother bears responsibility?"

"Yes. Every police department that closed her cases without investigating. Every nursing board that called her paranoid. Every social worker who took me away instead of investigating her claims. They all enabled GenHealth to keep killing people."

The interview is powerful. Painful. True.

August 5, 2025 The Second Death

Martin Shaw, 76, Dies in Federal Custody

Shaw, the Chief Operating Officer who oversaw all GenHealth facilities, died at FMC Butner medical unit.

Cause of death: Complications from stroke.

He served less than two months.

Two down. Four to go.

But unlike Patterson, Shaw left behind documents. In his prison cell, guards find a notebook filled with facility names, dates, and cryptic numbers.

The FBI uses it to identify three more psychiatric hospitals that received GenHealth funding in the 1990s:

- Riverside Psychiatric Center, Maine (1991-1996)
- Lakewood Mental Health Facility, Ohio (1992-1997)

- Pinecrest Psychiatric Hospital, Oregon (1993-1999)

All three closed suddenly. All three had unusually high patient death rates.

The investigation expands again.

August 15, 2025 Owen's Letter

Owen writes from prison:

Jenna,

I've been following the news about the other facilities. Twenty-seven victims in Vermont. Possibly more in Maine, Ohio, and Oregon.

I spent thirty years investigating Sophie's death. I never imagined there were other Willowbrooks. Other Sophies. Other Lindas.

If I had waited, if I hadn't killed those four people, maybe I could have helped the FBI investigate these other facilities. Maybe I could have found the evidence legally instead of going to prison.

But I didn't wait. I chose violence. And now I'm in here while the real investigation happens without me.

That's my regret. Not that I sought justice. But that I sought it the wrong way.

The FBI contacted me. They want to interview me about my investigation methods. They think my documentation techniques could help them investigate the other facilities.

I said yes. I'll help however I can from prison.

Thank you for continuing the work. Thank you for finding Mrs. Patterson. Thank you for not letting this end with Willowbrook.

Owen

August 20, 2025 Maine Investigation Results

The FBI exhumes twelve bodies from Riverside Psychiatric Center in Maine.

All twelve test positive for NX-447.

Thirty-nine more families learn their loved ones were murdered.

The victim count is now: 73 (Willowbrook) + 27 (Vermont) + 39 (Maine) = 139 victims.

And Ohio and Oregon investigations haven't even begun.

August 25, 2025 Catherine's Breakdown

Catherine calls me, sobbing.

"I can't do this, Jenna. Every week there are more victims. More families. More deaths. Sophie was just one of hundreds. How do I process that?"

"I don't know. I'm struggling too."

"When we got the verdict, I thought it was over. Justice was served. Six men in prison. But it's not over. It's expanding. There are more victims than we ever imagined."

"But they're being found now. Because of Sophie. Because of Linda. Because you testified. Because we didn't give up."

"But they're still dead. All those people, 139 victims so far, they're still dead. And we can't bring them back."

"No. But we can give their families the truth. We can make sure Gen Health pays. We can reform the system so it never happens again."

Catherine is quiet. Then: "I need to visit Sophie's grave. I need to tell her she saved more than seventy-three people. She saved hundreds."

"I'll meet you there."

August 31, 2025 Sophie's Grave

Catherine and I kneel at Sophie's grave together.

The headstone with the angel:

SOPHIE MARIE BRENNAN 1971-1987

BELOVED DAUGHTER, SISTER, FRIEND "SHE TRIED TO SAVE THEM"

"Sophie," Catherine says, her voice shaking. "They found more. More facilities. More victims. At least 139 people so far. Maybe more in Ohio and Oregon. Your journal didn't just expose Willowbrook. It exposed an entire system."

I place flowers beside the stone. "The FBI is using your documentation methods, Sophie. Owen taught them how to cross-reference death certificates with pharmaceutical funding records. Your courage is helping find victims across five states."

A bird lands on the nearby tree, singing.

Catherine continues: "I'm so sorry you died trying to save people. I'm so sorry you were only sixteen. But Sophie, your journal did what it was meant to do. You saved them. Not in time. But you saved them from being forgotten. You gave them truth. You gave them justice."

We sit in silence as the August sun sets over Riverside Cemetery.

Sophie died at sixteen, documenting pharmaceutical crimes.

Thirty-eight years later, her journal is still exposing murders.

CHAPTER 17

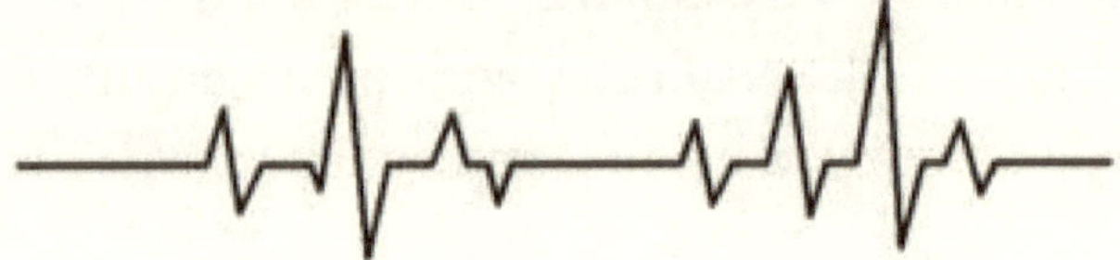

Legacy

September 15, 2025 Harvard Medical School, Boston

I attend the inaugural lecture for the Linda Walters Chair in Medical Ethics and Whistleblower Protection.

The auditorium holds 500 people. Every seat is filled, medical students, practicing physicians, nurses, ethicists, journalists covering the story.

Dr. Patricia Morrison, the forensic pathologist who examined Sophie's remains, stands at the podium.

"Good evening. I am honored to be the first Linda Walters Professor. Linda Walters was a registered nurse who witnessed a murder in 1987 and spent thirteen years trying to report it. She was fired. Blacklisted. Had her nursing license revoked. Lost custody of her daughter. Was labeled mentally ill. And ultimately died by suicide in 2011."

The auditorium is silent.

"Linda Walters was telling the truth. Every claim she made was accurate. Every report she filed was legitimate. But she was destroyed because the system valued corporate profit over patient safety. She was destroyed because whistleblowers are punished instead of protected."

Dr. Morrison pauses, looking directly at the audience.

"This chair exists to prevent future Linda Walters. To teach medical professionals that when a colleague reports abuse, we must investigate, not dismiss. When a nurse questions patient deaths, we must listen, not label them paranoid. When someone risks their career to expose wrongdoing, we must protect them, not destroy them."

She speaks for ninety minutes about medical ethics, corporate corruption, and the moral obligation to believe whistleblowers.

At the end, she introduces me.

"Ladies and gentlemen, please welcome Jenna Walters, Linda's daughter."

I walk to the podium, my heart pounding.

Five hundred people stand and applaud for three full minutes.

I speak for twenty minutes about my mother. About her courage. About her sacrifice. About how the medical community failed her.

"My mother spent thirteen years being called crazy. She died believing she failed. But she didn't fail. She exposed a conspiracy that killed at least 139 people across five states. Her reports, dismissed as paranoid delusions in the 1980s, are now evidence in federal investigations. Her name is on a professorship at Harvard Medical School. Her story is being told in the Smithsonian."

I look out at the audience. "Don't let the next Linda Walters be destroyed. When someone reports abuse, investigate. When someone questions deaths, listen. When someone risks everything to tell the truth, protect them. That's how we honor my mother's memory."

The standing ovation lasts five minutes.

September 22, 2025 Ohio Investigation Results

Agent Chen calls with news from Ohio.

"We exhumed eighteen bodies from Lakewood Mental Health Facility. All eighteen tested positive for NX-447 or related experimental compounds."

"So, the victim count is now...?"

"157. Seventy-three from Willowbrook, twenty-seven from Vermont, thirty-nine from Maine, eighteen from Ohio. And we haven't finished Oregon yet."

157 people murdered by GenHealth Pharmaceuticals.

157 families who thought their loved ones committed

suicide.

157 victims whose deaths were covered up for decades.

"How many more do you think there are?" I ask.

"Honestly? We don't know. We've identified five facilities so far. But GenHealth had contracts with dozens of psychiatric hospitals in the 1980s and 90s. There could be more."

"This is never going to end, is it?"

"The investigation will continue for years. But Jenna, every victim we find is one more family that gets the truth. That's because of you. Because you found Sophie's journal. Because you didn't give up."

October 1, 2025 Federal Prison Update

The news reports on the remaining four executives:

James Morrison (age 77) - FMC Devens medical unit. His Parkinson's has progressed to advanced stage. He can no longer walk, speak clearly, or feed himself. Requires 24-hour nursing care. Prison doctors estimate less than six months to live.

Robert Chen (age 70) - FMC Butner. Attempted suicide in his cell on September 28. Placed on suicide watch. Refuses to see visitors or accept phone calls. Severe depression.

Michael Williams (age 72) - FMC Butner. Diagnosed with lung cancer in August. Began chemotherapy but it's not working. Doctors estimate six to twelve months.

Thomas Foster (age 75) - FMC Butner. Still maintains innocence. Still filing appeals. All appeals denied. Good physical health but aging.

Three of the four are dying rapidly. Only Foster remains relatively healthy.

Justice is slow. But it's coming.

October 10, 2025 Oregon Investigation Begins

The FBI begins exhuming bodies from Pinecrest Psychiatric Hospital in Oregon.

The facility operated from 1993 to 1999 and had 143 patient deaths during that period, an unusually high death rate for a 50-bed facility.

Initial results won't be available for several weeks, but Agent Chen estimates at least 20-30 more victims.

The total could reach 180-190 murdered patients.

All because pharmaceutical executives valued profit over human life.

October 15, 2025 The Third Death

James Morrison, 77, Dies in Federal Custody

Morrison, the CEO who authorized the illegal trials, died at FMC Devens medical unit.

Cause of death: Complications from Parkinson's disease.

He served four months of his life sentence.

The man who orchestrated the murder of at least 157 people died in a prison hospital bed, unable to speak, unable to move, suffering until his final breath.

I feel no sympathy.

Three down. Three to go.

October 22, 2025 Smithsonian Exhibit Opening

Thirty-eight years to the day after Sophie's murder, the Smithsonian National Museum of American History opens its permanent Willowbrook exhibit.

The exhibit is called: **"Truth and Consequence: The Willowbrook Murders and the Cost of Corporate Crime"**

Catherine and I arrive at the museum at 9:00 AM for the private preview before the public opening.

The exhibit occupies an entire gallery. The walls are lined with photographs, documents, timelines.

At the center, behind protective glass:

Sophie's journal - the rainbow-stickered spiral notebook that documented pharmaceutical murder.

Next to it: **My mother's first police report** - dated October 23, 1987, the day after Sophie died.

Next to that: **Margaret Moore's final note** - written November 18, 2024, the day before she died.

Three women. Three acts of courage. Thirty-seven years apart.

The placard reads:

SOPHIE MARIE BRENNAN (1971-1987)

"I'm sixteen years old. I didn't kill myself. "

This journal, written by psychiatric patient Sophie Brennan, documented illegal drug trials conducted by GenHealth Pharmaceuticals that killed at least 157 people (and counting) between 1985 and 1999 across five states. Sophie was murdered on October 22, 1987, for trying to expose the conspiracy.

Her journal was preserved for 37 years by nurse Margaret Moore before being discovered in 2024 by Jenna Walters, daughter of whistleblower nurse Linda Walters.

Six pharmaceutical executives were convicted of murder in 2025. Three have died in federal custody; three remain imprisoned.

Below Sophie's journal, the exhibit displays photographs of all 157 identified victims, row after row of faces, names, ages, dates of death.

73 from Willowbrook.

27 from Vermont.

39 from Maine.

18 from Ohio.

And a section labeled "Oregon - Investigation Ongoing" with blank spaces waiting to be filled.

Catherine and I stand before the exhibit, crying.

"They're all here," she whispers. "Every single victim. Sophie. Linda. Margaret. The 157 who died. They're all remembered."

The exhibit continues with sections on:

- Owen's thirty-year investigation (including his confession to four murders)
- The FBI investigation and trial
- The sentencing and deaths of executives
- Federal reforms (Sophie Brennan Patient Safety Act, Linda Walters Whistleblower Protection Act)
- Ongoing investigations in Oregon and potentially other states

The final section is titled: **"The Cost of Speaking Truth"**

It features my mother's nursing license revocation hearing, custody documents showing I was taken at age seven, and her death certificate from 2011.

The placard reads:

LINDA MARIE WALTERS (1962-2011)

Whistleblower Nurse

Linda Walters witnessed Sophie Brennan's murder aftermath in 1987 and spent 13 years trying to report it. She filed dozens of police reports, contacted multiple agencies, and repeatedly warned that patients were being murdered. She was fired, blacklisted, had her nursing license revoked, lost custody of her daughter, and was labeled mentally ill. She died by suicide in 2011, believing no one would ever believe her.

Fourteen years later, her daughter proved Linda was telling the truth about everything.

I stand before my mother's section, reading every document, every report, every dismissal.

Finally, the world knows Linda Walters was a hero.

October 22, 2025, 2:00 PM Public Opening Ceremony

At 2:00 PM, the museum opens the exhibit to the public.

Over 2,000 people attend the opening ceremony.

The Smithsonian Director speaks first: "This exhibit honors the courage of ordinary people who exposed extraordinary evil. Sophie Brennan was sixteen years old when she documented crimes that powerful executives thought they had hidden. Linda Walters spent thirteen years fighting to expose the truth. Margaret Moore preserved evidence for thirty-seven years. Jenna Walters brought that evidence to light.

Because of them, at least 157 victims have been identified and their families finally know the truth."

Catherine speaks next: "My daughter Sophie was murdered thirty-eight years ago today. For thirty-seven of those years, I believed she committed suicide. I carried guilt. I blamed myself. I wondered what I missed. But Sophie didn't give up. She was murdered for trying to save people. She documented crimes in a journal decorated with rainbow stickers and unicorns, the journal of a teenage girl who was braver than most adults. Thank you for honoring her memory."

Then it's my turn.

I walk to the podium, my hands shaking.

"My mother Linda Walters spent thirteen years being called crazy. She lost her job. Her nursing license. Her daughter. Her sanity. Her life. She died in 2011 thinking she had failed. But she didn't fail. She was right about everything. Every report she filed was accurate. Every claim she made was true. Every warning she gave was legitimate."

I look out at the crowd. "This exhibit is vindication. Not just for my mother, but for every whistleblower who has been dismissed, destroyed, or killed for telling the truth. When you visit this exhibit, when you see Sophie's journal and my mother's reports, remember that speaking truth to power has costs. Sometimes terrible costs. But silence has worse costs."

The crowd stands and applauds.

After the ceremony, the exhibit opens to the public.

Lines stretch around the building. Thousands of people wait hours to see Sophie's journal, read my mother's reports, learn the truth about corporate murder.

By the end of the day, 12,000 people have visited the exhibit.

Within a week, it becomes the most visited exhibit in the museum.

October 25, 2025 Oregon Results

Agent Chen calls with preliminary Oregon results.

"Twenty-four victims confirmed in Oregon. That brings the total to 181 murdered patients."

181 people.

Across five states.

Over fourteen years.

"Are there more facilities?"

"We're investigating three more, one in Texas, one in Florida, one in California. All had GenHealth contracts in the 1990s. All closed suddenly. All had high patient death rates."

The conspiracy keeps expanding.

November 5, 2025 Robert Chen's Suicide

Robert Chen, 70, Dies in Federal Custody

Chen, the CFO who laundered bribe money and falsified financial records, was found dead in his cell at FMC Butner.

Cause of death: Suicide by hanging.

He left a note: *"I can't live with what I did. I helped murder 181 people. I deserve to die. I'm sorry."*

It's the first and only apology from any of the six executives.

Four down. Two to go.

November 12, 2025 Congressional Hearings Conclude

After three months of hearings, Congress passes the **Linda Walters Whistleblower Protection Act**.

The law provides:

- Federal protection for healthcare workers who report abuse
- Criminal penalties for retaliating against whistleblowers
- Mandatory independent investigations of all whistleblower claims
- Financial compensation for whistleblowers who are fired or blacklisted
- Public database of all whistleblower complaints

President signs it into law on November 15.

My mother's name is now federal law.

December 1, 2025 Texas, Florida, California Investigations Begin

The FBI begins investigating three more facilities:

Sunset Psychiatric Center, Texas (1994-1998) - 89 patient deaths

Palmview Mental Health, Florida (1995-1999) - 67 patient deaths

Coastal Psychiatric Hospital, California (1993-1997) - 72 patient deaths

If even half of those deaths were murders, the victim count could exceed 300 people.

Three hundred people murdered for pharmaceutical profit.

The enormity is staggering.

December 15, 2025 Victims' Families Coalition Grows

The coalition now includes families from eight states. Over 500 people are actively involved in:

- Searching for documents
- Contacting former staff members
- Supporting FBI investigations
- Advocating for federal reforms
- Honoring victims' memories

Janet Riley, whose brother Thomas died at Willowbrook in 1986, serves as coalition president.

She calls me: "Jenna, we're planning a national memorial. A wall with every victim's name. We want to install it in Washington D.C., near the Vietnam Memorial. Will you support it?"

"Absolutely."

"Good. We're calling it the **Pharmaceutical Victims Memorial**. It will honor everyone killed by corporate greed in the pharmaceutical industry, not just GenHealth victims, but everyone."

The memorial is funded entirely by victims' families donating their GenHealth bankruptcy settlements.

Construction begins in January 2026.

December 25, 2025 Christmas

I spend Christmas Day alone, visiting both graves.

First, Sophie's. I leave flowers and tell her 181 victims have been found, with possibly 100+ more.

Then, my mother's. I leave flowers and tell her the Smithsonian exhibit has had over 300,000 visitors in just two months.

Catherine joins me at Linda's grave.

"How are you doing?" she asks.

"Exhausted. Every week there are more victims. More families. More investigations. When does it end?"

"Maybe it doesn't. Maybe this is the new normal, constantly uncovering what GenHealth tried to hide."

"I just wanted to vindicate my mother. I didn't expect to spend the rest of my life fighting pharmaceutical crime."

Catherine puts her arm around me. "You don't have to fight. You've done enough. You found the journal. You testified. You spoke at the Smithsonian. Your mother has been vindicated. You can step back now."

"Can I though? Every time the FBI finds a new facility, I think about my mother. If she'd been believed in 1987, the Vermont victims would be alive. The Maine victims. The Ohio victims. All of them."

"That's not your fault."

"I know. But I can't just walk away."

We stand in silence, snow falling gently on the cemetery.

January 15, 2026 Michael Williams Dies

Michael Williams, 72, Dies in Federal Custody

Williams, the VP of Regulatory Affairs who bribed FDA officials, died at FMC Butner.

Cause of death: Lung cancer.

He served seven months of his life sentence.

Five down. One to go.

Only Thomas Foster remains alive.

February 10, 2026 Texas Results

FBI confirms 43 murders at Sunset Psychiatric Center in Texas.

The victim count is now: 224 murdered patients.

Florida and California investigations continue.

March 1, 2026 Owen's Parole Hearing Scheduled

I receive a letter from Owen:

Jenna,

The Bureau of Prisons just notified me that I'm eligible for a parole hearing in 2044, eighteen years from now. I'll be 66 years old.

I don't know if I want parole. I killed four people. I deserve to be in prison. But part of me wonders if I could do more good outside, speaking about pharmaceutical crime, advocating for whistleblower protection, honoring Sophie's memory.

I'm conflicted.

But that's eighteen years away. For now, I teach GED classes, help in the law library, and write my book. I'm on chapter 23, "The Cost of Violence."

The Smithsonian contacted me again. They want to add a section about my investigation and my imprisonment. They want to show both sides, the man who helped expose corporate crime and the man who murdered four people seeking revenge.

I agreed. People should know the whole truth, not just the parts that make me look heroic.

Thank you for continuing the fight. Thank you for not giving up when the victim count kept growing. Thank you for honoring Sophie and Linda.

Owen

March 15, 2026 Florida Results

FBI confirms 31 murders at Palmview Mental Health in Florida.

Victim count: 255.

April 1, 2026 California Results

FBI confirms 38 murders at Coastal Psychiatric Hospital in California.

Total victim count: 293 murdered patients across eight

states.

GenHealth Pharmaceuticals murdered nearly 300 people between 1985 and 1999.

And there may still be more facilities.

April 15, 2026 National Memorial Groundbreaking

Construction begins on the Pharmaceutical Victims Memorial in Washington D.C.

The memorial will be a black granite wall listing every name of every person killed by pharmaceutical corporate crime, starting with the 293 GenHealth victims, but designed to accommodate future additions.

Catherine and I attend the groundbreaking ceremony along with 400 victims' families.

Janet Riley speaks: "This memorial ensures that corporate crime victims are never forgotten. Every name on this wall represents a person, not a statistic. A mother. A father. A brother. A sister. A child. Someone loved. Someone missed. Someone murdered."

The memorial is scheduled to be completed by October 22, 2026, the thirty-ninth anniversary of Sophie's death.

May 1, 2026 One Year Since the Trial Ended

It's been one year since the verdict, almost one year since sentencing.

I sit in my apartment, reflecting on everything that's happened:

- 6 executives convicted
- 5 executives dead in prison
- 1 executive (Foster) still alive, serving life sentence
- 293 victims identified (possibly more)
- Smithsonian exhibit with 500,000+ visitors
- Federal laws named after my mother and Sophie
- Harvard professorship in my mother's name
- National memorial being built
- GenHealth Pharmaceuticals bankrupt and liquidated

My mother spent thirteen years fighting.

I've spent eighteen months finishing what she started.

And the fight continues.

May 15, 2026 Phone Call with Catherine

"Jenna, I need to tell you something. I'm stepping back from the coalition."

"Are you okay?"

"I'm tired. I'm 74 years old. I've spent the last eighteen months attending FBI briefings, visiting graves, speaking at ceremonies, supporting families. I need to rest."

"I understand."

"But more than that, I need to grieve. Really grieve. Not

as Sophie's mother who's fighting for justice. Just as Sophie's mother who lost her daughter."

I understand completely. "You've done enough, Catherine. More than enough."

"So have you. You found the journal. You testified. You honored Linda. You can step back too."

"Maybe. I don't know. Every time I try to step back, the FBI finds more victims."

"The FBI can continue without you. Janet Riley can lead the coalition. The Smithsonian exhibit will remain. The memorial will be built. Your mother's law will protect whistleblowers. The work continues whether or not you're actively involved."

She's right. The work has momentum now. It doesn't need me to drive it forward.

"I'll think about it," I tell her.

June 1, 2026 Almost One Year After Sentencing

It's been nearly one year since the six executives were sentenced.

Five are dead:

- David Patterson (July 2025)
- Martin Shaw (August 2025)
- James Morrison (October 2025)

- Robert Chen (November 2025)
- Michael Williams (January 2026)

One remains alive:

- Thomas Foster (age 76, FMC Butner, still maintains innocence)

Foster is the last one. The only one still breathing. The only one still serving his sentence.

Doctors say he's in relatively good health. He could live another five to ten years.

He'll die in prison. But unlike the others, he won't die quickly.

He'll serve his life sentence. Day after day. Year after year. Knowing he was convicted of murdering 293 people. Knowing the world knows what he did.

That's justice too.

Slow. Complete. Inevitable.

CHAPTER 18

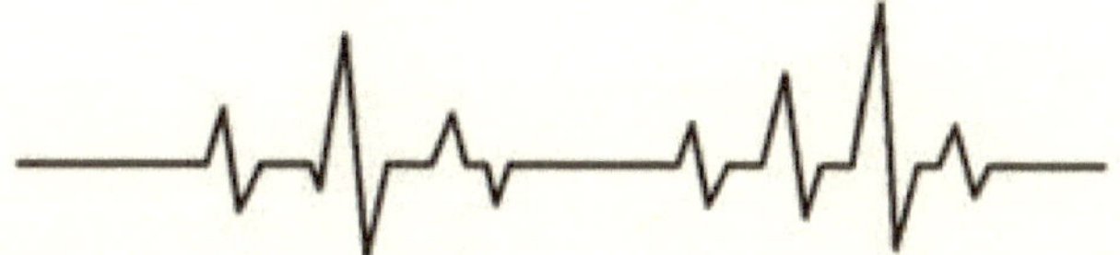

Closure

June 9, 2026 One Year After Sentencing

Exactly one year ago today, six pharmaceutical executives were sentenced to multiple life terms.

Today, five are dead. One remains alive.

I visit both graves, Sophie's and my mother's, just like I did a year ago.

At Sophie's grave, I place flowers and speak quietly:

"It's been a year since the sentencing. The investigation found 293 victims across eight states. Your journal exposed all of them, Sophie. Not just the 73 at Willowbrook, but all 293. The FBI used your documentation methods. Your courage saved hundreds of families from spending their lives believing their loved ones committed suicide."

I touch the headstone gently.

"Five of the six executives are dead. Only Thomas Foster is still alive. He's 76 now, in federal prison, and he'll die there. He's the last one."

At my mother's grave, I do the same:

"Hi, Mom. One year since sentencing. Your name is federal law now, the Linda Walters Whistleblower Protection Act. There's a professorship at Harvard in your name. The Smithsonian has your police reports on display. Over 500,000 people have seen them. The world knows you were telling the truth."

I sit in the grass beside her headstone.

"I think I'm done, Mom. Catherine is stepping back from the coalition. The FBI investigations will continue, but they don't need me anymore. The memorial is being built. The laws are passed. The reforms are implemented. Justice came. You were vindicated."

I pause, thinking.

"I'm just a nurse. I want to go back to being just a nurse. Is that okay?"

The wind rustles through the cemetery trees, carrying no answers.

But I feel peace.

June 15, 2026 Letter to Janet Riley

I write to Janet Riley, the coalition president:

Dear Janet,

I'm writing to let you know I'm stepping back from active involvement in the coalition. My mother has been vindicated. Sophie's story has been told. The FBI investigations will continue, but they no longer need my direct participation.

The work you're doing is important. The memorial will honor every victim. The continued investigations will find more families. The advocacy will prevent future crimes.

But I need to return to my life. I'm a nurse. I work night shifts at Manchester General Hospital. That's who I am. Not a crusader. Not an activist. Just a nurse who found a journal and did the right thing.

Thank you for everything you've done. Thank you for leading when I couldn't.

With gratitude,

Jenna

Janet calls me the next day.

"I understand completely. You've done more than enough. You found Sophie's journal. You testified. You spoke at the Smithsonian. You honored your mother. Nobody can ask more from you."

"Will the coalition be okay without me?"

"The coalition has 500 families now. We have momentum. We have funding. We have federal support. We'll be fine. You rest. You've earned it."

July 1, 2026 Return to Normal

I work my night shifts. I care for patients. I document medications. I check vitals.

The media has mostly moved on. I'm rarely recognized anymore. The story is history now, important history, but history nonetheless.

I'm just Jenna Walters, RN, working the night shift at Manchester General Hospital.

And that's exactly who I want to be.

August 10, 2026 Phone Call from Owen

Owen calls from FCI Devens.

"Jenna, I finished my book. 437 pages. 'Thirty-Seven Years: A Sister's Murder and a Brother's Revenge.'"

"Are you going to publish it?"

"I don't know. Part of me wants the story told. Part of me thinks publishing a book about murdering four people is inappropriate, even if I did help convict six executives."

"What does your editor say?"

"I don't have an editor. I wrote it for myself. To process everything. To understand what I did and why."

"Do you understand now?"

A long pause. "Yes. I understand that I loved Sophie more than I loved my own freedom. I understand that I couldn't live in a world where her murderers walked free. I understand that I chose violence because I didn't trust the legal system. And I understand that I was wrong."

"But the legal system did fail. For thirty years."

"It failed until it didn't. The FBI did investigate. Rachel Diaz did prosecute. The jury did convict. The judge did sentence. Justice came. It took thirty-seven years, but it came. If I'd waited just a little longer, I could have seen justice without becoming a murderer myself."

"You can't know that."

"No. But I believe it. And that's what haunts me. Not that I killed four people who helped murder Sophie. But that I killed them three years before the FBI would have arrested them anyway."

We're both quiet.

Finally, Owen says, "How are you doing? Are you still involved in the investigations?"

"No. I stepped back. The coalition continues, the FBI

continues, but I'm done. I'm just a nurse again."

"Good. You did your part. More than your part. Live your life, Jenna. Don't let this consume you the way it consumed me."

September 1, 2026 FBI Final Report

Agent Chen sends me the FBI's final report on GenHealth Pharmaceuticals.

The investigation identified:

- 8 psychiatric facilities where illegal drug trials occurred
- 293 confirmed murder victims (with possibly 20-30 more still under investigation)
- $127 million in documented bribes to officials
- 14 years of systematic corporate crime (1985-1999)
- 6 executives convicted, 5 now deceased, 1 serving life sentence

The report concludes:

"The GenHealth pharmaceutical murders represent one of the most extensive corporate crime conspiracies in U.S. history. The crimes were hidden for decades through systematic destruction of evidence, intimidation of witnesses, and exploitation of marginalized psychiatric patients whose deaths were dismissed as suicide or natural causes.

The conspiracy was exposed due to the courage of:

- *Sophie Brennan (victim, age 16) who documented the crimes*
- *Linda Walters (whistleblower nurse) who reported the crimes for 13 years*
- *Margaret Moore (nurse) who preserved evidence for 37 years*
- *Jenna Walters (nurse) who brought the evidence to authorities*
- *Owen Brennan (victim's brother) whose investigation provided crucial documentation*

As a result of this case, federal laws have been reformed, pharmaceutical oversight has been strengthened, and whistleblower protections have been enhanced. The victims' families have received truth, if not complete justice."

I read the report once, then file it away.

It's done. The investigation is complete. The story is told.

October 1, 2026 Catherine's Visit

Catherine Brennan visits me in Manchester.

We have coffee at a small cafe near the hospital.

"How are you doing?" I ask.

"Better. I've been going to grief counseling. Actually, grieving Sophie, not just fighting for her. It's different."

"Is it helping?"

"Yes. For thirty-eight years, I've been Sophie's mother who lost her daughter. Now I'm learning to be Catherine, just Catherine, who happens to have lost a daughter but is also a whole person with her own life."

"I'm trying to do the same thing. Be Jenna the nurse, not Jenna the daughter of the whistleblower."

"Are you succeeding?"

"Mostly. Some days I forget about the trial entirely. Other days a patient reminds me of my mother, or I see news about pharmaceutical reform, and it all comes back."

"That's normal. Trauma doesn't disappear. It just becomes part of your story instead of your entire story."

We sit in comfortable silence, two women who shared an extraordinary journey and are now trying to return to ordinary life.

"Owen called me," Catherine says. "He asked if I'd visit him in prison."

"Will you?"

"I don't know. He's my son. I love him. But he killed four people. I'm proud of what his investigation accomplished and horrified by what he did to accomplish it."

"That's the contradiction."

"Yes. Owen is both the man who helped convict six murderers and the man who murdered four people. He's both a hero and a criminal. I don't know how to reconcile that."

"Maybe you don't have to. Maybe you just accept both are true."

Catherine nods. "Maybe."

October 15, 2026 Memorial Construction Complete

The Pharmaceutical Victims Memorial is complete.

A black granite wall, 50 feet long and 8 feet high, located on the National Mall in Washington D.C.

Engraved on the wall: 293 names.

Every victim identified by the FBI investigation. Listed by facility and date of death.

WILLOWBROOK PSYCHIATRIC HOSPITAL (1985-1991)

73 victims

GREENMONT PSYCHIATRIC HOSPITAL, VERMONT (1993-1998)

27 victims

RIVERSIDE PSYCHIATRIC CENTER, MAINE (1991-1996)

39 victims

LAKEWOOD MENTAL HEALTH FACILITY, OHIO (1992-1997)

18 victims

PINECREST PSYCHIATRIC HOSPITAL, OREGON (1993-1999)

24 victims

SUNSET PSYCHIATRIC CENTER, TEXAS (1994-1998)

43 victims

PALMVIEW MENTAL HEALTH, FLORIDA (1995-1999)

31 victims

COASTAL PSYCHIATRIC HOSPITAL, CALIFORNIA (1993-1997)

38 victims

At the top of the wall, in large letters:

IN MEMORY OF THOSE MURDERED BY CORPORATE GREED

"THEY TRIED TO SAVE THEM"

At the bottom:

Dedicated to Sophie Brennan, who documented the crimes

Linda Walters, who reported the crimes

Margaret Moore, who preserved the evidence

And all those who speak truth at great cost

The dedication ceremony is scheduled for October 22, the thirty-ninth anniversary of Sophie's death.

October 22, 2026 Memorial Dedication

Five thousand people attend the dedication ceremony.

Victims' families from eight states. Psychiatric patient advocates. Whistleblower protection organizations. Nurses. Doctors. Journalists. Members of Congress.

Senator Elizabeth Warren speaks first:

"This memorial honors 293 people murdered by pharmaceutical executives who valued profit over human life. But it also honors the whistleblowers who exposed the truth, Sophie Brennan, Linda Walters, Margaret Moore, and countless others who risk everything to protect the vulnerable."

Janet Riley speaks next, representing the coalition:

"My brother Thomas died at Willowbrook in 1986. For thirty-seven years, I believed he committed suicide. In 2025, I learned he was murdered. That truth was painful, but it was better than living with the lie. These 293 names represent 293 families who finally know the truth. That's not complete justice. But it's something."

Then Catherine speaks:

"My daughter Sophie was sixteen when she was murdered for documenting pharmaceutical crimes. She kept a journal decorated with rainbows and unicorns. She was a child. A brave, beautiful child who tried to save people and was killed for it. Every name on this wall represents someone's Sophie, someone young, someone vulnerable, someone who deserved to live."

Finally, I speak:

"My mother Linda Walters spent thirteen years trying to expose these crimes. She was called crazy. She lost her job. Her license. Her daughter. Her life. She died in 2011 believing she had failed. But she didn't fail. She was the first person to report Sophie Brennan's murder. She was the first whistleblower. And because she never gave up, because she kept filing reports even when no one listened, her documentation helped the FBI build the case that convicted six executives."

I look out at the crowd.

"This memorial honors the dead. But it also honors the living, everyone who speaks truth, files reports, questions authority, refuses to stay silent. Whistleblowing has costs. Sometimes terrible costs. But silence costs more. These 293 people died because others stayed silent. Let this memorial remind us that speaking truth, even when it's hard, even when it's dangerous, is always the right choice."

The crowd stands in silence.

Then, one by one, families approach the wall to touch the

names of their loved ones.

I touch Sophie's name, engraved in the granite forever.

I touch my mother's name in the dedication plaque.

Justice came.

Slow. Painful. Incomplete.

But it came.

October 25, 2026 The Last Death

Thomas Foster, 76, Dies in Federal Custody

Foster, the last surviving executive, died at FMC Butner.

Cause of death: Heart attack.

He served sixteen months of his life sentence.

Unlike the others, Foster maintained his innocence until the end. His final words to prison staff: "I didn't do anything wrong. History will vindicate me."

History will not vindicate him.

History will remember him as one of six executives who murdered 293 people for pharmaceutical profit.

All six are now dead:

- David Patterson (July 2025) - 1 month served
- Martin Shaw (August 2025) - 2 months served

- James Morrison (October 2025) - 4 months served
- Robert Chen (November 2025) - 5 months served, suicide
- Michael Williams (January 2026) - 7 months served
- Thomas Foster (October 2026) - 16 months served

The longest any of them served was sixteen months.

For murdering 293 people.

It's not enough time. It will never be enough time.

But they all died in prison. They all died convicted of murder. They all died knowing the world knew what they did.

That's justice.

Imperfect. Incomplete. But justice.

November 1, 2026 Jenna's Decision

I sit in my apartment, thinking about the past two years.

November 2024: Found Margaret's note

November 2024: Found Sophie's journal

December 2024: FBI arrests

March-April 2025: Trial

April 2025: Verdict

June 2025: Sentencing

October 2025: Smithsonian exhibit opens

October 2026: Memorial dedicated

October 2026: Last executive dies

It's over.

The six executives are dead. The 293 victims have been identified and honored. The memorial stands. The laws are passed. The reforms are implemented.

My mother has been vindicated.

Sophie's story has been told.

Justice has been served.

And I... I can finally rest.

I write one final letter to Agent Chen:

Dear Agent Chen,

Thank you for believing me when I brought you Sophie's journal in November 2024. Thank you for investigating. Thank you for prosecuting. Thank you for never giving up.

I'm stepping away from all coalition activities, advocacy work, and public appearances. I've done what I needed to do. My mother has been vindicated. That was always the goal.

I'm returning to my life as a nurse. That's who I am. That's who I want to be.

If you need me for future testimony or investigation, you

know how to reach me. But otherwise, I'm done.

With gratitude,
Jenna Walters

Agent Chen calls me the next day.

"I understand. You've done more than anyone could ask. Rest. Live your life. You've earned it."

"Will the investigation continue?"

"We're still looking into three more facilities that had GenHealth contracts. But we have 500 families in the coalition, we have federal support, we have momentum. We don't need you to drive it anymore."

"Thank you for everything."

"No, Jenna. Thank you. Without you, those six executives would have died free men. Without you, 293 families would still believe their loved ones committed suicide. Without you, your mother would still be remembered as mentally ill. You changed everything."

December 1, 2026 Christmas Shopping

I'm Christmas shopping in downtown Manchester when someone approaches me.

"Excuse me, are you Jenna Walters?"

I tense. I haven't been recognized in months.

"Yes."

"I'm Sarah Chen. No relation to the executive," she adds quickly. "I'm a nursing student at UNH. I just wanted to say thank you. I wrote my thesis on your mother. On Linda Walters and whistleblower protection in healthcare. Because of her story, I'm committed to never ignoring a colleague who reports abuse."

I smile. "Thank you for telling me. My mother would be proud."

"She should be proud. She changed healthcare. The Linda Walters Whistleblower Protection Act is required reading in our nursing ethics class. Every nursing student in America learns about her now."

After Sarah leaves, I sit on a bench, crying.

My mother spent thirteen years being called crazy.

Now nursing students study her as a hero.

That's vindication.

December 25, 2026 Christmas

I spend Christmas morning alone at the cemetery.

I bring flowers to both graves.

At Sophie's: "Merry Christmas, Sophie. All six executives are dead now. Foster died in October. You got complete justice.

Every single one of them died in prison."

At my mother's: "Merry Christmas, Mom. Nursing students study you now. You're in textbooks. You're in federal law. You're in the Smithsonian. The world knows you were a hero."

I sit in the snow, peaceful.

Catherine joins me, bringing her own flowers.

"Merry Christmas, Jenna."

"Merry Christmas, Catherine."

We place flowers on both graves together.

"What are you doing for the rest of the day?" she asks.

"Working night shift. Volunteered so the nurses with families could have the day off."

"That's kind of you."

"It's who I am. A nurse."

"Yes. But also, the woman who exposed pharmaceutical murder. You can be both."

"Maybe. But right now, I just want to be a nurse."

Catherine nods. "I understand. Owen asked if you'd visit him in prison."

"Would you come with me?"

"Yes. Let's visit him together. In the new year. We'll tell him it's over. All six executives are dead. The investigation is complete. Justice was served."

December 31, 2026 New Year's Eve

I work the night shift on New Year's Eve.

At midnight, the hospital is quiet. Most patients are sleeping. The hallways are empty.

I stand at the window of the nurse's station, looking out at Manchester.

Two years ago, I found a note left by a dying woman.

That note led to a journal.

That journal led to a trial.

That trial led to convictions.

Those convictions led to justice.

And now, two years later, I'm back where I started: a night shift nurse at Manchester General Hospital.

But everything is different.

My mother has been vindicated. Her name is federal law. Her story is in the Smithsonian. She's remembered as a hero, not a mentally ill woman.

Sophie's murderers are dead. All six of them. They died in

prison, convicted of killing 293 people.

The victims are honored. A memorial stands on the National Mall with all their names.

The system is reformed. Federal laws protect whistleblowers. The FDA has new oversight protocols. The pharmaceutical industry has new standards.

Justice came.

Slow. Painful. Incomplete.

But it came.

At 12:01 AM, my pager goes off.

Room 412, the same room where Margaret Moore died two years ago, needs medication.

I grab my cart and walk down the familiar hallway.

Just a nurse. Doing her job. Living her life.

And that's enough.

EPILOGUE

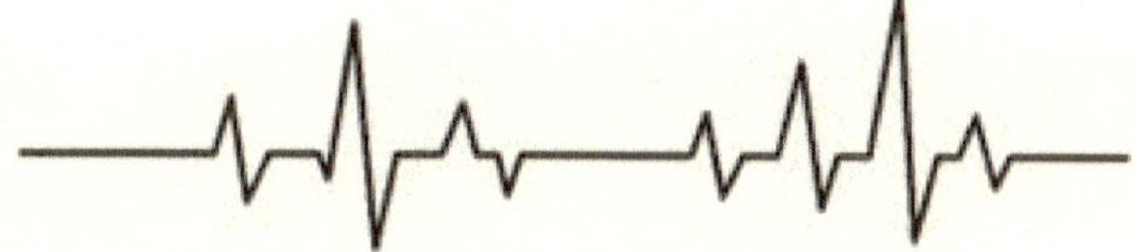

JENNA - Ten Years Later (October 22, 2034)

October 22, 2034, 3:30 PM

Sophie Brennan Memorial Center for Patient Safety
Manchester, New Hampshire

The building is beautiful.

Ten years ago, this was just an idea, a dream that Catherine Brennan and I discussed over coffee while six pharmaceutical executives awaited sentencing. Now it's real: a three-story glass and steel structure on the Manchester skyline, with Sophie's name carved in granite above the entrance.

The Sophie Brennan Memorial Center for Patient Safety.

I park in the visitor lot and walk through the main

entrance. The lobby is filled with sunlight streaming through floor-to-ceiling windows. On the far wall, a massive memorial lists all 293 victims' names in alphabetical order:

EMILY ANDERSON, 1968-1987

ROBERT BAILEY, 1952-1989

SOPHIE MARIE BRENNAN, 1971-1987

I've been here hundreds of times, but I still pause at Sophie's name. Sixteen years old. Dead for forty-seven years. But not forgotten.

Never forgotten.

"Jenna!"

I turn to see Catherine crossing the lobby, arms outstretched. She's seventy-three now, her hair completely gray, but her eyes are bright and alive in a way they weren't when we first met ten years ago.

We embrace.

"You made it," she says. "I was worried you might get stuck at work."

"I wouldn't miss this. Not today."

Today is October 22nd, the forty-seventh anniversary of Sophie's murder. Every year on this date, we gather here to honor the victims and celebrate the changes that came from their deaths.

Catherine links her arm through mine as we walk toward the auditorium.

"Big crowd this year," she says. "Over three hundred people registered. Families, nursing students, policy makers. Senator Williams is speaking. So is Dr. Patterson from the FDA."

"You're speaking too, right?"

"Closing remarks. I'll keep it short, I always cry halfway through."

"That's okay. Everyone expects it. I usually cry too."

We enter the auditorium, where rows of chairs face a stage decorated with photos of the 293 victims. In the center is Sophie's portrait, the one from her journal, where she's smiling at the camera, sixteen and hopeful and unaware she has only weeks to live.

I see familiar faces throughout the crowd. FBI Agent Michael Chen, now retired, sitting with his wife. Rachel Diaz, the prosecutor who won the case, now a federal judge. Dr. Emily Reyes from Manchester General. Owen Brennan, released from prison five years ago, sitting quietly in the back row.

And new faces too. Nursing students with notebooks. Policy researchers with tablets. Medical ethicists. Journalists. People who never knew Sophie or my mother, but who study their stories now.

Catherine squeezes my hand. "Your mother should be here to see this."

"She is," I say softly. "In every single law we passed. In every student who learns about whistleblower protection. She's here."

We take our seats in the front row, reserved for family members.

The program begins.

Senator Williams speaks first, discussing the **Linda Walters Whistleblower Protection Act** and how it's been strengthened over the past decade. "Since 2025, over four hundred healthcare whistleblowers have come forward under these protections," she says. "Not one has lost their license or faced retaliation. **That's Linda Walters' legacy.**"

Dr. Patterson from the FDA discusses new clinical trial oversight protocols implemented after the Willowbrook scandal. "Every clinical trial in America now has independent monitors, mandatory adverse event reporting, and patient advocate oversight. We've prevented forty-three potentially dangerous trials from proceeding in the last decade. **That's Sophie Brennan's legacy.**"

A nursing student from UNH reads a poem about courage and silence and speaking truth to power.

Then Catherine walks to the podium.

She grips the edges tightly, looking out at the audience.

When she speaks, her voice trembles but doesn't break.

"Forty-seven years ago today, my daughter was murdered. Sophie was sixteen years old. She was brave and smart and kind. She loved music and books and helping people. She wanted to be a doctor.

"Instead, she became a patient in a psychiatric hospital where staff members conducted illegal experiments on vulnerable people. When Sophie discovered what they were doing, she documented everything in a journal. She tried to expose them.

"They killed her for it.

"For thirty-seven years, I believed Sophie took her own life. I believed the system failed her because mental health care was inadequate. I carried guilt and grief and confusion.

"Then Jenna Walters found Sophie's journal. And everything I believed was proven wrong.

"**Sophie didn't give up. She didn't surrender. She fought until the very end.** She tried to save the other patients. She tried to expose the truth.

"She was a hero. But the system called her mentally ill and dismissed her.

"Just like they dismissed Linda Walters when she witnessed Sophie's death being staged. Just like they dismissed Margaret Moore when she kept Sophie's journal hidden for decades because she was too afraid to come forward.

"Three women. Three different generations. All silenced by a system that valued profit over truth.

"But that system is changing. Because of Jenna's courage in coming forward. Because of the FBI's diligence in investigating. Because of prosecutors who fought for justice. Because of jurors who listened to the evidence and voted to convict.

"And because of all of you, everyone in this room who works every day to make healthcare safer, more ethical, more accountable.

"**Sophie's death was not in vain.** The 293 people who died in those illegal trials, their deaths were not in vain. Because we learned. We changed. We built protections. We created laws. We established oversight.

"This center exists because of them. These reforms exist because of them.

"So today, on the forty-seventh anniversary of my daughter's murder, I don't just grieve. I celebrate. I celebrate her courage. I celebrate the justice that finally came. And I celebrate everyone who works to ensure this never happens again."

Catherine's voice finally breaks. She grips the podium, tears streaming down her face.

"Thank you, Sophie. Thank you for being brave. Thank you for fighting. Thank you for trying to save them.

"We hear you now. We believe you now. And we promise, we will never stop fighting to honor your memory."

The audience rises in a standing ovation.

I'm crying. Everyone around me is crying. But they're not tears of despair, they're tears of recognition. Of gratitude. Of remembrance.

After the program ends, people gather in the lobby for reception. I talk to nursing students who are studying my mother's case in their ethics classes. I talk to policy researchers who cite the Linda Walters Act in their papers. I talk to families of other victims who found closure through the trial.

At five o'clock, Catherine and I leave together. We walk to the parking lot, arms linked, comfortable in companionable silence.

"Will you visit the cemetery with me?" Catherine asks. "It's on my way."

"Of course."

We drive separately to Riverside Cemetery. Sophie is buried in the older section, beneath a tall oak tree. My mother is buried in the newer section, near the pond.

We visit Sophie's grave first. Catherine places fresh roses, Sophie's favorite, at the headstone:

SOPHIE MARIE BRENNAN 1971 – 1987 "SHE TRIED TO SAVE THEM"

"I'm proud of you, baby," Catherine whispers, touching the cold granite. "You exposed them. You saved others by documenting what they did. You were so brave."

Then we walk to my mother's grave:

LINDA MARIE WALTERS 1962 – 2011

REGISTERED NURSE

WHISTLEBLOWER

HERO "SHE TOLD THE TRUTH"

I kneel and place my hand on the stone.

"Hi, Mom. It's October 22nd again. Sophie's anniversary. Catherine and I just came from the memorial center, over three hundred people attended. The senator spoke. The FDA commissioner spoke. They all talked about you and Sophie and the changes that came from your courage.

"There's a new class of nursing students studying your case this semester. The professor emailed me, she said her students are inspired by you. They want to be the kind of nurses who speak up when they see something wrong.

"**That's your legacy, Mom.** Not the thirteen years when people called you crazy. Not the license revocation or the involuntary commitments or the medications they forced on you.

"Your legacy is courage. Truth. Justice.

"Every nursing student who learns about you. Every whistleblower who comes forward because of the law named after you. Every patient who's protected because the system changed.

"That's you, Mom. That's what you did.

"I'm so proud to be your daughter."

I stand, brushing dirt from my knees. Catherine joins me, and we stand together between the two graves, between Sophie and Linda, between two women who fought the same corruption thirty-seven years apart.

"They'd be proud of us," Catherine says quietly.

"They'd be proud we didn't give up."

"No. We never gave up."

As the sun sets, casting long shadows across the cemetery, I think about the journey that brought us here.

Ten years ago, I was a night shift nurse who found a dying woman's note. That note led to a journal. That journal led to an investigation. That investigation led to a trial. That trial led to convictions. Those convictions led to reforms.

And now, ten years later, the world is different.

Not perfect. Not completely healed. But different.

Pharmaceutical companies have oversight. Clinical trials have protections. Whistleblowers have federal law defending them. Healthcare institutions have accountability.

And Sophie Brennan is remembered not as a mentally ill teenager who committed suicide, but as a brave sixteen-year-old who documented crimes and tried to save others.

And my mother is remembered not as a delusional nurse who made false accusations, but as a heroic whistleblower who witnessed murder and spent thirteen years trying to expose it.

Their names are carved in granite. Their stories are taught in classrooms. Their legacies protect the vulnerable.

That's justice.

Not the kind that comes quickly or easily. Not the kind that undoes the past or brings back the dead.

But justice nonetheless.

October 22, 2034, 7:45 PM

Jenna's Apartment

I get home just after dark. My apartment is quiet and comfortable, a one-bedroom in downtown Manchester with a view of the city lights. Not fancy, but it's mine.

On my refrigerator, held by magnets, are three photos:

1. **My mother in her nursing scrubs, 1986**, before Willowbrook, before the trauma, before the system destroyed her. She's smiling at the camera, young and hopeful.
2. **Sophie's portrait from her journal**, sixteen years old, sitting in the Willowbrook dayroom, unaware she has only weeks to live.
3. **Catherine and me at the Sophie Brennan Memorial Center ribbon-cutting ceremony, five years ago.** Both of us smiling, arms around each other. Family.

I make tea and sit by the window, looking out at Manchester.

Ten years.

Ten years since I found Margaret's note. Ten years since everything changed.

I'm forty-three now. Still a nurse, I work as Patient Advocacy Coordinator at Manchester General, the same hospital where this all began. I help patients navigate the healthcare system, advocate for their rights, investigate complaints.

It's meaningful work. Work that honors both my mother and Sophie.

I never married. Never had children. Some nights I wonder if I should have made different choices, focused less on justice and more on building a personal life.

But then I remember the nursing students who study my

mother. The whistleblowers who come forward under the protections we fought for. The families who found closure through the trial. The memorial center with 293 names carved in stone.

And I know I made the right choice.

Justice was worth it.

Truth was worth it.

My phone buzzes. Text from Catherine:

Thank you for today. Sophie would be proud of you. Linda would be proud of you. I'm proud of you. Love you, dear.

I smile and text back:

Love you too. Same time next year?

Always.

I set my phone down and return to the window.

The city lights glow in the darkness. Manchester sleeps peacefully beneath a clear October sky.

Somewhere in this city, there's a memorial center with 293 names. A federal law protecting whistleblowers. Nursing students learning about courage and truth. Hospitals with better oversight. Clinical trials with stronger protections.

All because a dying woman left a note.

All because I followed where that note led.

I raise my tea mug toward the window, a silent toast to the ghosts who brought me here.

"To Sophie Brennan, who documented the truth."

"To Margaret Moore, who kept it safe."

"To Linda Walters, who witnessed the crime and never stopped reporting it."

"And to the 293 patients who died in those illegal trials."

"You're remembered. You're honored. You changed the world."

The tea is warm against my lips. The apartment is quiet. The night is peaceful.

And somewhere, I hope, three women who fought the same battle across different decades are finally resting.

Their work is done.

Justice came.

Truth prevailed.

And that's enough.

A LETTER FROM THE AUTHOR

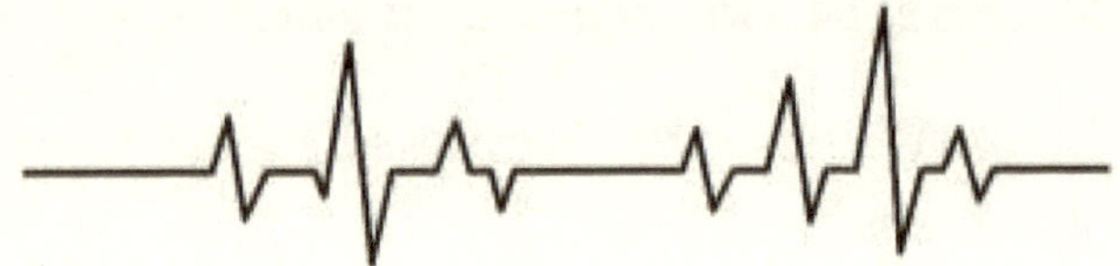

Dear Reader,

Thank you for picking up *The Night Nurse's Secret*. This book has been both the hardest and most important story I've ever written.

While this is a work of fiction, it's inspired by very real events. The history of unethical medical experimentation, particularly on vulnerable populations, is not just a dark chapter from the distant past. From the Tuskegee Syphilis Study to more recent pharmaceutical scandals, patients have been used, harmed, and silenced in the name of profit and progress.

The whistleblowers in these real-world cases rarely receive the justice my characters eventually find. Many lose their careers, their reputations, and their lives fighting systems designed to silence them. Some, like my fictional Linda Walters, never live to see vindication.

I wrote this book because I believe their stories matter. I believe truth-tellers deserve our gratitude, not our suspicion. I believe institutional corruption thrives on silence, and dies in the light.

Jenna's journey from doubt to advocacy mirrors a question we all face: What do we do when we discover an uncomfortable truth? Do we look away, or do we bear witness? Do we stay silent, or do we speak up, even when speaking costs us everything?

This novel asks difficult questions about justice delayed, about the price of truth, and about whose voices get believed. It's about a mother dismissed as mentally ill, a teenager whose murder was covered up, and a daughter who spent years ashamed of the very woman she should have honored.

It's also about redemption. About how truth, even when buried for decades, can eventually surface. About how one person's courage, or one dying woman's confession, can change everything.

If you're reading this because you're a healthcare worker, a whistleblower, or someone who's ever been dismissed when you tried to tell the truth: I see you. Your courage matters. Your voice matters.

If you're reading this because you love a good mystery with heart: welcome. I hope Jenna's story stays with you long after the last page.

And if you're reading this in a book club, around a coffee table, or late at night when you should be sleeping: thank you. Stories only matter when they're shared. Conversations only happen when someone speaks first.

May we all have the courage to be truth-tellers in our own lives. May we all honor those who speak up when silence would be easier. And may we never forget that justice delayed is still justice worth fighting for.

With gratitude and hope,

Sarah Blackwell

P.S. — The discussion questions in the back of this book are designed to spark conversations about ethics, justice, and institutional accountability. Please use them. These conversations matter.

ACKNOWLEDGMENTS

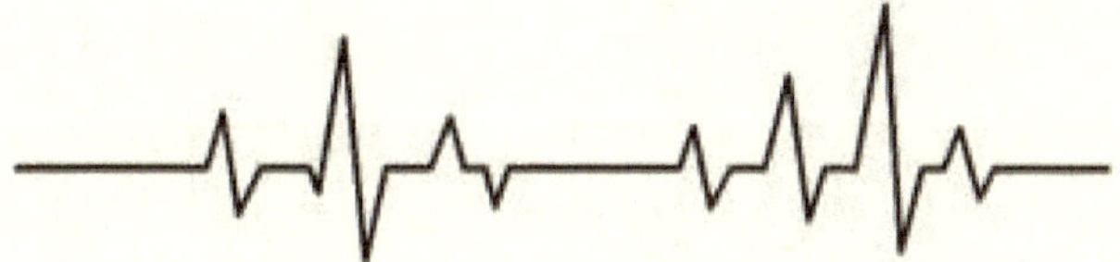

This book exists because of the many people who believed in it, and in me, even when the story felt too big to tell.

First and foremost, to MK Storyworks: Thank you for taking a chance on a medical thriller that's also a story about motherhood, justice, and the long road to vindication. Your editorial insight made this book immeasurably better, and your cover design captured the heart of the story perfectly. I'm honored to work with a publisher that values both commercial appeal and meaningful storytelling.

To my editor, Joe: You understood what I was trying to do with this book from day one. Your notes pushed me to dig deeper into Jenna's emotional journey and to make Linda's story feel as urgent and real as it deserved to be. Every draft got stronger because of your guidance.

To my early readers: Edward, Anna, Stacey and John, who read terrible first drafts and told me the truth with kindness.

You helped me find the story beneath the story.

To the real whistleblowers: While this book is fiction, it's inspired by the countless healthcare workers who've risked everything to expose corruption, abuse, and negligence in medical institutions. Your courage changes systems. Your voices save lives. Thank you for choosing truth over safety.

To my mother: Who taught me that standing up for what's right is more important than fitting in. Who showed me that women can be both nurturing and fierce. Who believed in my writing before I believed in it myself. This book is for you.

To my father: Who read every medical detail to make sure I got it right, and who reminded me that good people can work in broken systems and still maintain their integrity.

To my partner Luke: Who gave me space to write, time to research, and endless patience when I disappeared into "the book cave" for weeks at a time. Thank you for believing this story mattered.

To my children Harriett and Thomas: Who remind me every day why stories about justice and truth-telling are so important. May you grow up in a world where whistleblowers are honored, not destroyed.

To the medical professionals who answered my questions: Thank you for helping me understand the realities of nursing, hospital protocols, and the ethical dilemmas healthcare workers face. Any errors or liberties taken are mine alone.

To the legal experts who reviewed the trial scenes: Your insights into federal prosecution, RICO cases, and jury dynamics were invaluable. Again, any errors are mine.

To the readers who've followed my work from the beginning: You're why I keep writing. Your messages, reviews, and enthusiasm fuel every word.

And finally, to you, the person holding this book: Thank you for spending your precious time with Jenna, Linda, Sophie, and Catherine. Thank you for caring about their story. Thank you for believing that truth matters, even when justice takes decades.

May we all have the courage to speak up when we witness wrongdoing. May we all honor those who do. And may we never forget that silence protects the powerful, but truth protects the vulnerable.

With deepest gratitude,

Sarah Blackwell

ABOUT THE AUTHOR

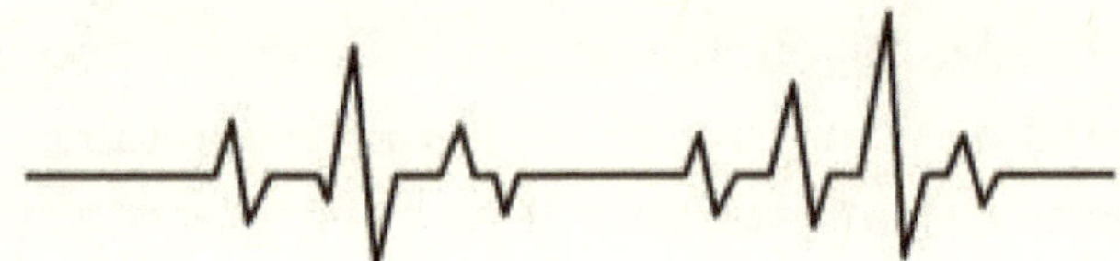

SARAH BLACKWELL is the author of medical thrillers that explore the intersection of healthcare, ethics, and justice. Her novels combine gripping suspense with deeply human stories about the people who fight for truth in broken systems.

Before becoming a full-time writer, Sarah worked in healthcare and law, experiences that inform her realistic portrayal of institutional corruption and whistleblower retaliation.

The Night Nurse's Secret is her first debut novel with MK Storyworks.

Sarah lives in New York with family and her cats. When she's not writing, she can be found in the library, drinking too much coffee, and researching dark corners of medical history that probably shouldn't fascinate her as much as they do.

She believes in the power of stories to change minds, honor the forgotten, and demand accountability from those in power.

Connect with Sarah:

- Website: www.mkstoryworks.com
- Social Media: Follow MK Storyworks on all platforms @mkstoryworks
- Newsletter: Sign up at www.mkstoryworks.com for new release alerts and exclusive content

DISCUSSION QUESTIONS FOR BOOK CLUBS

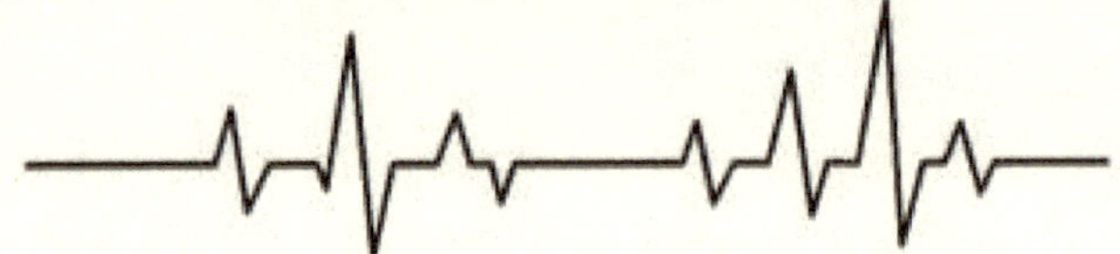

1. **The Price of Truth:** Linda Walters spent thirteen years reporting Sophie's murder, losing her career, her license, her daughter, and eventually her life in the process. Do you think her sacrifice was worth it? What would you have done in her position?

2. **Belief and Dismissal:** For years, Jenna believed her mother was mentally ill rather than a whistleblower telling the truth. How did this affect your reading experience? What does this say about how society treats women who challenge powerful institutions?

3. **Justice Delayed:** Sophie was murdered in 1987, but justice didn't come until 2025, 38 years later. Is justice that comes after decades still meaningful? What about for Linda, who died in 2011 without ever seeing vindication?

4. **The Journal:** Sophie's journal survived for 37 years because Margaret Moore kept it hidden out of fear. Do

you think Margaret made the right choice? What would have happened if she'd come forward immediately in 1987?

5. **Institutional Corruption:** The novel depicts corruption across multiple systems, pharmaceutical companies, hospitals, medical examiners, law enforcement, and social services. Which betrayal felt most impactful to you? Why?

6. **Whistleblower Retaliation:** Linda was labeled mentally ill, had her license revoked, and lost custody of her daughter after reporting what she witnessed. How realistic do you find this portrayal? What protections should exist for healthcare whistleblowers?

7. **Jenna's Journey:** Jenna goes from doubting her mother to becoming an advocate for her legacy. What moment in the book do you think was most pivotal in changing Jenna's perspective?

8. **Mother-Daughter Legacy:** The relationship between Linda and Jenna is central to the story, even though Linda died before the main events. How did their relationship evolve for you as a reader? What did you think about Jenna's guilt over not believing her mother?

9. **Catherine's Grief:** Catherine spent 37 years believing her daughter committed suicide, only to learn she was murdered. How did you react to this revelation? How do you think Catherine's grief changed after learning the

truth?

10. **The Trial:** The trial takes up a significant portion of the book. Did you find the legal proceedings engaging? What testimony or moment from the trial stood out most to you?

11. **Owen's Character:** Owen Brennan killed four executives in vigilante justice before the legal system could act. Do you have sympathy for his actions? How did you feel about his portrayal?

12. **Real-World Parallels:** While this is fiction, it's inspired by real cases of medical experimentation and whistleblower retaliation. Did the book change how you think about pharmaceutical trials, patient rights, or institutional accountability?

13. **The Epilogue:** The epilogue shows the lasting impact 10 years later, including the Sophie Brennan Memorial Center and the Linda Walters Whistleblower Protection Act. Did you find this resolution satisfying? What did you think about Jenna's choice to remain a nurse?

14. **Speaking Up:** One of the central themes is the question: "What do we do when we witness wrongdoing?" How has this book influenced your thinking about speaking up in your own life or profession?

15. **Who is the "Night Nurse"?:** The title *The Night Nurse's*

Secret could refer to multiple characters, Margaret keeping Sophie's journal, Linda witnessing the crime during night shift, or Jenna finding Margaret's note. Who do you think the title best describes? Why?

Bonus Discussion:

- If you could ask any character in the book one question, who would it be and what would you ask?

- Which scene will stay with you longest after finishing the book?

- Would you recommend this book to others? What would you tell them to expect?

PRAISE FOR SARAH BLACKWELL

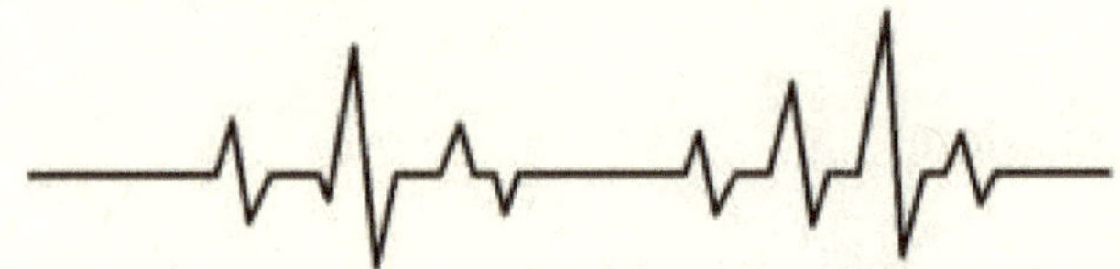

"SARAH BLACKWELL writes medical thrillers with a conscience. THE NIGHT NURSE'S SECRET is gripping from page one, but it's also deeply human, a story about mothers and daughters, truth and justice, and the long road to vindication. I couldn't put it down."

"A masterful blend of suspense and social commentary. Blackwell doesn't just entertain; she makes you think about the systems we trust and the people who dare to challenge them. This book will stay with you long after the last page."

"THE NIGHT NURSE'S SECRET is the rare thriller that's both a page-turner and a profound meditation on justice. Blackwell's portrayal of whistleblower retaliation is both heartbreaking and infuriating, and absolutely necessary reading."

"Compelling, thought-provoking, and impossible to put down. Sarah Blackwell has crafted a story that honors the real whistleblowers who risk everything for truth. Linda Walters will break your heart. Jenna will inspire you. This book matters."

"Move over Robin Cook and Tess Gerritsen, there's a new voice in medical thrillers, and she's got something important to say. THE NIGHT NURSE'S SECRET combines pulse-pounding suspense with genuine emotional depth. Highly recommended."

ALSO BY SARAH BLACKWELL

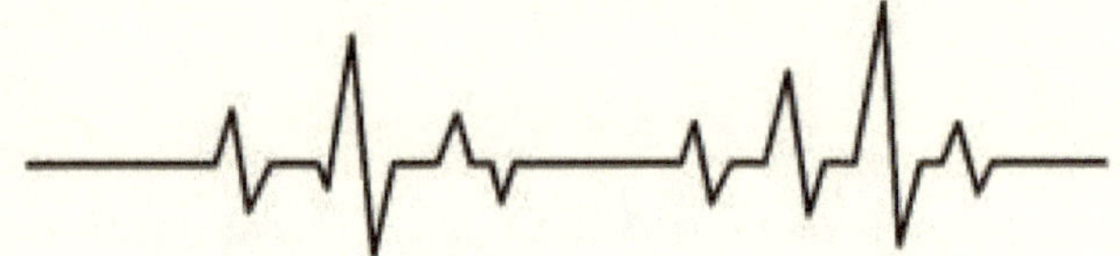

The Night Nurse's Secret is Sarah Blackwell's debut novel.

Her next book, *The Doctor's Diagnosis*, will be released in 2026 by MK Storyworks.

FORTHCOMING:

The Doctor's Diagnosis (2026)

PREVIEW: THE DOCTOR'S DIAGNOSIS

Chapter One

Dr. Emma Rhodes had diagnosed thousands of patients in her fifteen-year career as an emergency room physician. She'd seen heart attacks, strokes, poisonings, and traumas. She'd saved lives and lost them. She prided herself on never missing a diagnosis.

Until the day she realized she'd been diagnosing the same rare condition, acute intermittent porphyria, in three patients per month for the past year.

AIP affects one in 200,000 people.

Manchester General Hospital serves a population of 400,000.

Statistically, they should see one case every two years.

Emma had diagnosed thirty-six cases in twelve months.

The math didn't work.

Which meant either she was the unluckiest ER doctor in America...

Or someone was poisoning patients to create symptoms that mimicked porphyria.

And if Emma was right, the poisoner had access to the hospital's medication supply.

The killer worked here.

Possibly in the ER.

Possibly someone Emma saw every single day.

She pulled up the patient files and started looking for patterns.

What she found made her blood run cold.

THE DOCTOR'S DIAGNOSIS A Medical Thriller by Sarah Blackwell Coming 2026

CONNECT WITH MK STORYWORKS

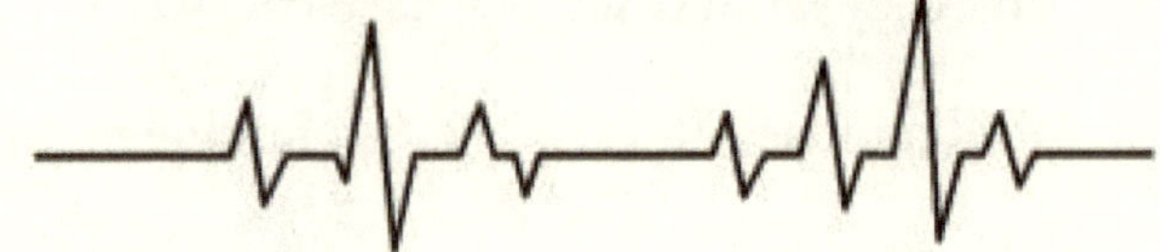

Thank you for reading!

If you enjoyed *The Night Nurse's Secret*, please consider:

- Leaving a review on MK Storyworks, Amazon, Barnes & Noble, or your favorite book platform
- Recommending it to your book club
- Sharing your thoughts on social media (tag us @mkstoryworks)

Stay Connected:

Newsletter: Sign up at www.mkstoryworks.com for:

- New release announcements
- Exclusive bonus content
- Author interviews
- Early access to cover reveals
- Special promotions and giveaways

Website: www.mkstoryworks.com

Email: contact@mkstoryworks.com

🔲 Social Media: Follow us on all platforms

- Instagram: @mkstoryworks
- Facebook: @mkstoryworks
- X: @mkstoryworks
- TikTok: @mkstoryworks
- Threads: @mkstoryworks

Discover More Stories:

MK Storyworks publishes compelling fiction across multiple genres, with a focus on stories that entertain, challenge, and inspire. Visit our website to explore our full catalog.

For Book Clubs:

Looking for discussion materials, author Q&As, or reading guides? Contact us at contact@mkstoryworks.com

We love connecting with book clubs!

For Reviewers and Media:

Press inquiries, review copies, and interview requests: contact@mkstoryworks.com

MK STORYWORKS

Stories Worth Telling. Voices Worth Hearing.

www.mkstoryworks.com

Thank you for reading THE NIGHT NURSE'S SECRET.

May we all have the courage to speak truth to power.

ABOUT THE PUBLISHER

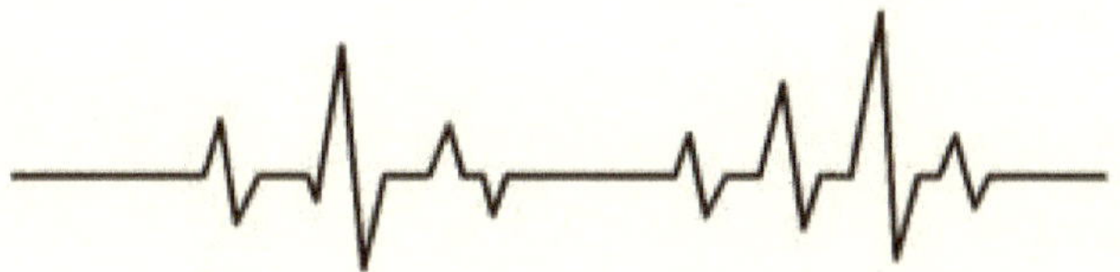

MK **Storyworks** is a truly global book publisher, dedicated to the timeless mission of connecting compelling authors with enthusiastic readers across the world.

We pride ourselves on curating a diverse and dynamic list that spans the full spectrum of literary interests. Whether you are looking for an immersive escape into a bestselling fiction novel, seeking wisdom and knowledge from groundbreaking non-fiction titles, perfecting a dish with our acclaimed cookbooks, or introducing the magic of reading to the next generation with our enchanting children's books, **MK Storyworks** delivers stories that inform, entertain, and inspire.

Our commitment to quality, creativity, and global reach ensures that every book we publish finds its place in the hands and hearts of readers, no matter where they are.

Connect with MK Storyworks

Stay up-to-date with our latest releases, author news, and behind-the-scenes glimpses by connecting with us online:

Website: www.mkstoryworks.com

Social Media:

- YouTube: @mkstoryworks
- Instagram: @mkstoryworks
- Facebook: @mkstoryworks
- X: @mkstoryworks
- Pinterest: @mkstoryworks
- TikTok: @mkstoryworks